EVERY PROMISE

ANDREA BAJANI

EVERY PROMISE

Translated from the Italian by
Alastair McEwen

MACLEHOSE PRESS
QUERCUS · LONDON

First published in the Italian language as *Ogni promessa*
by Giulio Einaudi editore, Turin, in 2010
First published in Great Britain in 2013 by

MacLehose Press
an imprint of Quercus
55 Baker Street
7th Floor, South Block
London W1U 8EW

A CIP catalogue record for this book is available
from the British Library.

ISBN (HB) 978 0 85705 146 2
ISBN (TPB) 978 0 85705 147 9
ISBN (Ebook) 978 0 85705 148 6

10 9 8 7 6 5 4 3 2 1

Designed and typeset in Sabon by Libanus Press
Printed and bound in Great Britain by Clays Ltd, St Ives plc

EVERY PROMISE

1

WHEN SARA AND I FIRST LIVED TOGETHER, SHE USED TO accompany me to the school every morning to see the children. We had just arrived in the new house, the move had been fairly hasty, and like all moves it had been an audition; the neighbours looking at us from the window while we tried to say and do nothing that might irritate them. All we wanted was to be accepted right away. So, at first, we only put striking flowers on the balcony, we only hung out our best clothes, and we only showed ourselves to be the closest of couples. When we argued we would close the windows so we couldn't be heard, and blow our rage out indoors. The room would swell with our fury, its walls would curve. It became a cave, every shout another puff, the walls bulging outwards, and the ceiling rising. And we used to think about the signora who lived above us, and her grandson, who would see the floor suddenly swell beneath their feet. Then, when we stopped fighting, and we would open the windows again, our anger would escape in a single, pulsating blast, and the walls and floor would again become straight. And we would go out onto the balcony all smiles, and if we saw someone we would say *Good day, how's it going?* On the stairs we used to say hello to everyone, I would introduce myself and shake our neighbours by the hand, and Sara always said *We*, because saying *We* was more reassuring. It was romantic, too, it was like getting back together again every time, like choosing ourselves once more. Finally, and above all, that *We* expressed a hope.

*

Sara's *We* held all the life we would have led together, like a suitcase filled to the brim with so many words that you had to sit on top of it to close it. For that *We* to exist it was necessary to have children. Because her *We* was: now there are only two of us, but then there will be three or four, if not five of us, and we'll fill the house with children who will cry a bit at first, then they'll go out on the balcony with someone who will teach them how to walk on tiptoe and you can say hello to them if you wish. And then they'll play on their own on the balcony as they cram their faces with some snack. Then you'll see them going out the front door holding their mother's hand to go to school. Then you'll see them go out on their own, walk a few yards, look round, turn the corner and light up a cigarette. Then you'll hear us arguing with them and you'll hear doors slamming, yelling that will spread from room to room. Then you'll hear us arguing, mother and father, because we won't agree on the best way to bring them up, and you'll see one of us coming out onto the balcony for an edgy smoke and going back inside and coming out again. And one of our children will go out every afternoon while another will always stay at home. And down in the courtyard you'll see them change the way they walk, thrusting their backsides out or scampering along like monkeys – some will straighten their shoulders arrogantly and others, fearfully, will hunch them up. And then they'll start to bring home boyfriends and girlfriends, and when you get used to one suddenly he or she won't come anymore. And then they'll go to university and you'll see them leave with a big bag on Sunday and come back on Saturday with the same bag, only more crumpled. And then you'll see them take away what little they possess when they move out, only to come back every so often for Sunday lunch and Easter and Christmas. And then you'll see us, the mother and the father, suddenly bereft of children, sitting for hours and hours on the balcony without exchanging a word, only to dash into the house when the telephone rings so we have something new to talk about after the call, and then back across the courtyard you'll see bellies growing as they cross the courtyard together with our sons and everything will begin anew. And again you'll hear crying in the house as we grow old all at once, in a sudden crash, smiling at each other, contenting ourselves, busy with the children our own children will have given us in exchange for themselves.

Yet we made love and no child came along. It was our *We* that fell to the ground every month and broke in two, and by dint of gluing it together again it couldn't be fixed anymore. The first months had been normal, going down the whole route every time, getting past menstrual cycles without wondering about anything, not even thinking about it, just making love because we couldn't do anything but search for each other under our clothing as soon as we were a little close. Then that thought of children had come along, a thought that at first was a nice one, the one with which we embraced before sleeping. And so making love had become a way of trying to inflate our *We*, the two of us trying to make it become three and then four, like a balloon in the form of a rabbit that you blow into hard and nothing happens and then one ear suddenly pops out. In that period Sara often accompanied me to school in the morning, and she would greet the children in my classes as if they were our children. She would take some of them in her arms and ask me, *How do I look?* Every month it was the same illusion. For a few weeks we believed in it, Sara used to say she could feel it. And we would go around disguised as a family, both of us showing off her belly, seeing the world as if we were three. And there was an immense strength, Sara would say to me I'm afraid of nothing and nobody. When we came across pregnant women, Sara would find a way to approach them, without exchanging a word, just to stand close to them, leaving the bellies to talk to one another. But then every time nothing changed, and the months began to pass, and neither of us wanted to know about medical tests, least of all to share the blame. Sara no longer wanted to come to school. Every morning she would invent a different excuse to stay at home. She would say goodbye on the doorstep. Every time I heard her opening the drawer where she kept her sanitary towels in the bathroom, I knew I would see her come out biting her lip. She would have sat down beside me, without saying a word for hours. Then, in the evening, she would have frantically sought me in bed. We began to make love in a rough way; she would fling herself at me, her feet clenched in anger, her eyes half shut in her frenzy. Then we would remain there, each in our own part of the bed, breathing, eyes open, each with an anguish we couldn't share, and for which the other could provide no consolation.

2

THERE WAS A LONG PERIOD IN WHICH THERE WAS NO MORE talk of a child. We circled around it warily, as if it were stretched out somewhere in the house, invisible and foetal, and we had to be careful not to trip over it. We moved round the house the way you do at night, your skin tense, your whole body on the alert, first setting down the heel of your foot and then the sole, with your hands outstretched before you. And if we sensed its presence, lying stretched out there invisible, we would step over it, lifting one leg to the other side, then the body would follow, and when the other foot was lifted over we would set off again. Then nothing more would be said and the more those invisible outstretched presences grew in number, the more difficult it became to move around. Little by little, our house filled up with those bodies on the floor; the hall was full of them, as was the bathroom, the living room, and the kitchen. Sometimes it even seemed that we saw them by the front door, from where we would have to shift them bodily or resign ourselves to not going out, sitting there and waiting for them to go away by themselves. So we would sit and wait, looking at the floor, our feet cramped and motionless in the few free spaces left in that cluttered house.

Even when we talked it was as if that child who didn't exist was always in front of us, as if he had sat down between us and, in order to talk, we had to lean to his left and then to his right, the way you do on a bus. And when we didn't talk we would look at each other, clinging to each other's eyes, guilty and reproachful at the same time. Each of us would have liked to enter the other, into the other's eyes, first to get through and then to throw ourselves down, letting ourselves slip along the ducts of the body until we got to the place where everything was blocked. There, somewhere, we might have known which of the two wasn't working, which of us had jammed. And above all, from there we might have been able to help ourselves, we might have combed the area, centimetre by centimetre, we might have managed to identify the error, intervene, disentangle the wires, invert the contacts and go back up quickly, come out and finally breathe. But in any case we couldn't enter each other's eyes, and all that was left for us was this silent intermittence of blame and pleas for forgiveness. We still made love, but it had become a hesitant replica, like high-jumpers who take the run up and then, at the last moment, don't make the leap. And Sara had also stopped weeping, only sometimes she would come to me and give me a hug, my chest becoming her pillow, and you could see that she couldn't stand it any longer. She would stay there for a while and then she would ask me *What shall we do?* without letting me go. I felt her question warm up a precise point in my chest, as if we were obliged to talk to each other through that hole she was hollowing out with the breath of her words. And in that question, in that *What shall we do?* there were many things. There was the *We* that was peeling away, there was her, there was me, there was the house, the name on the intercom, and there were our parents sitting on the balcony.

So we bought a dog. It came into the house like a professional; it took a quick look around, went from one room to another with the look of someone who needs no more than a glance to realize what needs to be done, then it came back to us and curled up on the rug. Sitting on the sofa, we looked like people who say *Money is no object*, and so the dog remained on the rug, already bored after the first minutes of work. But we hadn't given him a name, because sitting down at the table and piling up columns of names on a sheet of paper struck us as making the dog play the part of a child. So, the whole time, he wandered around the house like a question mark. The only one who was happy the dog had no name was the baby in the flat above. From the balcony he gave him a different name every day, but you could see that all the dog needed was to be called, and he would wag his tail and half close his eyes when we stroked him. In any event he had understood his job, the first thing he would do in the morning was to go around the house looking for those invisible bodies, those silent presences that made our flat a storehouse of obsessions. One after another, he would use his teeth to take them by a flap of clothing and drag them along delicately, making them slide across the floor and gathering them all in the room at the end of the hall, the one that had been left free in the event of a child coming, and which over time had become the room with the ironing board and things that weren't to be seen. Then he would go back to being a dog, he would let himself be taken for walks on the lead, run after birds, wear his claws down on the tarmac, chew on slippers and sleep on our bed breathing all his boundless love in our faces.

But in the room at the end of the hall there still slept those presences that we didn't want anymore. When I used to go for a pee at night I would pass in front of that closed door and it seemed that I could hear them, all that breathing, a draught that froze my feet. Once Sara and I walked past each other in front of the door, and there was no need to say a word. She was wearing my T-shirt, her eyes shut, and I just gave her a kiss on the forehead. Then we found ourselves back in bed, Sara clinging tight to my back, glued to me in an embrace, her body forming a parallel line with mine, her arm thrown like an anchor over my other side. Everything that the dog managed to rid us of would later emerge in dreams we didn't tell each other about, and we continued to run after him, up and down the town. The dog had become our jailer, his lead the cord that united us. We would watch him chase the pigeons, and every time he disappeared inside a bush, every time he left the park behind another dog, every time he went out of our sight, we hoped that he wouldn't come back.

3

ON THE LAST MONTH BEFORE SCHOOL BROKE UP WE RECORDED sounds. Using little tape recorders, we would capture every sound, even those we seemed not to hear. The children in my class moved around in groups with their little machines, they ran them along the walls of the janitor's room, under the teacher's desk, over their classmates' schoolbags, inside notebooks, in the wastepaper basket, and rubbed them against the schoolmistresses. Watching them act like this, upending chairs on desks the better to breathe in the sound beneath, it seemed like watching the cleaners at work. The sounds fascinated them, they emerged from where they thought there were none. When they were inside, they didn't hear them. Before this experiment, they hadn't noticed the alternation of silences an hour long and the sudden roars of voices, almost immediately swallowed up by another silence and the umpteenth roar, and so on all day. Our primary school struck the hours for everyone. It was the time of the neighbourhood. It was a cuckoo clock from which, at every hour, three hundred children's faces popped out in unison, opening their mouths wide before disappearing back behind closed windows.

We catalogued all the sounds the children recorded in an archive. There were weekly sessions in which teams of children formed a queue, three or four per group with a representative who held the tape recorder. I would take it, insert a cable into it, connect it to the computer and we would wait for the sounds to be poured from one machine to the other. During the transfer the children didn't look at either the computer or the tape recorder but at the cable, as if it were there that everything was happening, as if the janitor and the schoolmistresses were really passing through that flex, along with my desk, the wastepaper bin, Caterina, and Matilde's purple pencil case. They looked at it waiting to see it change shape, like a snake that has swallowed a mouse. Then when the sounds were all in my computer I would unplug the cable and they would heave a sigh of relief. At that point we had to give a name to each of the sounds, to catalogue them without muddling them up. On the computer we had created four sections, four folders entitled *People*, *Places*, *Objects* and *Animals*. For the children this was a source of lengthy discussions and quite a few arguments, but they didn't last long. The children would move away from me, gather into a scrum like rugby players, talk intensely for a while, and then return with the name to give to a sound. Then, taking it in turns, they would sit down and type the name on the keyboard, each finger hovering over the letters like a bird of prey. And so at the end of these sessions we would file our recordings in alphabetical order: *emptyjanitorsroom*, *Mattiasshoes*, *redpizza-withanchovies*, *Silviaslongnose*.

There was one day, usually a Wednesday, when we would listen to everything we had recorded during the week. We moved the desks against the walls, closed the blinds until the darkness was complete, and we all sat on the floor in a circle. The children would sit motionless in that darkness, invisible at first, and then as we gradually got used to the dark their outlines would begin to emerge. The last things to appear were their eyes, and everyone kept theirs wide open, which was their way of not drowning in the darkness. Like this, we would review the staffroom with the moped below that would not start, Mattia's shoes that mysteriously made the sound of the sea as if they were shells, the janitor's room and the sound of coffee percolating. And we would hear the bedlam that was playtime, how the gym in the first hours of the afternoon seemed suspended, and the birds on the tree in front of our classroom (who had ever heard them?) and a pneumatic drill that was breaking up the street and the janitor in the corridor saying *Give me back my broom you scamps*. After a while the children no longer kept their eyes wide open against the dark. In fact, everyone was looking at a part of their body, some at a foot, some at a finger, others at a knee, and others again sat staring into space, mouths and eyes half open with a film of emptiness above them, and that was the screen on which they projected the sounds they saw.

*

The day before school broke up, each child made the others listen to the sounds of their house. Each of them, behind the darkness of the closed blinds, presented their homes to the class, describing the street in which their building stood, what floor their home was on, and how many people were in the family. Some children had already been in their classmates' houses, but most of them hadn't. I had asked them to do everything on their own, without anyone's help, in fact, if possible, to record without being seen by their parents, far less by their brothers and sisters. So we entered other people's houses, even I who had never been to any of their homes. There was Simone's house, where the neighbours were renovating their flat, or maybe demolishing it with pickaxes. There was Melissa's place where there was always someone coming in and going out of the room and you could hear the the air moving. Matilde's home with a T.V. on in every room and nobody watching the same thing. And Silvia with her mum who was singing an old song I hadn't heard for decades. Giacomo with his sister flirting on the telephone with her fiancé even though you couldn't hear the words very well. Giulio who had recorded his father snoring because his dad denied that he did so and he now finally had proof. Luca's, where there was total silence, and when I asked him why he said that it was because he was always alone at home. Beatrice who didn't hear a thing because to avoid being seen by her parents she had kept the recorder in her trouser pocket. Then there was Michele's house, his parents yelling terrible things, doors slamming, and I imagined him and his blue glasses wandering around holding his tape recorder while all around the world was falling apart.

4

FROM THE FLOOR ABOVE US EVERY SO OFTEN WE WOULD
hear the little boy running, his mum used to leave him with his
grandmother in the afternoons. In the evening she would come
back to pick him up, they would leave with him carrying his
schoolbag over his shoulder. I used to see them cross the courtyard
in the dark. Sometimes he would come down to my place. His
grandmother would warn me of his arrival from the balcony. I
would open the door, hear hers opening upstairs and shortly afterwards I would see him come in. He would sit down on the sofa and
switch on the television. I would shout to the grandmother from
out the window to say he had arrived, I would close the door and
hear hers closing too. This was our agreement with his grandmother; if I was at home she could send him down, he was no
bother to me. If I had time, I would stay with him, if I didn't have
time, he was independent and didn't disturb me. He was six and
knew the T.V. remote control and the fridge by heart as they were
the two things that really interested him in my house. But more
than the fridge he was interested in the freezer, which he would
open with an expert gesture after having climbed onto a stool taken
specifically for this operation. Then he would slip his hand into the
box of ice cream cones, choose one according to the day and his
mood, and head for the sofa. Sometimes I would find him standing
on the stool studying the boxes of frozen food, with the freezer
breathing all its cold on him. And he would stand there, turning in
his hands the boxes of peas, the packets of spinach with the photographs of serving suggestions, the pancakes, the transparent bags
with three or four loaves saved from going stale. He would look at
them with curiosity and suspicion, and then put them back. He
studied them as if they wanted to cheat him. He would take fish

fingers out of their packets, scrutinize them and you could see he was thinking, *Anyway, I know you're not an ice cream.* The frozen foods kept him very busy and took up a good deal of the time he spent in my house. Once I heard a noise and, frightened, I ran into the kitchen and saw he had dropped a box of rissoles. He was next to the fridge blowing on his hands. *It was boiling*, he said.

The first time the grandson of the signora upstairs came to my house was the day when Sara took the furniture away. Before then, the grandmother had let me talk to him from the balcony. He would put his hands on the balustrade and his face between the bars. He would ask me *What are you doing?* even if I wasn't doing anything, and if I said *Nothing* then he wouldn't ask anything more. I had begun to do things on the balcony specially to tell him about them, to teach him tricky words. *I'm watering the tulips, I'm pondering, I'm sipping a glass of bitters, I'm nibbling a few grapes, I'm humming*, and when I said these things he would laugh. So every time he went back indoors with a word he showed it off as if he had found it playing. Then he would repeat it running through the rooms, he would breathe in air and when he let it out it had become a word that floated upwards. One room after another, he filled the house with words. I would see them coming out the windows like soap bubbles. Then, every so often, he would come out onto the balcony, call me, and say he had forgotten a word. *Trampoline.* And off he would go jumping on it for hours, putting it in his mouth, turning it around, losing it somewhere and then seeing it appear again.

He had seen Sara's entire move from the balcony. He stayed up there, watching people coming in and going out with furniture on their shoulders, and he greeted them all. *Hello*, and they would stop, put down the furniture, look up, say hello, pick up the furniture and carry on. His grandmother, who had understood all there was to understand, constantly called him back inside, but he paid no attention. He asked for explanations, kept a count of the things, said who was the strongest among Sara's friends who were giving her a hand, and expected a greeting every time someone went in or came out. Before leaving, Sara only waved her hand to say goodbye. He, who at that point had understood, looked at me to see if he could return her gesture. I asked him *Aren't you going to say goodbye to her?* and he gave her a hasty *Bye*, which was immediately swallowed up and didn't even come to touch the rest of his face. That's why his grandmother also came out onto the balcony, leaned her elbows on the balustrade and looked at me. *Shall I send him down?* she asked, and I said *Good idea.* So I opened the door, and she shouted *Here he is*, and I saw him coming down the stairs with one arm on the handrail.

The boy came into the house where the walls revealed the holes left by the furniture they had taken away. They were like recesses mined by an explosion. Every room had its empty spaces, Sara's furniture that had stood there until a short time before, squashed up against the wall among my own. The boy came in and turned round, looking at me with the expression of someone who is a little desirous and a little afraid. I gestured at him to go ahead, and he ventured forward. Every room, to see it from the doorway, was a spoiled mouth, every niche that opened up, a tooth removed. I watched him standing still in the doorways, I saw him move among incisors and molars, walking on tiptoe over the tongue. He kept on turning to look me in the eye, and with my eyes and a gesture of the head I told him to carry on; only children can walk into the mouths of monsters. At that point he wasn't afraid anymore, it was enough for him to trust me blindly. He looked at the gaps in the middle of the gums, those violent holes against the wall, with a face distorted by disgust. Then he went to slip between those teeth that were still standing up. He stood there and looked at me, and I thought that even if the monster had closed its mouth, he would have saved himself by staying there in the middle.

5

SARA LEFT ON THE DAY SCHOOL BROKE UP. OUT OF THE BLUE, the summer burst open. It swallowed my children in one gulp, it emptied my house, and I was left there, a car hanging on the edge of a cliff. The school day had begun at eight with a cathartic yell on the stairs. It was one of those days in which it was pointless to raise your voice, to patrol the desks, ask to see the homework notebook or call kids to the blackboard. Every year, I would try to counter the chaos of that holiday that began before it should. I would change trick every time, counting on amazement and then on fright, but it was useless. The kids couldn't manage to stay seated, staying only a few moments on their chairs before they would slide off, elbow their neighbour, run their hands through their hair, rub their eyes with closed fists, try all the colours without ever making a drawing, toss something in the wastepaper basket. In the end I would shout, beat my hand on my desk, and all of them would look at me speechless, as animals do when they sense a danger or a sound. And just like animals, they would suddenly stop, only stretching out their necks and raising their heads, as if their silence and immobility made them invisible. But obviously I saw them, still as statues there in front of me, frozen in the act of pulling their hair, chasing one another or throwing a ball, the sole object that amid the general paralysis continued to cross the room only to hit a wall and bounce back on the floor. So there was this prolonged moment of silence, my ibexes all standing still in the middle of the stony ground. And then all someone had to do was sneeze, or the ball would roll back to me, and chaos returned to the classroom.

The day Sara left you could feel it. It was one of those days when the air vibrates for everyone, one of those days when there is a contagious fever. It's as if electricity had struck you, as if there were someone who gets the shock first and then leans against the person next to him and that's where everything begins. And so, one after another, the charge runs through all the bodies in the city, street by street, house by house, spreads through shops and markets, swimming pools and restaurants, enters the buses and the underground, men and women kissing one another, embracing, and the electric charge runs through them, reaches the pews in the churches, the barracks and the post offices, and then enters the cars of the driving schools, the same electrical charge that threads one body after another as if they were beads, and goes on into the museums and the underground parking lots, men and women looking at one another, faces distorted by spasms that instantly disappear, and the charge enters the judo gyms, the libraries and the retirement homes, until, after having crossed the entire city, that irritation, that electrical shock, discharges itself at a single point: earth. It does this with a hiss and a flash, and all that there was in that point then becomes dust, and if there were grass there would always be a hole. And that point of discharge, that day, was my house.

Before setting the children free for the summer we had taken them to the gym, a party, with plastic cups and everyone saying goodbye all together. There was a teacher who photographed the classes. She did this every year with an old Polaroid, standing in the middle while each class waited its turn for the photograph that in September would be pinned up behind the teachers' desks. Each photograph was a quarter hour of false starts, everyone posing and someone making a rude gesture, and then the others all laughing, the teachers leaving the group and shouting, and everything back to square one. The teacher behind the camera would gesticulate, herding back those who had wound up outside the picture. She looked like a goalkeeper organizing the defence. The other classes stood to one side, motionless and silent, watching, some shrieking, many holding their breath and trying to imagine themselves in the place of those who were posing. After every photograph there was a shout. Even the teachers finally laughed and bent over the children to comment, some they would take to one side, *That's no way to behave*. Then it was our turn, they had left us till last, there was no-one left in the gym, balloons everywhere. We took up a pose, all twenty of us in front of the volleyball net, and I said *Don't make me look bad*. They were impeccable, the teacher said *Children, smile please*, and all of us widened our mouths, the teacher pressed the button and the camera stuck out its tongue. The photograph emerged from the front. Then we all went towards the teacher, who was laughing and saying *Behave now*. She had left the photograph with Michele. So all the kids gathered round him. Michele was holding it in his palm as if it were an injured bird. The children stood there, their faces over his hand, some were shoving, the others pushed them back out of the group. At first there was only a dark outline, a class photograph that looked like a mountain chain. And yet, bit by bit, the faces emerged too, revealing themselves on the paper that had been blank shortly before. Matilde yelled *Ghosts!* They appeared as if they had come out of the water. Michele, who was holding the photograph at arm's length, was almost frightened of them. And we were all in it, each one ready for the summer, three months of emptiness ahead. There was the volleyball net behind us, the green flooring of the gym, and I was standing tall in their midst, the only one not smiling.

When I went back home, all I found was the dog curled up on the other side of the door. Sara wasn't there. I saw that there was nothing on her table, and in the hall a nail was sticking out, a nail from which one of her friend's paintings used to hang. She was intending to come and get the rest later on. The dog was no longer in the hall, the door was still open, and he had gone out. He had gone down the stairs, someone had opened the street door for him and let him go. I threw open the shutters and let in some air, as if the entire house needed to take a deep breath. On the kitchen table there was a note and on that note it said *Your mother called, Mario is dead.* A few lines below she had added with another pen *Mario?* with a question mark. At the foot of the page Sara had written her name and the date, which she never added. Mario was my mother's father, and for at least fifteen years no-one had mentioned his name.

6

MY MOTHER'S FATHER WAS A MAN FROM WHOM TIME HAD stolen everything, even his face. I had met him only a few times, and then he didn't show up anymore. It wasn't enough to earn the title of grandfather, yet his absence was too awkward to turn him merely into a gentleman who passed by from time to time. So we had found this middle way of calling him, to make him only my mother's kin while I had the choice of what to do with him, repudiate or recognize him. When his name happened to come to her mouth she would keep him there, hidden in her palate. To say *Your grandfather* was only a desire and to say *My father* was a moat between me and her, raising the drawbridge in the middle of a sentence. But every now and then she might happen to say *Grandfather*. This required double the effort: seeking a reaction in my face, as well as trying to have faith in her father, to entrust him with his grandson if only within words. And then worrying, wringing her hands, hoping to see me return safe and sound.

In reality, I had seen him a few times, almost always with my mother and sometimes even just me and him alone. Every so often they would come to pick me up at school, the first years in primary school. The same school I was to teach in many years later. I would come out and see them there, next to each other, a little apart from the other parents. So, suspiciously, I would join them, unwillingly, and I would make them wait a bit. Sometimes I pretended I had forgotten something in the classroom, I would run back inside and stop just beyond the doorway, I would lean against the wall, hoping they had gone away. But when I came out he was always there by her side. They would talk without looking at each other, both of them searching for me among the other children. So then I would arrive and say hello to my mother, keeping him out of my gaze. But she would say *Give grandfather a kiss*, and I hated her. You could see she wasn't doing it for herself, but above all for us two, so that he could have a grandson, and for me, so that I could try to believe I had another grandfather. He would bend over and pick me up in his arms, a movement that brought on a sharp pain in his back, and he would hold his breath, screw up his eyes and lift me up. I let myself be lifted up, but I would move my face away. It was an instinct, not wanting to smell him because his was a foreign smell which had nothing to do with me. The smell of his skin, his hair, his aftershave. And his bristly clothes, his rough grey jacket, I could feel them prickling my hands, and I would brace myself hoping to get away. Even his height, he was so much taller than anyone else, was foreign to me when I was in his arms. It was a new distance from the ground, seeing my mother from up there made her a fragile thing I didn't recognize. I would look at this man and I was frightened of his sunken features, his cheeks gnawed away, his skull squatting below the skin, the bones embedded in his cranium. And his eyes, which didn't seem to be there, darkness in the back of two caves. We would stay there like that, and I would hope that it wouldn't last long and he would look at me in the darkness. Then he would give me a big hug, I could feel the vice of his arms on my back, and I didn't breathe until he had finished.

I would let them walk a few metres ahead, father and daughter. He would take my schoolbag and sling it over his shoulder. Sometimes my mother would try to put me in between them, she would say *Give grandfather your hand*, but shortly afterwards I would let it go. And every second that passed in that grip was an effort I didn't want to make. I didn't feel that it was only my hand in his hand, but it was me, confined inside the rough darkness of a fist. I felt like a prisoner, his calluses that scraped my skin, scanning the walls in the darkness, running my fingers along the lines of his hand in search of an opening. Then I would find the gap and come out, one jerk and I would escape. To see them from behind, my mother so small beside her father who was so tall, it looked as if she were the little girl he had gone to pick up after school. Yet, at the same time, he seemed like the little boy, his uncertain gait, his balance regained almost by chance at every step, and my red schoolbag on his back. He would slip on both the straps like a schoolboy. You could see it was tight over his jacket, creasing it, and so he would pull it up. They spoke quietly in those ten minutes of road between the school and my house, above all it was my mother who spoke to him. She looked up at him from below, sometimes she would bring her face close to his as if she were spoonfeeding him with words. Every so often they would stop, my mother would detach her arm from his and then they would turn towards each other, she gesticulating and he always with that eyeless gaze of his. I could hear some words, but there were too few of them to be able to understand. They were words that shot out like cigarettes thrown from a car window, which cut through the air only to burn out further away. At times I would see him hold an arm out towards her, extending his bones towards his daughter's shoulders. But he would stay that way for a short time, and with too much fear for it to be considered a real hug.

Then when we came to the house we would stop for a little longer. He would hand me back my schoolbag and my mother would ask me to show him my exercise books. We would sit down on the steps and he followed my finger over the sheet, every now and then he'd say *What a good boy* and run his rough hand over my hair. Then my mother would get up and say it was time to go, my father was waiting for us upstairs. In the lift she wouldn't talk, you could see that she was entirely inside the thought of her father. I wondered how I could leave his smell outside the door, together with our lined-up shoes.

7

MY SCHOOLMATES CALLED HIM *THE SKELETON*. THEY SAID HE was bones covered with clothes, and that when he walked it sounded like the knocking of wood. And, in fact, it seemed like he wasn't anything else, seeing him standing there motionless near the school gate, a jacket draped over a clothes hanger, and above it a skull that never smiled. Some even said this out loud, shouting it in everybody's face when they saw him from the window. They would yell *The skeleton!* and they would all clack their teeth together, twenty sets of teeth chattering, a constant clack-clack, a beating of sticks on the floor that would come down the stairs from our classroom, cross the entrance hall and throw itself outside. And, filled with shame, I would clack my teeth furiously, making more noise than anyone else, and push myself forward. Then when we came outside it seemed to me that I could see him tremble with fear, I thought I could see a wind slip among his bones and jumble them up. But he said nothing, and when I arrived he would reassemble himself, put his skeleton in order and get ready to walk, even with a smile on his face. He had come to pick me up alone three or four times, when the new term began, and my mother had accompanied him at first as far as the gate to see if he could handle it. She had accompanied him only to see us go away, to tell me *Be good, please,* and follow us with her gaze from a distance. She did this without letting my father know, because he didn't like this man. Every time his name came up in conversation his glass would quiver with anger. He used to say that if that man had hurt my mother, he would hurt me too. So my mother didn't talk about those few visits, and there hadn't even been any need to ask for my complicity – let alone tell my father that she had left me with him, the two of us together for a couple of hours, as she waited on a bench with a book and her watch.

The first time had been a disaster. I had cried the whole time, and he didn't know what to do, he even got scared. I saw him bending over me, staring at me through those holes in his face. He bent his bones and looked at me a bit powerless, like a bit of a failure, as if I were a broken cogwheel and he didn't know what part to get his hands on. He hoped for a miracle, that I would start to function again by myself. But that miracle hadn't happened: one hour of inconsolable tears, my throat strained with sobbing. For an hour he had pushed me on a swing, I went back and forth howling out my pain and he hoped that the wind would at least spare him the torment of my weeping. Embarrassed, he turned, checking to see that no-one was coming to witness that scene, a skeleton pushing a swing with a desperate child on it. For the entire hour that my weeping lasted, that first time, I saw the buildings in front of me coming towards me and moving away disassembled inside the prisms of my tears. And like the buildings, the people who were facing us were disassembled in a mosaic of hexagons, and the cars, the pigeons and his face, a face split into many pieces that in the end let me get off. He had stretched out his arm and stopped the swing with a grip that took my breath away, the buildings suddenly stopped. Then we had gone back to my mother, the feeble echo of my tears still upon me. He gave me back to her with an embarrassed look, like someone bringing back a car that had been scratched.

The other times it went better, I found him at the entrance and handed myself over in resignation, my hands in my pockets so that he wouldn't ask me to hold his. He always took me to see a duck that swam in a fountain, a couple of bus stops away, one hundred metres inside the park, and then a seat on a bench. In the bus we didn't even sit down, the journey was too short. He would hang on to the rail high up and I would try to keep my balance without holding anything. I would move my legs, shifting my weight forwards or backwards according to the swaying, the bends, the braking and moving off again, as if I were travelling on my own skateboard and not everyone's bus. But every so often I would lose my balance, and so I would hang on to him as if it were a defeat. In the park he would walk along beside me, tall as could be, his shadow a long stick that made way for us. Around the fountain there were lots of benches, and we would choose one. There was this enormous pond with a fountain and in it a single duck, and dozens of people with eyes only for it. Sometimes the duck would make a concession, it would come haughtily towards us, look at us, and then go off showing us its back, merely a flick of the tail. Other times instead it would stay in the middle of the pond, careless of the children's shrill calling and the things they threw, first generously, then impatiently, then a bit vexed, and then it became like a fairground target under a volley of biscuits. We would spend a long time sitting there. He didn't say much and his words were always the same, scrambled conversation about Russia, the war, the cold, walking, imprisonment. But then he would realize that I wasn't listening, and so he would give me a hand with the duck again. He would put his fingers in his mouth and this strong sound would come out, full-bodied, like a shepherd's whistle. I really wasn't expecting it the first time, it seemed to me that he couldn't have made it, as he spoke little and quietly. So when it happened my head jerked up at that call. I saw him standing near the edge of the pond, I heard the whistle come out and the others turning towards him. And it made me get up, and stand closer to him, to let everybody know we were together.

8

SUDDENLY HE WASN'T THERE ANYMORE, AND IT WAS AS IF HE had only been a bad dream. No skeleton outside the school, no procession of kids clacking their teeth like a firing squad coming down the stairs, and no duck to court in the park. Even my mother stopped talking about him, no longer mentioning his name or referring to him for any reason. When I came out of school I would find her as always among the other mothers. She would wave her hand, and then she would take my schoolbag. At first, I used to look for him from the classroom window, partly out of fear and partly because of the whistle that only he could make. I also looked for him inside the windows of the buses, the ones that went towards the park with the fountain in the middle. And all the tall men I saw seemed like Mario to me, with heads that stood out above the rest. But he wasn't there anymore, simply, and I knew I shouldn't ask. So, bit by bit, I tried to forget him, drive the thought out when I felt it was coming, not to expect to see him outside the school, not to think of my mother walking beside him.

But he would come back to me in the evenings, in my room, as soon as my mother said goodnight and closed the door, leaving the rest of the world outside. There was a rectangle of light, above the wardrobe. The street lights slipped in through a gap in the blinds, passed over my bed and ended up high against the wall. I liked to know that above me there was that secret passage of light. It was secret because you could see it only if you put something into it. Otherwise it would stay there, a luminous overpass, invisible to the naked eye. I used to raise my arm to look for that gallery of light, I would see my hand appear on high, glowing, as if it had been detached from my body. Sometimes I would throw a book up, or raise a foot, a slipper, and they would appear, and I would wiggle my toes to assure myself that that foot was still part of me, I would try to tickle myself to hear my laughter in the darkness. Before I went under the blankets, I would bring a few objects close to the bed, my ruler, a shoe, the football, a toy car. Then, as soon as my mother closed the door, the apparitions would begin. It took me a while to realize that those ghosts also ended up in the rectangle of light that opened wide above the wardrobe. And I was afraid of them. They were huge, much bigger than they really were, my foot a menacing shadow, my hand so large it almost completely filled that rectangle, casting the room into darkness. It was precisely there, in that window above the wardrobe, that my mother's father would appear. No-one in the house talked about him, but I used to see his shadow, his lanky skeleton, a big hat on his head, standing motionless in the same place until I fell asleep. I thought about him in the street, upright and still, looking up at my window. It seemed I could hear his whistle, perhaps he wanted to talk to me, and I stayed there in hiding. So I slept badly, tossing and turning all night beneath the blankets, I would shut my eyes so as not to see him and then open them again to check if he was still there. He would also return in my sleep, with those two big holes inside his skull, those cavities that in my dreams were always the school windows, I would see my schoolmates looking out of them and shouting *The skeleton!* sticking their arms out of his skull and waving. Luckily, the next morning he and the rectangle of light had gone. We would leave to go to school, I would pass the lamp post without looking at it, holding my mother's hand, and not even a glance, or a suspicion.

No trace remained of him, of his sudden fading away, even in my mother's gaze. I searched her face for a sign or an understanding, for some complicity, a trace of the secret grandfather. But I found nothing, I could think I had invented him. Then I finally forgot him and he went away, as if I had gathered all his bones scattered around the house, put them in a sack and thrown them in the river during the night. There were no photographs of him anywhere. And even in my mother's album, the one with her name on the first page, he never appeared. Even when she was only a few years old she was always alone with my grandmother, on the beach with a handkerchief on her head and a parasol clumsily planted in the sand, on skis with her legs snowploughing, at a restaurant with other people I didn't know, then together in the distance by the Mole Antonelliana, and years later on bicycles, both of them at a standstill, both with the same leg on the ground, and cooking together, my mum all stained and looking like someone who is learning and who has already had enough, and with grandmother again walking along a street full of shop windows, my mother wearing her first heels. At a certain point my father also made an appearance, inside the album, with his jacket, shirt and the wedding lunch, three really long tables, all the men with their ties already loosened, napkins thrown down on the table, glasses opaque with drinks, cigarettes in the ashtrays.

Finally there was my album that was still slim, but to which I devoted all the time I had, I wanted it to be big like my parents' one. So I arranged the photographs, and the first was one of my mother pregnant, and my grandmother beside her. I forced anyone who came to the house to look at my album, though my father always asked me to wait a few moments. I would look at the clock in the kitchen, and when ten minutes had passed I would close in, my album at the ready, under my arm. We would leaf through it together, my explanations always more fanciful, articulated, picturesque, and the visitor's comments. But it quickly came to an end, the photographs of my birth, my first bicycle and then right away school, the series of class photographs. And all those who saw the class photographs would say the same thing. They would look at the pictures of me in the album, and then at my parents sitting in the living room. And they would wonder how it was possible, with such a small mother and father, that a boy like me had come along. With my broad, taut smile I towered above my classmates who only came up to my shoulders.

9

I FOUND THE FIRST PHOTOGRAPH OF RUSSIA INSIDE A BOOK, a group of youngsters with my mother's father in the middle. It was during a break when we were moving house because they were building another one in front of our window. We saw the building rising up, a shadow that grew a bit higher every day, it seemed to us that it was flooding the house and soon we would be drowned. My father and mother had protested with the manager of the flats, then they had started looking for a new home. So I spent long afternoons alone, the menacing shadow of the building climbing up the walls, at first only a few centimetres, then as far as the little table in the living room, the sofa, the dining table. I decided to measure the rising shadow. I made pencil marks on the wall, and I would write the date alongside. The wall was the same one on which my own heights were marked, although in different colours, the building and I growing together. Every so often I would look out and watch the workmen, I saw them walking along the scaffolding, shouting orders followed by vertical movements, pipes moving upwards, empty buckets coming down, hanging from ropes. It struck me as a contest, between them and my parents, the workers building a house and my parents looking for another one. In the evenings we would go out onto the balcony and lean against the parapet to look at the building site, the upturned buckets, the piles of scrap metal, the odd glove on the scaffolding together with a coloured hard hat. We would stay there until late, my parents bringing each other up to date on the houses they had visited, while I tried to imagine those houses, and all three of us were comforted by the fact that the building wouldn't grow any further until the next day. And we looked at the mountain in the distance, as if it were shrinking day by day.

Then we found the house. It was a flat, three blocks from where we lived, and they couldn't build in front of it because there was already a low house there. We were safe unless they decided to demolish it. It was so close to our house that my father said we could have carried our furniture over there by ourselves. I did my bit above all at home, putting things into crates, slotting them in so as to make them hold still as much as possible. Then I took newspaper and wrapped up glasses, plates, cups, photograph holders, collected all the instruction manuals in a single container, all the bunches of keys in an envelope, a single box for my mother's perfumes and creams. The one I liked best was the crate for the shoes, because they could be put in higgledy-piggledy, it was the only crate in which the entire family stayed together, feet large and small, high heels, flip-flops, football boots, wellington boots, slip-ons and moonboots. When I asked to see the new house they said I would only see it on the day I went to live there, like a bride and groom who only see each other dressed up for the first time at the altar. So I devoted myself to subdividing the house into crates, I would break off only when my father and the three young men who were helping him came to take away some item of furniture. Every time they came in they were dirtier. They passed through the house giving one another instructions and went out talking in gasps under the weight. I would close the door behind them and go to see the hole in the wall where a piece of furniture had been. Then I would go back to my task of subdivision, in the company of those new smells of sweat that made me think that this was already not our house anymore. When I got tired of putting things inside crates I would go out onto the balcony and lean over, I would watch the men moving along the street with the furniture. I followed them with my gaze, as they swerved through the people, the ladies with their skirts and handbags, lugging sofas and chests saying *Excuse me*. They carried the heaviest pieces in four, like coffins, two on each side, the funeral of our old house.

I found the photograph of Russia when leafing through a book I was about to put in the crate. Gathering up books was the easiest job. No anomalous bulk, no projections, only parallelepipeds to be stacked one on top of the other, and the slimmer volumes to fill the gaps. Yet it was the job that took longest to finish, I always ended up with my nose inside the books, leafing through them, to see if something had been left inside. My curiosity was aroused above all by the dog-ears my parents had made while reading, you could see the folds. My mother's big dog-ears, casual, sometimes half pages folded over, and then my father's tiny, always identical, decorous triangles. They alternated if they had both read the book, her excess and his meticulousness. Sometimes I would find them on the same page. From the distance between the dog-ears I understood the sequence of days and hours. Two dog-ears at a distance of two pages were my father's evening reading, until a dream began to seep its way into the story. Instead, two dog-ears very far apart were my mother's Sunday afternoons, the sofa, the blanket and her legs drawn up underneath her. When there were lots of dog-ears in the first pages then usually there wouldn't be any more, you could see that no-one had ever opened the second part of the book. Every book, before being filed, was all an expert auscultation, and only after that would it end up in the crate. Then sometimes post-cards would fall out from between the pages, a few lines filled with exclamation marks and the illegible signatures of men and women friends whose names I had never heard mentioned. There was a postcard from Calabria where it was written *This is where we're staying*. In passing, my father told me to get a move on, and so I took a few books in a pile, put them in the crate and said *You're right*. Then he went away, and I went on again as before.

The photograph emerged from a huge recipe book that had fallen along with the shelf when I removed the books that served as its counterweight. I put the book away and only afterwards did I see the photograph, there on the floor in the middle of the hallway, while the helpers passed by taking my bed which was still made up. So I took the photograph and slipped it in my pocket. I looked at it when everyone had left. It was a small photograph, black-and-white, a bit dirty and worn. The photograph showed a group of young men posing in the snow. There were eight of them, and he was among them, already with a skull in place of his head. On the back of the photograph there was written in ink *The Don Front, Russia, 13 December 1942*. Below that, it said, in a hand identical to my mother's, *The dots are for the missing, the cross for the dead, and those with no mark are the living*. And then the signature, *Mario*. So I turned the photograph over and I saw that above the head of each person there were marks in ink. Of those eight men, five had a dot, two a cross, and he had nothing.

10

FOR ALL THE YEARS IN WHICH HE HAD NOT SHOWED up, my mother's father had therefore been left hidden inside the books in our house. Every so often I would find him among the pages, the first times because I looked for him, years after because I had begun to read. At first, retrieving the photographs had been a bother, and as soon as I was alone at home I would take the books down from the shelves one after another. I leafed through them, shook them, turned them upside down, and waited until the photograph fell out, parachuted onto the carpet. But there were few photographs, more than anything else what fell out were the notes my parents had left inside over the years. I would study their handwriting, that script that struck me as so youthful, the slender stems of the tall letters, full of pride and shame. Unlike my father, in each of the notes my mother had a different handwriting, she looked for new shapes for it by pressing the pen against the paper. Sometimes it was full and curved, the capital letters inflated, the crosses of the *t*s like plumes in almost all the words, the legs of the *p*s that invaded the line beneath. Other times it was threadlike, the words like metallic insects, each letter on its own, as if it didn't want help from anyone. But even there the legs of the *p*s eluded control, betrayed my mother, swooping down on the words written below and defacing them. When I shook the books, all the notes would fall down one on top of the other, piling up on the carpet like rubble from a house that had collapsed. There in the middle there were also some recent notes, written in the hand I knew. It was clear that among the many possibilities open to her, my mother had chosen only one, the enfeebled synthesis, devoid of any enthusiasm, of the others.

Every time I found a photograph of Mario I would hastily put it in my pocket, looking around, hoping no-one had seen me. I always found him, hidden in our house without letting himself be discovered, lying down between the pages of a book as if it were a bush. It struck me as a secret between us, knowing he was huddled down on the bookcase observing us while we ate. I had even tried to change the places at table, I had begged my mother to sit in the front of the bookcase, I wanted him to see her. At first she had been against this as she had to walk round the table to get to the kitchen, but then she resigned herself to it. So I imagined her being looked at from between the pages, his two fingers spreading the pages apart, and then her face as she was eating, talking, laughing, getting angry, blushing, thinking things over, her place empty in between courses, and I would sit there for a moment with the excuse of saying something in my father's ear. But sometimes we would eat in the kitchen, when time was running short, and the table stayed that way, with a cover and a vase standing on it all day long. When I was alone at home I would liberate Mario, I would take him out of the books and let him get some air, I would put the photographs on the little plastic table on the balcony, laid out one beside the other. They were all very similar, the same rectangle soiled by the years and these groups of seven or eight young men all together, in army uniforms. They were always in formation, looking like a football team in disguise, the first row kneeling down in front and the others standing behind, all with the expressions necessary for their role, some wearing a smile. Sometimes behind or beside them there was a cannon, and someone leaning against it as if it were a comrade's shoulder. More than half the photographs were in meadows. The men had their shirt sleeves rolled up or were bare-chested, their stomach muscles firm, an oblique gaze, all playing the man together, each one for the woman who was to receive the photograph. The other photographs were in the the snow, the men were more imposing in their winter jackets, beards, but the smiles they sent home were a bit gloomier. On the front of those photographs, *Russian steppes* was written in ink. Behind, he had written only the dates, between July and December 1942, and then the usual phrase. *The dots are for the missing, the cross for the dead, and those with no mark are the living, Mario. The dots are for the missing, the cross for the dead, and those with no mark are the living, Mario. The dots are for the missing, the cross for the dead, and those with no mark are the living, Mario. The dots are for the missing, the cross for the dead, and those with no mark are the living, Mario.* And just as in the first photograph I had found, the only one without a mark was always him and him alone.

*

Then there was a period in which the telephone would ring at night. I used to hear it ring for a long time in the darkness, the house vibrated with that sound, a cold draught that seized us all. The first time my father went to answer, with my mother and me in the doorway watching him. All he said was *Hello*, and shortly after *Yes*. Then he had laid the handset down on the table, looked at my mother and there was no need to tell her anything. Since then it happened often, first that long ring, then my parents' bedroom door opening, my mother's heels on the floor and finally the ringing would finish. They talked like that, my mother always in the dark, I would hear her begin speaking softly and then raising her voice without realizing. She constantly said *But Papa*, and *Everything's all right*, a few words all in a rush. Sometimes she would suddenly burst into tears, I could hear her sniffing, saying *Don't you understand that it's all over?* Once she yelled *We're not in Russia*, and the house remained impregnated with that yell for weeks, my father and I with staring at the ceiling in our beds. Those nocturnal calls could last for a few minutes or for hours, my mother sitting on the floor, her legs curled up under her dressing gown, the nape of her neck against the radiator. I had seen her one night, I had got up with the pretext of getting a glass of water, but she shooed me away with her hand. The beginning of every telephone call was difficult, she would talk to him agitatedly, as if to disarm him, first to attack him and then to embrace him, to feel that he was letting himself go. In the end she would lower her voice and speak to him kindly in a soft voice, as if to send him her warm breath, to make him fall asleep. Then she would hang up. The heels went back across the room, the bedroom door would open and then close behind her. And in the morning she would say nothing, as usual, and I would look at the radiator, to search for the point that caused pain, to see if her head had left a mark.

THEN, FOR YEARS, NO MORE TELEPHONE CALLS IN THE NIGHT, and after a while I too stopped looking for him. Christmas and Easter always meant family reunions, the convergence of relatives from the surrounding district, and those who called to say they had just woken up, they needed time to get dressed, drink a coffee, but in the meanwhile everyone should just go ahead and start without them. The cars were all parked below the house. Someone would have a new model and the others would walk around it, looking inside with their noses pressed up against the windows, opening the doors, sitting in the driving seat, sometimes taking a spin. Then they would spread out around the house, I would take everyone's coats and carry them to my parents' bed, a mountain that grew a little every time the doorbell rang. There were always new arrivals, someone's second marriage, cousins' fiancées, embarrassed to be taken round the house. I would watch them walking about staring, dressed up for the occasion, always saying the same thing after introducing themselves, sitting down at table, hoping to meet someone nice, helping themselves to a glass of wine. Then there were the new bellies. Someone would pull up her jersey for the others to place a hand on the bulge. And children who hadn't even been born before the previous party – their pushchairs left outside next to the first bicycles – were passed from arm to arm across the dining room. Finally there were those you never saw, who worked far away, and who on the few occasions during the year when they did show up wore jackets, ties, looked at their watches and said *Excuse me*, then disappeared. At Christmas they would arrive with an orange sweater, two-day stubble, and tell everyone how their company was doing, and everyone would look at them open-mouthed except for the odd ignored brother-in-law. And so we would sit down at the table, the volume of conversation having increased because of the aperitifs and the children, the new arrivals seated in safe positions, those who argued seated in strategic points, and the adolescents all together to complain. It would begin with a toast, and my uncle would get to his feet already a little tipsy after the aperitif. Then he would always say *This year, too, we're all together, thank goodness, Merry Christmas*, and everyone clinking their glasses. But Mario was never there.

They treated my grandmother as if she were a widow. One Christmas she even arrived with a man. He was a real widower. She had said he was only a friend who was still a bit sad about his wife's death. She asked us to keep him company. So we took turns sitting beside this sad gentleman. We children were sent forwards by way of consolation, and with us was one of my mother's cousins who had lost her husband and she already knew how to handle this. She talked to him reassuringly and we watched her, she said *One small step at a time, take it calmly*. She used her hands a lot, she seemed like a physiotherapist. She explained what to do, she told him *The first year is the hardest, every anniversary is another death, and then the birthday, her shoes in the house, and learning to do the things that only she did. But then it passes and things get better*, she told him. *The second year you sigh without realizing it, you empty the wardrobes, you cry, but without being surprised by this anymore, only a few icy moments of awareness, but sporadic.* Then, she told him, *with the third year irony comes*. She spoke to him slowly, as if giving him time to memorize the moves. But after that Christmas, my grandmother's friend didn't show up again. And so the following year she went back to being the family widow, sitting unaccompanied among her relatives. Every so often someone would ask her *Why don't you marry again?* but she would wave those words away with one hand as if they were flies above her plate. And when someone mentioned the war everyone would look at her as though she were a war widow – her husband blown up by a landmine, one of those with a cross or a dot inked on the photograph. When they looked at her that way her face would take on a worried look, and for a few moments she would vanish from her own eyes, as if she had left her body on the chair and had gone to cry elsewhere. Shortly afterwards she would return to herself, look out from herself, and would say *They murdered him*, but my mother had already changed the subject.

Changing the subject was pointless. Because everybody knew that he wasn't dead, that he had come back from the war, but that his head had been blown up by a mine. Everybody knew, but I didn't yet, that he was locked up somewhere, that they made him walk in a park, listen to the birds, talk about Russia. The first years had been complete reclusion, then they had let him out, let him take the tram and go into town. And they calmed him down when he was seized by fears, they took him to the river, if he yelled they put him to sleep, his muscles slowly yielding. And if he was good they would let him go out again, take the bus, go to visit his daughter and grandson, and if he was bad they would not let him make telephone calls, *You're not at home for anyone anymore*. And at Christmas they ate cake, there was a tree with lights, the nurses wore red caps, there was music and a man dressed as Father Christmas would raise his glass and say *Are we all here? Well done*.

12

HE REAPPEARED, BUT ONLY FOR AN AFTERNOON, WHEN I WAS seventeen. In the meantime, I had eliminated him, as my mother had, and no-one even mentioned the war anymore. I had also started to say that he was dead, when they asked me about my grandparents, who they were and where they lived. At first I had tried to explain, but it was difficult, they looked at me as if that grandfather were a lie. Then I tried to add details, to sum up, then I stopped. I would say *It doesn't matter, forget it*. I should have talked about the night-time telephone calls, my mother with the nape of her neck against the radiator, and the photographs in the books, the Russian steppe, seeing him without letting my father know, but all these things were grievances. I knew they would not have understood me, they would merely have looked on as I got flustered, and I would have felt ashamed making them think they were right. So I gave up, and saying he was dead was the easiest thing to do. I threw him away, bodily, I threw him on top of the bodies of my friends' grandparents, all piled up together in a discourse that was over by then, and even if he were alive they wouldn't have noticed, another body would have arrived on top shortly afterwards, and another one after that, and after that others again, and even if he had cried out they wouldn't have heard him.

I saw him again one afternoon when I was no longer thinking about him. He was walking along the riverbank with my mother. It was on the days after the rains, the river had overflowed, the water brown and swollen, the branches floating downstream, and along with them tin cans, beer bottles and then a single shoe, its companion arriving a little later, watermelon rinds, and a dead pigeon, all together in a procession of detritus, going all the way, ready to run aground or make the leap. I was on the opposite bank when I saw them. My helmet was already on my head, the visor lowered, my motorbike pushed off its stand. I was about to leave and then I saw them walking close to the wall to avoid getting their feet wet. I followed them from inside the rectangle of my helmet, my eyes only on them and my breath in my ears, watching as the visor condensed up in front of my nose. To see him from up there, Mario was more of a skeleton than ever, his head even bigger, his empty clothes, his long shoes. He threw his feet forwards as if they were anchors and then his legs would follow. But my mother didn't give him her arm, I saw her walking with her hands in her pockets and looking at her feet, her shoulders hunched up in an embarrassment I had seen her express only a few times. I didn't know what to do, join them or leave them to it. After all this time we should have introduced ourselves, or pretended unnaturally that nothing had happened, or sought what we were in our faces, words borrowed from the vocabulary of affection. So I crossed the bridge on my bike, if they had seen me I would have dismounted, I would have said something from inside my helmet, or I would have removed it without turning the engine off. I crossed slowly, I wanted to give them at least a chance to see me as I passed by. Mario raised his head towards the bridge and looked at me, I had stopped behind a queue of cars and had one foot on the ground. I raised my arm, waved it in the air, but he started walking slowly again, and I raced off.

Then I went back home and I found a crowd below the house, a dozen people in front of the door. I left the bike on the other side of the road and crossed, my helmet slipped over his arm. On seeing me arrive, one man left the others and came towards me, with an expression that held fear but was meant to reassure me too. I heard him tell the others *The son is here*, and everyone turned round. He took me by the arm and led me away, and I tried to free myself of his grip, I could hear the yelling. He said to me *They were talking and suddenly your grandfather started to raise his voice, he didn't stop, he hit her*. Then I wriggled free, I ran towards the main gate, and he shouted *Wait*. And so I saw all three of them, Mario, my mother and my father, and the others who were no longer saying anything. They were gazing at the look on my face. My mother was sitting on the pavement, crying, with her head between her hands, staring at the space between her feet, tears dripping and plunging down. She sat there, closed up inside that suffering, watching the drops falling and then exploding on the tarmac one after another. In front of her, standing, was my grandfather, he was looking at his hand, the holes of his eyes, a trembling of the head that wouldn't stop. A man was holding him back, he had almost taken off his jacket. And there was my father who was yelling, and two fellows who were struggling to hold him back too. Suddenly I saw him shrug them off and throw himself at Mario with his hand balled into a fist, and my mother cried out the longest cry, her mouth gaping. And then there were the sirens, the lights flashed against the walls of the house for a while. They took Mario away in a car, in the back seat. My mother remained on the pavement in silence, someone's jacket draped over her shoulders. And there was me. I had sat down beside her, even though I was of no use.

13

AND SO THERE WAS THIS SHEET OF PAPER, FIFTEEN YEARS LATER. *Your mother called, Mario is dead.* In the meantime there had been nothing, only a bruised silence the next day, my parents sleeping separately, as I moved quietly around the house. In the building, too, they didn't talk about it, the others kept their distance from us, partly it was the embarrassment of not knowing what to say, and partly also the risk of contagion. They kept us in quarantine on the sixth floor. If someone was standing in front of the lift I would take the stairs two at a time, leaping up the steps, the light appearing at each floor. When I had to use the lift, everyone would stand against a wall, only offering a greeting on getting in and out, and they slipped inside the building holding their breath and exhaling on leaving. It was as if the one who hampered movements, outside and inside the house, was always Mario, and you had to dodge him every time. But, little by little, that silence had faded, at first only a few phrases, everyday manoeuvres, then the word that rescued everyone, a quip from me, and we all came together again thanks to laughter. This was what happened that time, too, one word and everything got moving again, like when you put a token in a merry-go-round. A sound, a click, and then the lights come on, the music, everything turning again. My mother went back to sleeping with my father, the neighbours started to say hello again, I began racing around on my motorbike once more and got ticked off because I came home late. The cost of that token had been a deprivation, my mother's loss of a father, my loss of a grandfather, not wondering whether it was right or wrong, and the promise not to talk about it ever again.

When I found the note that Sara had left me on leaving and I had read it, I sat down. *Your mother called, Mario is dead*, and further down the extra word *Mario?* with a question mark. I sat still for a bit, my eyes shifting from Sara's note to Mario and from Mario to Sara, and then up and down, up and down, until I felt an intense pain, I bent over against my knees. I ran to the bathroom, just in time, slipping my trousers down to my ankles, then a violent discharge into the toilet bowl. I sat there for a long time, fierce cramps biting into my belly, sweat running down my forehead and between my shoulder blades, pins and needles in my legs. I sat staring at the tiles on the wall, reviewing them, my arms folded over my belly. During the few moments of respite I breathed with relief, and then I shut my eyes again, clenching my teeth. At a certain point I realized that it was coming, a contraction, and I felt it coming slowly. Until with a yell it came out, first one piece then all the rest, Mario's body left in there for fifteen years, the instinct to hold it back and let it go, let it breathe. So I pulled the flush, switched off the light and shut the door. I went out onto the balcony and looked at the sky above the buildings, my hands at my midriff as if I'd just got up and needed to stretch. Then I went back inside, picked up the telephone and dialled my parents' number. It rang for a long time, the ring moving from room to room, seeing if the occupants were at home, warning them that someone wanted them. No-one's at home – please leave a message. On the answering machine there were the voices of my father and mother, they changed the message every month. My mother would make my father go through this torment, to say stupid things together. The recording began, my mother's voice saying *What if we didn't feel like calling you back?* and my father's voice in the background, embarrassed, saying *Come on, not like that, that's not nice*, but then he was interrupted by the beep. I remained silent for a little while, undecided whether to hang up or try and reach them on the mobile. Then I said *Nothing, it's me. It was only to say hello, I'll call you tomorrow.*

I hung up because the grandson of the signora upstairs had been calling me from the balcony for some time. He was yelling *Pietro* as if it were an alarm, maybe it had been recorded on my parents' answering machine, along with my message. When I went out he was making a toy aeroplane fly with his hands. He carried on calling me in automatic mode, without realizing it, my name had become the roar of the aeroplane. I called out to him, shielding my eyes against the sun with one hand. Days before we had made a small pulley that connected the two balconies, a little basket hanging from it in which to put things and make them go up and down along the rope. At first it had been hell, he would call me all the time and send playthings and soft toys down to me. I had to send them up to him again. So one afternoon there was this chairlift of puppets that patiently travelled up and down between the ground floor and the first floor, and after the puppets we moved on to his toothbrush, shoes, tennis balls, his grandmother's mobile. Until his grandmother herself appeared, laid one hand on his head and said *We're going out now*, and to me she said *And you stick up for yourself*. Luckily, after the first days the boy calmed down and only called me now and then. Like that day, in fact, a siren, an aeroplane in his hand and goodness knows what he wanted to send down. So I said *Send it*, he put a sheet of paper in the basket and said *Pull*. When it arrived I saw that there was a photograph inside, and it was of his grandmother and him at the seaside. He was at the water's edge with flippers on. I told him I hadn't thought he had such long feet, he said *They're not my feet, they're flippers*.

He asked me if I had a photograph with my grandmother. I thought about it for a while, I told him I didn't have one, but I did have one of my grandfather. I took one of the photographs of Russia and went outside. Back inside, I put a cross in pen above Mario's head and went back onto the balcony. *The dots are for the missing, the cross for the dead, and those with no mark are the living*. I put the photograph in the basket, and then I told him *Pull*. I watched the basket slowly rising, Mario's funeral.

14

BEFORE BUYING A HOUSE TOGETHER, SARA AND I HAD BUILT a miniature one with scissors and paper. We had tried to imagine how a life together would have been, how much room we would have had. We were still living in separate houses, but every evening she would come with a new piece of furniture and set it on the kitchen table. They were items of paper furniture, light boxes held together with glue and sticky tape. She would take them out of a bag and lay them out, one beside the other, and from then on the rooms gradually came into being. So first of all came the sofa, with blue cushions already in position, and a red armchair beside it. Afterwards, a T.V. table arrived, a carpet and a big bookcase that stretched up to a nonexistent ceiling. Sara would appear, show me the items, placing them at the edge of my plate. I would eat, my glass in front of me, and close to stood the bedroom wardrobe, just as tall, or the desk, four toothpicks for legs. Then all it took was a row to throw everything out of joint. She would take a cupboard, roll it around between her fingers, a tremor, her lips taut with a rancour that always showed itself there. With a sudden outburst and a violent squeeze she would scrunch the cupboard up between her hands. I saw it disappear under that crude pressure, the two doors vanished in a flash. The clothes that until a short time before had only been imaginary were now crumpled, crushed in that furious vice. I looked at her and heard the wood snap, a forest coming down, and I saw the pieces of furniture attempting to save themselves by seeking a way out through her hands. I knew, however, that each of those pieces was me. I was that crushed sofa, and the blue bedside table, and those sounds I heard were bones, the fear I felt when she tossed me in the rubbish basket.

I rediscovered our house in miniature on top of the wardrobe. We had put a cover over it so it wouldn't get dusty. At first, Sara had wanted to keep it on display, on the table near the front door. Every item we bought she would add there, too, she would construct it with paper in the evening. I could hear hear her cutting and colouring, the tearing of the sticky tape. Sometimes she would talk to me with her pencil in her mouth, she seemed as if gagged. Then she would appear, show me what she had done and go to add it to the landscape that we had built day after day. She would bend over our life with cautious and delicate movements, a tenderness entirely in the tips of her fingers, breathing slowly, shifting the bathmat with her fingertips. She would concentrate on only one point, with the firm precision of a surgical procedure in an operating theatre. Then she would straighten up, look at that house of ours inside our house and turn to me. And there was a wholly futile determination and tenderness in that scrupulous construction of an imperfect *matrioska*, in that world of paper, sticky tape and glue – the overly tall bookcase that would sometimes topple over, in the morning we would find it crushed against the floor. In the evenings we would go to sleep and our paper house stayed there, unroofed, the kitchen and bathroom sunk in shadow. There was the faint light of the room that barely touched it, first our two night-lights, then only mine that would stay on until late, and then a click and even in that flat without people night would fall. It remained there on the table in the hall like a flawed manger scene, the manger that would always remain empty, just like that room at the end of the corridor near the bathroom.

It was by chance that I found the miniature apartment on top of the wardrobe. I was looking for an old bag, Sara had gathered them all up there. Every time she would take the stepladder and climb up to fetch one. We had put the paper house in a safe place when the dog arrived, at least to save that from its teeth. But we hadn't really succeeded, we got there too late. And in fact on looking at it now, re-exhumed from under the cover, it looked like a looted house, the armchair eaten, the T.V. set ripped off its table, and even our bed had ended up in the grip of its jaws. It stayed up there like an ancient village clinging to a mountain. I took it down and put it on the kitchen table. I wanted to see the effect it would have on me without Sara. The cover had crushed all the furniture, I straightened it up, blew off the dust. Sitting there, in front of that dilapidated flat, I seemed to go back in time, with Sara still in that house, coming in, opening the windows, letting in some fresh air. I glanced around the rooms like an intruder, it seemed as if I didn't have the right to do so. I ran a finger along the hall to clean it, I stuck a piece of tape on the dishwasher, the piece that was already there was splitting in two. The kitchen had remained exactly as it was, the colours were only a little faded, and in the dining room the red sofa was no longer there. But there was the window and on the window she had written *River*, because every time she had tried to draw it it didn't come out well. The thing that had come out best for her was a small piece of furniture we had put in the hall, on it Sara had also constructed the telephone, but that was peeling off. So I removed it and I put a spot of glue on the little table. While I was holding it, the telephone rang. I let it ring and the answering machine started, *We're not in, leave a message after the beep. Thanks.*

15

OLMO ARRIVED JUST LIKE THAT, SUDDENLY. I FOUND HIM inside the apartment block we had lived in for years, the door half closed, revealing a slice of wary face. He observed me from behind his glasses, lenses so big that they also covered his eyebrows, his lips already prepared to say *I don't need anything,* We looked at each other for a while, without saying anything. I stood on the doormat, and he a little further back, as if I were looking for something through that chink, and the more he saw me looking for something, the more he pushed the door shut. I saw his slice of face become narrower and narrower, first two eyes, then only one, finally only a ray of light that separated the jamb and the door. I had been passing by for days, below that house we had left many years before, and every time I thought of ringing, but didn't. Over the years the building across the street had grown, it had shot up straight, even taller than our house, six or seven floors and a terrace, onto which someone would occasionally emerge. It stood on the other side of the street, stock-still, a facade of mirrored glass, a son grown taller than his father, and with the same upwards thrust and embarrassment at standing there gawking. To see it there, with the building opposite, our house seemed to have aged all at once, a defeated yellow interrupted only by the windows, rust on the railings and metal storage cabinets on the balconies, every so often someone would come out, take out a broom, go back indoors. So now the house stood there definitively vanquished, the mountains in front gone, and in their place there was only that wall of mirrors, the house destined to see itself succumb to time, the yellow to get dirty, the rust to corrode the balconies, and someone sitting inside.

One day I rang the intercom, but then I heard the voice, a gritty voice that said twice *Who is it?* I remained down below without speaking. I sat for a while on the pavement, the place where I used to stay with Mario when he came to pick me up from school, sitting there until my mother said that it was time to go, not to irritate my father, Mario's bones moving into the distance, the sound of sticks beating against sticks. Then a man came out of the street door, his face seemed to belong to the voice I had heard. His gait a struggle, he passed me by, crossing the road with one hand raised to slow the cars. I shouted *Excuse me*, certain that it was him, but he didn't hear me, I shouted *Excuse me* again, but my voice weakened before I got to the end. He had stopped under the tram shelter, he got on the first one and then he was gone. In his place there was a girl talking on her mobile, and after that a bus and even she was gone too. So I went back to the intercom, I rang my bell with two letters above it separated by a full stop, and from inside there emerged the same gritty voice as before, again *Who is it?* And I looked at the little holes in the intercom and right after that the tram shelter. There was that voice that came out, as if the man who had crossed the road had left it at home before going out.

One day I finally went in, a young woman with a pushchair was coming out of the street door, I held it open for her, then I slipped up the stairs. And there was that smell, still the same after all the years, most of the names and surnames had vanished from the bells and yet that smell had survived all the losses. When I rang my doorbell, he was in the house, he opened the door only a little, and poked his face out. Once again he said to me *Who is it?* looking at my shoes, as if he thought he couldn't be seen, lurking there behind the gap in the door. I told him that when I was a boy I used to live there with my parents. I told him this in a quiet voice, reassuring him with my expression, not putting my hands in my pockets, and he opened the door only to get a better look at me. He ran his eyes over my entire body, he looked for my truth in my clothes, to trust my socks or not, the crease in my trousers, and I had instinctively rolled up my shirt sleeves, a button missing on one cuff. We stayed for a long time in that position, as I told him that once I used to live in that building, with the mountains in front of it, and his trust of me came and went. With trust the door would open a little, then close a little again, triangles of house appeared and then disappeared, the peg with a hat on it, the mirror, a telephone on a little table, and all of it blocked by Olmo. Then the door of the neighbouring flat opened, a young man in slippers came out, a tattoo along his neck. He asked *Everything O.K.?* He looked Olmo straight in the eye and he said *Of course* and flushed, saying *He's a friend, he's come to visit me*. Then the guy looked me straight in the eye, to check if this was true, before taking his slippers and tattoo back into his house. And when the neighbour's door closed Olmo smiled at me and said *Would you like to come in?*

So I saw my house explode in a few moments, the flat turned upside down by renovation, and where my room had been there was now a bathroom, and the kitchen was no longer in its place, there was a living room that had taken a piece of another room. I roamed around that flat looking for my old house behind the walls. I didn't find it, and felt a kind of death rattle inside. I was there as if before the body of a dead relative, recomposed inside the mortuary, looking at him and not recognizing him, feeling him really die for the first time under my gaze. Olmo stood still in a corner of the entrance, next to the clothes peg, he made himself as small as possible to counter my dismay, his expression that of someone apologizing for being there, as if it were still my house. Then he opened the window for me. We went out on the balcony, and I finally breathed. We leaned our elbows on the balustrade, and I gazed up. We were reflected in the mirrored glass of the building opposite. Olmo said *Look*, and pointed to us with an outstretched arm.

Before Olmo, that house had been occupied by a couple. They were the ones who had renovated it. Olmo told me this to justify himself, spreading his arms out a little, and I pointed to the bathroom and said *My bed was there in the corner*. In the middle of the kitchen I said *Here there was a broom cupboard*, then pointing at the building on the other side of the road I said *the mountains*. He followed me docilely from room to room, then he stopped, his eyes behind those large spectacles. He stared at things to follow their transformation. But every time he would say *I don't understand anything now*, I saw him shake his head in vexation. And so his kitchen remained his kitchen, and on the building in front the snow didn't fall, and no matter how hard he tried, my fridge and the gas rings my mother cooked on did not appear in his bedroom. In the end Olmo roamed around the house ill at ease, even a little fear in his eyes, that other house hidden below, walled up alive inside his own walls. I said *Here we would have breakfast on Sunday mornings*, and *My father would sit on the balcony with his feet against the balustrade, and my mother and me on the sofa*, and suddenly those presences came out of the walls, my mother, my father, and me as a child, all sitting round the kitchen table, or on the sofa, looking at the view. Olmo couldn't see us but he heard us, like someone walking on the floor above. We went in and out of the walls, we passed through them, and he ran his gaze all over, he turned suddenly, but he didn't find anyone. In the end I told him *But it's really nice like this, too,* and he looked at me with a smile that was also something of a plea, to leave him the house in which he lived. Then my mother, my father and me as a child got up from the kitchen table, all lined up, and went back inside the walls. And Olmo said *Thanks, you're very kind.*

He offered me a coffee, he wanted us to drink it right there, at the kitchen table. He prepared it carefully, carrying out each step as if it were for the first time, the water up to the safety valve, then the coffee: tamp it down, put the pot on the ring, light the flame, turn the heat down to minimum, adjust the coffee pot above the gas, to avoid burning the handle. When he sat down, he said *When my wife was alive she used to make it,* and pointed to a little glass display cabinet, behind it was a photograph of a lady. He used to sit there on purpose, to be able to see his wife and the television at the same time. He spoke quietly when he spoke about his wife, lowering his voice as if it were a secret. He said *In fact my coffee isn't good*, then he got up and took away the cups, a widower once more. When he came back he added *And we didn't have children.* Suddenly the kitchen was filled with a violent light, Olmo said *It's seven o'clock*, and without turning round he pointed at the building with mirror glass. I looked at my watch, it was seven, the sun struck the hour against the facade, the collision, and then the ray crossed the road, passed high above the cars stopped at the traffic light, above the lampposts, it pierced the window, spreading out against Olmo's kitchen. But all it took was a few minutes and the shadow returned, and the light flowed outside like water when a dyke is opened.

16

OLMO DIDN'T SLEEP WELL AFTER MY FIRST VISIT. HE TOLD ME a few days later on the telephone. That afternoon we had taken our leave with a little embarrassment, he said *Don't disappear*, and then he closed the grille of the lift, his fingers poking through the metal mesh. Before pressing the button I told him *This is still a bit my house, however,* and I looked at his face divided up by the mesh, each square a piece of a smile. When I pressed the button for the ground floor, the cage made a sharp sound and pulled away, it plunged down abandoning itself to gravity, trusting in the resistance of the cables, with me closed inside. Olmo raised one hand as the lift began the descent, his farewell stuck in the air, watching me sink down. I also raised one arm, I repeated *Bye.* Shortly after, I heard his door close behind him, a thud and four turns of the lock. The ground floor came suddenly, too quickly, my first journey alone in the lift of that building. With my mother that descent had always seemed so long, five floors to finish getting dressed. I would enter still half-dressed, and she would get a little more irritated with every passing floor, shoving my jersey forcefully into my trousers, buttoning them up, threatening me through clenched teeth *If you don't get up earlier tomorrow,* and fretting with the zip, getting my underpants or my T-shirt stuck in the middle of it. By the end of the descent we would always be on time, a hand run through my hair a second before the lift stopped. And both of us would emerge impeccably dressed. She would cup her hand and I would slip mine into hers, and we would say *Good morning* if someone was waiting to go up.

When I left the building, after that first meeting with Olmo, there was a woman outside speaking into the intercom, she turned round in all directions and said *Look, there's no young man here.* She was a small woman, seventy or so and a lampshade of grey hair on her head, all backside and spectacle frames. She was standing still beneath the intercom, looking at it with a beseeching, almost desperate air, she said *Bear with me, but I really have to go now.* I had found her there, on leaving the building, she was leaning against the wall, I could hear Olmo's voice coming down saying *Take a better look, try a bit harder.* And when she saw me her eyes opened wide behind her glasses, she yelled *Here he is,* dragging me bodily under the jet of her voice. Then she went away almost at a run, her backside and her bag jiggling beside it, and he said to me from the intercom that I had left my wallet in the house, he would put it in the lift. Then he gave a yell from up there, shouting *Press the button,* the cables began to run upwards, and shortly afterwards the lift cage came down by itself. He had put the wallet inside a bread bag, closed with an elastic band. I returned his shout up the stairs, *Got it,* my yell went up flight after flight, and a *Come back soon* came back down to me.

I showed up before ten days had even gone by. In the meantime he had called me two or three times, always at the same time, half past seven. All he said to me was *Hi* and then he would keep quiet, he wanted to see if I recognized him. Knowing that I had lived in the house was making him have strange dreams, there were lots of people, he would find them all in the shower, and also in the glass display cabinet, all in their own frames, near the one with his wife. That's why he asked me about my mother and father, the jobs they did, their characters, but above all their measurements, height and weight, in order to try to insert them in those spaces, and when I had said that my mother was a petite, slim woman he had replied *Just as well*. In the background of Olmo's telephone calls there was always the sound of the television, low but constant, and if he kept quiet it would carry on, occasionally he would silence it, he would say *Keep quiet*, and switch it off with the remote. The calls always finished suddenly, never after eight, and he would hang up saying *Goodnight*. So when I went back to visit him we already knew each other a bit better. The first time, he came to meet me at the bus stop, he was standing there in the shelter and when he saw me he raised a hand in greeting. Perhaps he did this also to be recognized, out of fear of seeing me get off the tram and walk straight on. So when I arrived in front of him he smiled at me, offered me his hand, and I drew him into a hug. He made just a hint of resistance, but only out of virility. Alongside us there was a woman, she said *Good day Olmo, how's things?* He gave a rather embarrassed smile, he said *Hello Rosa, let me introduce my grandson*. The lady shook my hand, she looked at my face seeking some resemblance, then she said *What a strapping young man*, albeit with a little puzzlement. Olmo held me back by one arm, he told me *The world is full of nosey parkers, they want to know everything*. Then we walked over the road, he stopped in the middle of the zebra crossing, looked at me and asked *Does it offend you if I say you're my grandson?*

17

THE FIRST TIME MY MOTHER ENTERED MY HOUSE AFTER
Mario's death I had to tell her that Sara didn't live there anymore,
that we had left each other. We were standing in front of the door,
and she scanned my face, I saw her eyes run all over me, piece by
piece, to check whether everything was still all there, hair, forehead,
ears, nose, mouth, and then go back to look me in the eye – she
smiled, everything was all there. She merely said *Yes*, and looked
down because she didn't want me to see all the things that were
inside her, sadness for me, the worry about having to tell my father
that evening, a grandchild gone up in smoke, and that relief a
mother cannot confess to. Only Sara wasn't there in that face of
hers, in an instant she had ceased to be her daughter-in-law, despite
the bond there had been between them. Then she looked up again
and there was no longer anything there, only a caress to claim her
rights as a mother. So she went indoors and pretended that nothing
had happened, all she said was *It's a bit untidy*, and sat down in the
kitchen. I could sense her behind me as I was making the coffee,
looking at my back, the nape of her neck resting against the wall.
Then I told her about school, the children, but the conversation
died out by itself, no-one was interested. In the silence you could
hear the grandson of the signora on the floor above. They had given
him roller skates. Loud rolling and suddenly a thump and nothing
else, we looked up at the ceiling.

Before leaving, my mother left me a metal box, an enormous tin,
it looked like one of those you use to keep biscuits in, but much
bigger. She shoved it against my chest when she was already at the
door, all she said was *Your grandfather*, as if his ashes were inside.
Then I went back inside, washed the cups, sat down where she had

been and opened the box. Inside, there was a bit of everything, buttons, medals, coins, a cast of his teeth, a watch stopped at ten past nine, a pair of glasses with only one lens, shoelaces, a trouser belt. In a transparent envelope, there was his wedding ring, inside which the date 5–3–1941 was engraved. And there were other photographs of Russia, different from the usual ones. In the photographs there was Mario in shorts, a soldier, in the middle of a group of women and children, he was the only one who was smiling, his arms stretched out over the others, all of them under his wing. In the background, the steppe, and a few huts to interrupt the plain. These photographs were almost all the same, the same women, the same children with serious expressions. Inside the box there was also a yellow folder, with X-rays. I took them out and immediately put them away again, the ghost of Mario's skull frightened me, I saw it light up against the window, appearing in the middle of the kitchen. I didn't have the courage to look at the others, I closed up all his bones in the folder, and put them back inside the box.

That evening I went to bed with a booklet I had taken out of the box. It was a brown pamphlet, damaged by time and wear and tear. The title was *This is how you say it in Russian*. It had been printed in September 1941, and it was given to the soldiers who went off to war. On the first page there was an introduction, it said *If it is not excessively presumptuous on our part we would like to dedicate this booklet to the heroic troops of Fascist Italy who on the Eastern front are writing pages of imperishable glory in the struggle for civilization and Europe.* Then it went on: *To our Officers and Soldiers, above all we would be pleased, in this historic moment, if this practical manual of Russian nomenclature and conversation were of some use, helping them – on occasional contact with the populations freed from the yoke of Bolshevism – to understand and make themselves understood*. The feeble light of my bedside lamp obliged me to hold the book very close to my nose, even the ink had faded over time. Upstairs, the signora's grandson had stopped roller skating, the ceiling hadn't collapsed and, judging by the silence, they had gone to bed. The booklet opened by itself at page 34, because there was one of Mario's photographs with the crosses and the dots, lying crosswise between the pages. *The dots are for the missing, the cross for the dead, and those with no mark are the living.* As usual, except for him, the others were dead. So, sunk in my bed, in the semi-darkness of that feeble light, I read the exercises on page 34 of the Russian manual for *Officers and Soldiers*. They were phrases to be learned by heart, to be used on the Eastern front to communicate with the Russians. *Which are the finest buildings in the city?* the soldiers sent to wage war were supposed to say. And then *In this gallery there are many famous pictures and many beautiful statues. Is there an entry fee? Are there important sights to see in this city? Go straight on along this street until the fourth intersection. Is the riverside far away? Take the number 50 tram to get there.*

18

AT FIRST, I SAID NOTHING EITHER TO MY MOTHER OR FATHER about the fact that every so often I would go into that house. I would go to visit Olmo on the quiet, I would always get off at the stop after my parents' one, then I would hurriedly cross. I would reach the other side of the road almost without breathing. I tried not to think of my father sitting on the balcony, of all the time he stayed there, of the risk of him seeing me from up there. When I got to the door to the building, every time I hoped that Olmo would reply quickly, just to hear the click of the door, not to have to shout out my name in reply to his *Who is it?* Once inside, I would start breathing again, with the street remaining outside and with me inside Olmo's home, a bit exhausted already. I would sit down in his kitchen, the television on, the photograph of his wife always in the same place. And the afternoon would pass that way, in my old house, but surreptitiously. Olmo would talk and I would keep an eye on the time. I tried to make sure that my mother's visit to the supermarket or my parents' strolls did not coincide with the moment in which I set foot outside again. But every time it was the same challenge to fate, to say goodbye to Olmo hurriedly, go down in the lift and out into the street. It was my Russian roulette, to get away with it or meet them in a random accident of fate, to get away or bump into them on my way out of the door.

Once I met my mother on the tram as I was going to Olmo's. I felt a tap on my shoulder, and there she was, smiling at me, she stretched out her neck to give me a kiss. I looked at her, shut my eyes to receive her kiss, and inside I hid all my embarrassment, sitting on top of my lie. When I opened them again she took a medical report out of her bag as if it were nothing and handed me a sheet of paper with lab test results on it, *Your father's heart* she told me. She had the look of someone who wants to hear *It's not that bad*. I ran my finger over those figures, one after another, then I gave her back the sheet. I said *Come on, it's not that bad*. She smiled and said *Indeed*, then I turned round, I turned my back on her. We crossed a bit of the city that way, one behind the other, the tram jolting on the tracks, over the points, my mother talking incessantly. I felt her blowing in my ear, telling me about my father, his pension, and the pains in her feet, the massages he would give her as they watched the television. She talked quietly, her mind straying in the spaces between one word and the other. She was talking and yet she was also looking outside, she would break off in the middle of a sentence and then pick it up again. And in those empty spaces between her words there passed the buildings, the pavements, the advertising hoardings, and the people standing at the stops, and the cars speeding alongside us. There was one with a black cocker spaniel at the window of the passenger seat, a woman sitting alone in the back. Then my mother rested her chin on my shoulder, her head appeared next to mine, I felt its warmth. After many years I was giving back to her the shoulder she had given me, my chin resting on her many times of an afternoon, on the same tram. And from there behind me she said *What a nice surprise, your coming to visit us.* So we got off at the stop before, and when I arrived at Olmo's house, an hour after the time I had arranged, he asked *Did you forget about me?*

So I started dropping in on my mother when I went to Olmo's. Sometimes I would go before, more often after, three blocks on foot and then in through the door to their building I would sit there with them, a half-hour, sometimes for dinner, always with the fear that they would smell the old house on me – my mother who at every smell would wrinkle her nose and follow it until she could give it a name. I would sit there, with the temptation to tell, but I didn't say anything, out of fear of spoiling everything for them, too, knocking down the walls of memory. So I continued to keep quiet about those afternoons, and about Olmo, our two cups always ready on the tray, and the coffee pot on the ring, which he would light as soon as I came in. Then one day when I dropped in to see them, my mother asked me to help her fold the sheets. We spread them out in the dining room. I pulled from one side and she from the other, the sheets opening as if someone were about to throw himself off a building. When I was a little boy I used to jump inside them too, she and my father holding the sheet at either end. Every sheet was

63

the same choreography, that great dance for two, opening out and folding, then opening out and folding again, until we came together, united. I would let go of the sheet and my mother would take it and put it away. At the last sheet she held me by the hand, my face a few centimetres from hers, she asked me *Are you hiding something from me?* And only an hour before Olmo had shown me a photograph of his, in it was a young man who was laughing, he had said *Did you know I was in Russia?* Then he had added *This photograph was before, after Russia I stopped laughing.*

19

OLMO AND MY MOTHER ONCE CAME ACROSS EACH OTHER AT the foot of the building, late one afternoon. I was still on the tram when I saw her, I had just got up, the time to press the button for the next stop and head for the door to get off. My mother was a few metres from her door, her bicycle chained to a pole and she was standing to put her handbag in the basket, tucking it up like a baby in a cradle. There was a moment in which she raised her head, I was framed in the tram window, I looked at her, my face against hers on the other side of the street. But she didn't see anything, her eyes were entirely inside her thoughts, the tram passed by without her even noticing. I saw her get on the bicycle, adjust her skirt on the saddle, give a push with her foot, and finally lift her feet onto the pedals and take off. She went along the pavement for a while, towards Olmo's house, while I arrived at the stop, unsure whether to get off or carry on. Then with a puff the tram doors opened and four of us got off, me, two girls with piercings on their bellies and a fat lady who stepped off backwards, clinging to the rail and lowering herself onto the street the way you get into a swimming pool. Then when the tram set off again, Olmo was standing at the door on the other side of the road, his hands in his pockets, looking first one way and then the other, my mother approaching with her usual pedalling style, four thrusts before letting the bike go. Olmo saw me when I was about to cross, standing at the traffic light, half-concealed by two pedestrians. So he took one hand out of his pocket, raised his arm, a greeting and also a sign that he was coming to meet me. My mother had to dodge him, a sudden wide swerve, I saw the fear in her face, one hand on her bag to prevent it falling from the basket.

In the meantime Olmo's house was becoming Russia. All you had to do was ask him one question and he wouldn't stop talking. At first it was only a map, then every time I returned there was one more hanging from the wall, the kitchen walls gradually vanishing as Russia made room for itself inside the house. He took the first map from a cupboard and spread it out on the kitchen table. With the tip of a pencil he showed me the route he had taken to return home, he would constantly repeat *It was so cold*, and he joined his hands over his mouth and blew on them to warm them up, despite the heat of the house. Then he asked me to stay to dinner with him, the map left open on the table, and he said *Anyway we can carry on later*. So we set the table on top of it, plates, glasses, cutlery, and the two of us sitting down to eat in the middle of the steppe, the enemy lines on the far bank of the river, the Don flowing between, protected and waiting, ready to fire, one evening almost seventy years ago. As we were eating, somebody rang the doorbell, Olmo got to his feet to open. His tail wagging, a dog came into the kitchen, short paws and a heavy backside. Immediately after, a girl entered holding a plate. She was under thirty, dark hair shaved very short. She came into the kitchen in her flip-flops, springing back on her heels, a gecko tattoo ran up from her ankle towards her calf.

65

Olmo asked her if she wanted a glass of wine, she replied *Thanks, but Sandro's waiting for me.* The girl looked at me, without turning her face. And then she asked *Who's he?* pointing at me with her finger. Olmo said *He's Pietro, he used to live in this house.* In the meantime the dog had gone out onto the balcony, and it was barking furiously, its muzzle between the bars, angry at seeing itself on the other side of the street between the railings, the same as Olmo's. The girl laid a plate covered in tin foil on the table, she said *Enjoy your meal*, and added *If you need anything at all we're at home.* Then she called the dog, which walked past us swinging its backside behind it, and shortly after that the door closed, and we heard the one next door open and bang shut right away.

We cleared the plates away, liberated Russia from the breadcrumbs. A red sauce stain had spread out in the middle of the countryside. Olmo tried to clean it with a sponge, the red spread out all over, blood spilled in the middle of the steppe. Then he resumed his march with the pencil – a little graphite soldier struggling to walk amid the white, each stride a sharp blow made with the pencil point against the map, risking making a hole in it every time. By the end of the evening there was an anthill of black dots, all the soldiers who had passed by there, including Mario. I looked for him in the midst of the group, he was one of those dark points. And many died in the snow. They had been shot in the head, others were left on the road, frozen, others had gone mad. He came home, but only with his body.

20

SOMETIMES OF AN EVENING I WOULD LISTEN TO THE TAPES OF
the sounds I had made with Sara. I would lie down on the couch,
switch off the lights, and stay there listening to the holidays sweep
by. We kept them in an album, one C.D. for every trip, with dates
and destinations written on them. At first, Sara felt embarrassed at
being recorded. She would talk as if she were holding a conference,
she would say *Before us stands Mont Blanc, On the right, Lake
Trasimeno stretches out*, she would say *Motorway tollbooth, Vehi-
cle* and *A short break*, then she would start to laugh and say *I can't
stand that machine any longer*. But gradually she got used to it and
no longer noticed it. The first trips were all about talking over each
other, confidences, interruptions, then laughing and arguing, and I
would always want to drive. Sara would sing and I would complain
that she didn't know the songs. When we stopped at a motorway
café we would leave the tape recorder on guard inside the car. You
could hear car doors banging and afterwards this uncertain silence
unfolding, scraps of conversation from passers-by, someone parking alongside, a lorry manoeuvring and the background noise of
the motorway. Until the doors opened again, and it was us. Over
time the journeys changed. The trip in which we were happiest was
Brittany, at times we would talk, first a lot then nothing at all, Sara
would say *Look*, when there were windmills, and we would open
the windows to let in the ocean, it howled in unison with the
wind. And then there were those half-hours without words, with
only the sound of the rain on the car roof, and she would sing a
song, but not too loud, looking out at France as it passed by. On
the last trips we almost always forgot to record, or we would
switch the machine on and leave it in the car, whole days of nothing
but traffic. Of Berlin I had only the recording from the hotel

balcony, with me calling Sara repeatedly. She had gone down to the bar, but hadn't told me. The last C.D. was a trip to Austria, a silence wholly different from that of Brittany. Sara had stopped singing by then.

For weeks Sara had been leaving messages on the answering machine in which she didn't say a word. I would come home, sit down in the armchair, and listen to them until a beep interrupted her silences. Often she would stay there breathing into the handset, a long breath that poured into my house. I had no clue where she lived, only that it was a fourth-floor flat, with a telephone number, lots of light and not much room. After every message she left I would try to reconstruct that space. At times she would walk, her steps coming towards me, then she would sit down on the chair, shift it and make it creak, then she would clear her throat and say nothing. Her telephone must have been in the kitchen, she would call me and after the beep she would start cooking, water in the pot, gas sputtering on the ring, and the table being set, the glass, the cutlery, and then the guillotine of the time expired, two beeps, *You have no new messages.* The only times I heard her voice was when her mobile rang in the background, she would say *Hello* and then the line would go dead, a conversation cut off sharply. Just as I was beginning to see her house I was left at the door. And once a storm broke, I heard it explode in her kitchen, reach as far as me, the windows banging, her voice yelling *Enough,* as if it were sufficient to shout to calm the sky, and then she burst into endless sobbing, at first desperate, afterwards only a moan floating amid the thunderclaps. But the next message held a defenceless silence, and the windows were open again. There was a tree nearby, the birds were chirping in the kitchen, and two women were looking out and talking, one said *It was like a bombardment.*

*

One day she asked me to meet up. A message on the machine in curt and worried tones, *I need to see you*. In the background bells were ringing, three peals and then Sara hung up. Beep, and her side of the city closed up. All that remained was me, sitting in the armchair looking at that black box from which voices emerged. I called her back, certain I wouldn't get hold of her. And in fact no-one was there, I let the telephone ring. There was only the giddiness of entering her house treacherously and spying, each sound was information dictated in code: the dishes still to be washed, the dressing gown hanging up in the bathroom, the bed hurriedly made, and all the books she was reading left open around the house, sitting like butterflies on the furniture. And then the big box in which she had collected all her shoes. I stood looking at it for a while, in the middle of the hall, as the telephone rang inside the house, those interwoven feet, the soles, the heels submerged by other heels, and many shoes again on top, thrown one on top of the other as if in a common grave. When the ring of the telephone returned, empty-handed, the answering machine cut in, and I said *It's me*, then I started sneezing, I couldn't stop, I hung up.

21

THE MORE I WENT TO SEE OLMO, THE MORE HE TALKED ABOUT Russia and the dead, and the more I would end up in dreams that made me wake up with a yell. I only realized I was safe when I heard a car go by in the street. In the evenings I would go to sleep already condemned, I would get into bed the way you sleep in prison, I would lower my eyelids and hear the warder's keys turning, his steps fading. Then I would stay alone in the deepest darkness, lying down, behind my closed eyelids, trying to fight off sleep, to resist it by putting other thoughts before it, the faces of my pupils on holiday, the mothers who would come to pick them up at school over the year. I would call the roll, beg them all to stand around my bed and not let me sleep, talk to me, form a barrier against the sleep I felt coming on. Then suddenly I would see them fall silent and stand aside, pulling away from the bed together, turning and leaving, the mothers holding their children by the hand. From far off I saw a tide of people, all with holes on the right and left sides of their noses, I would see the tide rise more and more, until it reached the foot of my bed. In front of them all there was always Mario, his blind man's face gaping in the emptiness, he would come close and and say in my ear *We're a bit cold.* Then I felt them slip under the blankets, they would pile up everywhere, between my feet, thousands of them, they climbed up on me, I could feel them clambering up on my face, hanging on to my ears, walking on my eyes, and the first who went into my mouth would make me yell with all the breath I had in my body.

I started seeing Olmo almost every day, his was a presence I kept inside me from morning time, it followed me through the city. He was still a secret, my mother would call me every so often when I was with him and I wouldn't tell her where I was. Then, on the telephone in the evenings, I would invent my day, since Sara had left my mother wanted to know my every move. Every time, it was a torment, keeping silent. But then we began to talk about it, inventing a game, I became a son again and she a mother. One evening I said to her *Do you know I see your father now and then?* She started to laugh, I heard her blowing into the handset, she asked me *And is he well?* I told her *Of course.* So at times she was the one to bring up the subject, she would say *Do you still see Mario?* And I would talk to her about Olmo and his house, without telling her it was the very place we had lived in for years. But I would tell her about his kitchen, about his wife who was dead, and the cups with the gilded handles, the stories of the dead frozen in the middle of the snow, the tank that had almost run over him but hadn't killed him, the chaplain who was the last man to tell the corpses things about God. He was an imperfect Mario, Mario who had returned after his imprisonment at the end of the war while Olmo almost died returning home on foot. My mother listened without saying a word, these never-ending telephone calls slipping directly inside the night. My father, around one in the morning, would take the telephone from her only to say hello. *You talk, I'm going to bed*, and his voice was that of someone who had already fallen asleep several times in front of the television. Then she would take the telephone again and talk more quietly, a delicate breath, we would carry on with this game that amused and frightened her. Once she told me that Mario had never said anything to her about what had happened to him over there, when he came back everyone thought he had died. Then she added *He talked about Russia without saying anything, and then would immediately start to weep*. So on the telephone I would talk at length, filling Mario with Olmo's words, I poured them out a few at a time, very slowly so that they wouldn't spill over, my mother in silence, I knew she was in the kitchen, the light on above the rings, sitting on the floor with her legs tucked up under her dressing gown, the back of her neck against the radiator.

In the meantime every day in Olmo's kitchen there was a map that hadn't been there before. Little by little the room became the steppe, an expanse of map divided into millimetres spread out to the south of Russia. When I went in I would find him busy hanging up the maps on some part of the wall. He would take a few steps back to get an overview, then turn towards me already blind, his face caved in, his eyeballs sunk inside his head. Every map was different, some were small, others instead took up half the wall, there were dozens of them, goodness knows where they had been kept hidden. He would hang them on the wall methodically, systematically covering what had been there before, the framed views of Salerno and Otranto, Saint Peter's lit up at night. Olmo rolled the maps out on top of them like a blanket over a blaze. I watched the room disappear, swallowed up, piece by piece, by that obsession. Until there was nothing left but the window and one map, Olmo took it out of the little cupboard next to his bed and asked me to give him a hand putting it up. And so we pasted over the last hole, too. I stood on a chair in my socks and he showed me the place to bang the nail in, a bit further to the right, a bit more to the left. The map unfurled downwards like a rolling shutter, I got off the chair and went towards the door still in my socks, and turned the light on the Russia of 1943.

22

SARA DIDN'T WANT TO COME IN, BUT ONLY TO RING, TO PRESS her finger on the intercom to realize she no longer lived there, her name removed with the haste with which you free a house of a dead body. I went out through the door onto the street and Sara turned, I said *Here I am* so as not to have to touch her. All the rest was walking along the riverside, hands in pockets, hers in her jacket and mine in my trousers. There was us two and our reflections on the water, a metre away from us. Seagulls, flying high at first, suddenly plunged down against the river. I saw them vying for the water, initially watching it from high up, tracing vague curves, picking a point and then plunging down, attacking, tucking their wings alongside their breasts, piercing the air in between metre by metre. There was a moment in which above us, high over the water, a flock gathered, twenty or thirty seagulls flying in a circle, forming spirals. They looked down from under their wings and waited for the moment to come. Sara had looked up to see where that darkness had come from, like a cloud set crosswise between men and the sun. And when she saw they weren't clouds but seagulls she was afraid, she narrowed her eyes and said to me *What do they want?* I looked at her first, then at the air above us. But there was no longer enough time to say anything, the flock launched itself against our two silhouettes reflected in the water. They came down like a single falling body, they swooped on our figures mirrored in the water, and all together they began to strike our faces, to peck our eyes out of their sockets, one peck at a time until they were emptied, filling the river with foam. One of the seagulls vomited, and then they all went away, just as they had come. All that remained was that yellow stain, which continued to shimmer for a while.

Then we saw a group of people, a few women, a girl and a little boy. They were all standing against the railings, looking down. The boy had climbed up, his mother kept one hand on his back, while he leaned over. He was pointing at the water, yelling *Down there*, thrusting his arm forwards. One of the ladies saw us passing, she said *Excuse me*, and when she saw our faces, and all the pain inside them, it was too late to withdraw. So she repeated *Excuse me*, but in a completely different way. Then Sara smiled and asked her *What's going on?* pointing at the boy who was hanging on to the railings and yelling. The lady took courage, she said *Nothing, a trifle, but we wanted to know if you could see it, too.* So we looked over, alongside the boy who was still yelling and waving his arms. On the bottom of the river you could see a bicycle, mud covering one wheel, and fish swimming above it. Sara said *Down there* too. It was a woman's bicycle, new, a green frame and a wicker basket, the sunlight slipping into the water made a pedal shine. It was lying

73

on the bottom, almost in the middle of the river, the boy turned towards me and asked *Where did it fall from?*

Sara and I sat down on the bank a hundred metres further on, our legs dangling, my feet a few centimetres from the water, Sara's a little higher up. And we sat there without knowing what language to use, no longer able to talk about what we had invented, suddenly finding ourselves inside Italian. We spoke with rented words and used them like that, to move from one point to another. But we were ready to give them back once the conversation was over, to see them return to the shelves like empty ice skates. And I told her about Mario, that written question she had left in the house after taking everything else away. I told her who he was, a summary that was rather rushed, for fear of hearing her say what she had come to tell me. And so I told her about the clinic, the war, Russia, those visits at school when I was little, and the skeleton. And then my father's punch and the police sirens, my mother's wail, and the silence that followed. As I talked, Sara was looking at her hands, our tempo was that of the rowers who were following the river, the cox's rhythmic shouts, the panting, and the oars moving the river a little further backwards with every stroke. I told her that now my mother went to the cemetery every day, I often used to see her bicycle tied to one of the poles at the entrance, its basket holding the leaves that had fallen off the bunch of flowers. And once I had seen her come out and she was more beautiful. She had tied her hair back and had set off, standing up on the pedals. But Sara had stopped listening to me, I saw her eyes disappear, and where I was seeing my mother pedalling on the water she was seeing something else, and in the middle of my sentence she broke in abruptly. She told me *I'm pregnant*, and there was no need to say that it wasn't by me.

*

First I heard the piercing shrieks of the seagulls, ferocious, and after that a sudden silence, like the roof of a school that had fallen in. And then only the water, the cox's rhythm, and an oarsman who was saying that he, on Sunday, was going to give up if they didn't win, he was going stop his training, it's not worth it, all that effort, ruining your hands, for what?

23

TOGETHER WITH SARA I WAITED FOR THE TRAM. WE STOOD there, looking at the end of the street, hoping that every tram to appear from round the bend would have the right number. There we were, our faces pretending that nothing had happened, crouched inside us two different feelings, guessing the arrival of the tram by the electricity sizzling on the wires. I wasn't going to ask her anything and wouldn't have done, either to know the father's name or when the baby would be born. There I was with all my imperfection, not functioning and finally having proof of that. And we said nothing to each other, Sara with her full belly and I feeling as if I had a hole in mine, like the first hole made in a wall, with the bricklayer's face appearing on the other side. I stood motionless at the tram stop and I felt like covering myself with both hands, for fear that someone might slip an arm into that hole, that a passing child would look inside it, like a lion leaping through a ring of fire. For her part, Sara was quite the opposite, her body doubled at a stroke, with two feet poking at her inside, as if searching for the way. There were two of them, before me, and hands and eyes that were taking shape, I against the wall and they lined up in front of me, the cannon and the ball that had come out of it to pass through me. Then the tram arrived, first the current running through the wires, then the orange front with the number 15 above it. And Sara got on and went to sit down between two ladies, one of them smiled at her and removed her bag from the seat. Sara crossed her arms and didn't look at me, the doors closed, and when the tram moved off she had the look of someone bearing a secret.

On returning home I found a man there, he was standing in the middle of my garden as if it were the most natural place to be. A pile of rubble, green boots, a cigarette freshly lit. We looked at each other like two intruders, he had come from behind the wall of the house to the back of my home, it began where my garden ended. He said *The signori next door want to open up two big windows, after many years of darkness.* On the other side of the hole you could see a section of house, a basketball hoop, a television, a table-football game, a long table, chairs. Everything was covered by large nylon tarpaulins, like bodies of dead furniture. Then another workman appeared, he too climbed down into my garden, he offered me a calloused hand and said *Pleased to meet you.* He said that if there were any problems I should talk to the *signori next door,* but they were on holiday in the Balearic Islands. And so I went inside, and all day long I heard them hammering away loudly, my windows shook, the bricks of the wall falling down a piece at a time. I stood behind the window, I could hear the workmen occasionally saying something, answering the telephone, stopping for a smoke, sitting down on my chairs. I looked at my flowers, the rubble falling ruinously on top of them. Every time, the men would turn round, see me standing still on the other side of the window and shrug their shoulders, then they went back to smashing the wall with their pickaxes.

At six o'clock they went away, they clambered into the hole, I saw them disappear, swallowed up by the wall, and the wall would have given them back the next morning. I imagined them getting changed and going off, coming out of the door of that house, in the street parallel to mine. Before leaving, they covered up the holes in the wall, they sutured them with sheets of nylon. Late in the evening I went out into the garden, the sheet flapping in the wind like the sail of a moored boat. I walked among the debris, the rubble scrunching under my soles, and bent over to see how the flowers were, I removed them from beneath the stones and put them inside a black bin bag. Then I went out into the street, tossed them in the skip – early in the morning the dustcart would pass, with its reverse and motion alarm, a thump, and then it would set off again before stopping a little further on.

24

OLMO KEPT ALL THE PHOTOGRAPHS OF RUSSIA IN THE wardrobe in his bedroom. There was a door, the last one on the side of the window, behind which he kept that entire piece of life. For some time that place had been a secret. He would wait until I turned round, for my telephone to ring, and when I turned to look at him again there would be something that hadn't been there a few seconds before. I didn't ask, he didn't say anything, but on the bed there was a book, a medal for valour, a photograph. Nearby, he would be sitting down, waiting for me. He would look at the object as if it had suddenly appeared, a magic trick. Every time, I pretended nothing had happened. As I turned round I would hear the key in the wardrobe a first time, the second time I could start looking again. But after a while it was clear that he wanted me to see that hidden place, too. So he began to take longer and longer to look for things, I would stand at the window with my back to him and he would say *Where can it have got to?* Sometimes I asked him if he needed a hand, his answer would come muffled from inside the wardrobe, *No thanks, I'll find it now, don't worry.* Then he would carry on talking. Once I turned round and saw his legs sticking out of the wardrobe, I was afraid I'd see him swallowed up altogether in front of me. Finally, one day, he decided to show me what there was inside. He opened the wardrobe before me as if it were a secret door. He said *Look at this*, and he pointed at a uniform hanging up. To see it there, standing inside the wardrobe, the arms drooping down, the two legs dangling beneath, it looked like a hanged body. It looked at us from inside that darkness, our two faces in the window, in the light, side by side trying to see.

Then, when he shut the wardrobe again, that hanged body in uniform would disappear as if it had never been there. The door closed, but he stayed inside there, hanging by the neck from an iron rod. A turn of the key, and for the rest of the day he remained in the middle of the room like an upended coffin resting against a wall. Olmo paid no heed to this, sometimes he would lean his back against the wardrobe, the nape of his neck against the wood, sometimes he would punch the door talking, to emphasize a passage. For my part, I would look at him, against the wardrobe, and I couldn't help thinking about that hanged body inside it, which felt those punches coming, spreading out in the darkness. Since I had seen it, I felt like talking quietly, always trying to make Olmo move away, to make him sit down at the table, my head next to his to prevent him from shouting. But Olmo wasn't bothered. I thought about all our words, mine and Olmo's, and about how they arrived in there, having overcome the wooden barrier, distant, sometimes mistaken, transformed into something else: they slipped into the sleeves, into the trouser legs, first they puffed up the chest and the thighs, then the shoulders, the backside, the genitals, the back. They gave a form to the empty garment inside the wardrobe. And I thought about when I wasn't there, when no-one was talking, the voices on the television, or not even those, only the sounds of Olmo making something to eat far way in the kitchen, the frizzle of the gas lighter, and then the plates put in the sink, the water pouring down, and the tap that was suddenly turned off. And finally night-time, Olmo turning over in bed, the house in silence and his head sunk in the pillow, a few centimetres from the wardrobe. His breathing, which made his chest rise and fall, and on top of his chest the sheet, and on top of the sheet the blankets. He was breathing against the wood, warming it, and that body was there inside.

Then one day he wanted me to put the uniform on. He told me he no longer had the courage to do so, too many bad things had happened inside it. And also too many good things, he added. This was said with a blush, but he raised his face to look at me, as if to reveal all his shame. So he took the uniform out of the wardrobe and accompanied it to the bed. He laid it out on the blanket keeping one sleeve behind the back to the last, unfolding it only when the uniform was completely opened out. Then he looked at the floor, my trousers deflated on top of my shoes, and especially my vest, as if my body had suddenly dissolved. Actually, my body was standing alongside in underpants, Olmo in front of me, ready to hand me the uniform trousers and then the jacket. I saw him looking at my legs, his eyes running inch by inch over my knees and thighs. He said, *I don't know if it will fit, tall as you are.* I put my legs into the trousers, I felt my knees scraping against that thick, coarse material, I struggled to close the trousers, holding my breath. And after the trousers I got inside the jacket, first one arm and then the other, a jacket that was so heavy that I rounded my shoulders. Olmo was in front of me, he was buttoning it up with the care of a tailor, two buttons and a step back to see how it suited me, then he went back to work. It was so tight that every new button meant a little less air, but he persisted and forced the buttons into their holes. He wanted to contain me inside his measurements, and I was twenty centimetres taller. Then, when he had done the last button up, he moved away and sat on the bed to look at me. He said *Perfect*, as if he had built me, though my breath was reduced to a draught. And then he wanted to take a photograph of me, using a camera that still worked with a roll of film. Every now and then he would get hold of it and take a shot. Weeks later, that photograph was inside my parents' house, in the hall, my mother had framed it and put it beside Mario's. We were both in uniform, a grimace of suffering on my face, the sleeves too short, the trousers not even touching my ankles. On closer inspection you could also see a man, reflected. It was Olmo taking my picture. But my mum hadn't noticed, or she had chosen not to mention it.

25

EVEN THOUGH IT WAS ONLY A GAME, EVER SINCE MY MOTHER had known that her father was once more around town, somewhere or other, she took out some photographs of Mario. She put them here and there around the house, I saw them one afternoon on arriving at their place, the first was in a silver frame in the lobby. It was impossible not to notice that new presence. But she pretended that nothing had happened, she stood on her tiptoes to give me a kiss, took my jacket and hung it up on the stand by the door. Then she led the way to the kitchen, passing in front of the frame without looking at it. This was how Mario appeared in my parents' house, behind those little windows that had opened in all the rooms, he looked at us like someone passing by in the street, looking in from the outside to see the life on the other side of the windows. When I went to visit my parents, we always took coffee in the dining room, Mario's face inside his biggest frame, it seemed to me I could see his breath spreading out over the glass. From one minute to the next I expected to hear him tapping his fingers on it. One day we heard a loud noise in the hall, a violent blow and glass crashing to the floor. We ran to see, it was a bird that had wound up against the window by mistake, it had broken the pane and was lying on the floor with folded wings, blood dripping from one eye.

The photographs of Mario that appeared were all from before he left for Russia, he was a youngster. In each he wore his uniform, and to see him looking out from behind the silver frame it seemed as if the war had broken out. There were no photographs taken after that, my mother was happy about that, she said she didn't want to see the face that had come to him, a face gnawed by dogs. But despite the photographs around the house, she still didn't want to talk about Mario, if I mentioned his name her gaze would cloud over. So it was easier to talk about Olmo instead. She asked me for information about him, constant updates; worried and curious, she plied me with questions. I would look at her, not knowing what to say, that secret about Olmo who lived in our old house, every time I was on the point of telling her, but said nothing. There was a period in which she began to prepare things for him to eat. The first time was almost by chance, a slice of cake left over and a sudden pause as she cleared the table, *Do you want to take it to him?* That's how she put it, without even saying his name, only looking at my face with that new idea that had come to her. *Goodness knows what he makes himself to eat*, and I shrugged. She said *Precisely*, and a few minutes later the cake was wrapped in tinfoil. Then every time I went to visit them, she always cooked abundant quantities of food. There was a portion left in the pan, I would see her divide everything into four before asking us for our plates and bringing them to the table full and steaming, three of us around the table, the fourth portion in the kitchen. After lunch my father would go to bed, my mother would go to the cupboard and take out plastic containers I had never seen before, each of the covers in a different colour. We talked quietly so as not to wake my father. I would sit at the kitchen table with a heavy head while my mother washed the dishes and put the portions she had set aside in those opaque boxes. In them there were our weekend lunches, from the pasta to dessert, the roast steeped in sauce, the carrots already cooked in butter, and my mother would say *All you have to do is warm them up*. Then she would put them in a green bag, along with a cloth napkin, identical to the ones we had used at table.

So those boxes from my parents' kitchen arrived all the way inside Olmo's house, a few blocks away. All I had to do was go down to the street, walk along the wall, go up to Olmo's. I went in and put the green bag on the table, a bag that had already once been in that house. Then, one after another, I took out the containers and put them on the shelf beside the stove. I took a pan, melted some butter in it and little by little the room filled with the smell of my parents' house. The first times, Olmo would look at me in puzzlement, I told him *My mum is sending you these things*, and he thanked me without asking questions. But it was clear that he didn't understand, his face looking down into his plate, these people who all of a sudden had come into his life, and the way I would come almost every day to see him with boxes that arrived in a bag, the napkin inside a plastic ring. Then after a while that puzzlement left his face, he grew fond of the smell of the napkins, the smell of a house that was somewhere else. He always told me to thank my mother when he saw me take my jacket and prepare to leave, he would repeat this all the way to the door, sometimes he accompanied me to the lift. He liked to make a list of his favourite dishes, lasagne was always first, tiramisu a close second, and chicken breast last. So gradually chicken breast vanished from the plastic containers, my mother made him only the things he ranked highest, plus a few new dishes that she would first try out on us and then send to him in the bag I would find all ready at the door. One day there beside it I found a package inside a large plastic bag, it contained a microwave oven she had won with her supermarket points. She said *He might find it useful, if you explain how it works*, and Olmo and I would watch the lasagne turning round and round behind the glass like a ballerina in a carillon, until the bell rang.

26

MY MOTHER BEGAN TO THINK ABOUT OLMO ALL THE TIME, even though she didn't admit it, and when I asked her if she wanted to meet him she said no, a rather frightened look on her face. She said she did it only for me, that a mother loves the people her son loves, she makes war on his enemies, and forgets his woman the day she leaves him. The truth was that since Olmo had come into her life her face had changed, a few extra kilos filled out her clothes. When I went into the house you could see that she had kept all her thoughts to one side, she had me find them all ready, a list of questions jotted down on a sheet of paper, both of us at the kitchen table running through them, item by item. They were columns of words on the backs of the long receipts for the weekly shopping. She had written them on different days, with the pen nearest to hand, sometimes blue, other times red, or the black felt-tip she used to write the names on the bags of food before she put them in the freezer. They were things she had thought, the title of a magazine that Olmo might have liked, a film worth seeing, and questions about what there was or wasn't in his house, the usual electrical appliances that first she would ask me about and then leave me to find, sometimes new and sometimes those she didn't use anymore, the box kept over the years, put back in order with a bit of sticky tape. So I would imagine my mother going round the house carrying that new thought along with her, putting it in her bag among the handkerchiefs and keys before going out. And these little sheets that she would take out, maybe in the middle of the street, the cars alongside her, the horns of the buses, the people bumping into her as they passed, and she suddenly stopping, removing the cap of the pen, writing, and then starting to run again alongside everyone else.

Olmo's house gradually filled up with objects that had previously belonged to my parents, and that had now come back home after a long time away. Old prints that had been hung up for years before winding up in the cellar, the lamp that had stood on my bedside table for as long as I had lived with my parents, the heap of corkscrews we had, and a few pots worn by use, knife scars across the bottoms, loose handles, screws that could no longer be tightened. I would arrive and arrange these things with Olmo, nails and a hammer to hang up the frames, the maps of Russia stored for a while in the cupboard. I would look for the place where they had been before, even though the house was now completely different. Olmo would follow me, a few paces behind, as I vainly tried to reconstruct the old house, every object back in its place. Olmo helped me zealously, rapidly clearing the table if I had to set down a box full of things. He handed me the hammer when I asked him for it, he told me if the pictures were straight, taking two steps backwards, as I raised or lowered them by a few centimetres until he said *That's perfect*, even though in the end they were always a bit askew. Then he took the pictures with the views of Salerno and Lake Garda and piled them on top of one another in a corner, and would look at me and laugh, still a little bemused by all those changes. So, day after day, the doilies that had been in my parents' kitchen ended up on his table, and the blue bedspread I had slept beneath for years ended up covering his bed. We hung up the old curtains from our dining room, and we put my stereo on a shelf, with Olmo looking at the crackling red lights of the bass as if they were flames in a fireplace. And at the end of each day we would go to the door, glance back and get an overall view of that house that every day became a little less his, but also a little less ours. Both of us would look at it in dismay, the flat before us like a face distorted after an operation gone awry.

Then one afternoon Olmo said that he wanted to write a note to my mother, to thank her for all that she was doing for him. I told him that it would have made her happy, that it was a kind thought. So he tore a sheet out of an old brown diary he had taken from the table drawer, the leather cracked by time. He said it was a diary that the bank used to send him, he never knew what to write in it, now they didn't send him one anymore. But he had kept it, it might always come in handy, and in fact now it did. For a while he stayed with the pen hovering in the air, its shadow trembling on the paper. He asked *What shall I write to her?* I said *Whatever you feel like, call her by her first name if you want.* I got up so that he wouldn't feel uncomfortable. Suddenly he stopped, I heard him crumple the paper in his fist, saying *I can't do it*, his back still turned towards me. I told him not to worry, it was nothing important. I changed the subject, and he let it change. After a bit he laughed. Then that evening I dropped in on my parents, to say a quick hello. At the door, before I left, I gave my mother the note Olmo had written. I said *Open your hand*, I put the ball of paper in it, then I closed it. Then I gave her a kiss and pulled the door to behind me, I sensed her standing behind it as I waited for the lift. On the note was written *Dear Giovanna, thank you, the lasagne is always good, the rest too, and also Pietro, sometimes things come along when you don't expect them, instead, when you do expect them.* And he had broken off there, had stopped writing, the date was that of the diary, *3 March, 1987, Santa Cunegonda Imperatrice.*

27

FOR ALL THAT TIME MY FATHER HAD KEPT HIMSELF TO HIMSELF. He had been able to fight against Mario, with Olmo he could do nothing but look on. So every time Olmo appeared in our conversations he felt authorized to remove himself. He would leave his chair and sit in the armchair, put on his glasses, lift up the newspaper. All we heard was him clearing his throat, turning the pages, that paper that was also a sort of private room of decency. Every so often he would lower it onto his lap, and look at us for a few seconds from over his glasses. Then he would raise it once more and start coughing again and my mother and I would go back to our talking. From inside that private room the answer to a question I had asked my mother would sometimes arrive, only a brief comment, we would see the words spurt out from behind the newspaper. But he was never tactless, he would say them from his hiding place so that we could pretend we hadn't heard him, carry on with our conversation, talking about Mario and calling him Olmo. Sometimes he would leave us alone, go out for a stroll around the neighbourhood. We would hear him whistling as he went down the stairs, a sound that dwindled with every turn on a new landing.

When he came back home, my mother and I were often still sitting where he had left us, the table still set, the remains of our three napkins, the bread beginning to go stale on the tablecloth, the cutlery gathered together in a plate.

We never talked about what had happened that day many years before, my mother sitting on the pavement, the way my father had waded into Mario, and then the sirens. But every so often I would still find that expression on his face, those eyes I had seen when he had raised his fist at Mario. Maybe only because of an unpleasant thought that had come to him, or if he had had an unusually heated argument, and that look would return to possess my father altogether. When this happened I would lower my face, look at my hands and wait for it to go. But with the years it didn't take much for that expression to disappear, because death gave him back his eyes, and filled them with gaze once more. One day I even saw him pick up a photograph of Mario, one of those in silver frames placed throughout the house. He stood still for a while looking at it, the two faces confronting each other. I had come up from behind him, I laid one arm over his shoulder, I felt him tense up. Then he understood it was me, he carried on looking at the photograph of that boy in the frame, he lifted it up and put it next to my face, against my ear, I felt it icy cold. He looked at both of us, his eyes moving from one to the other several times, then he lowered the photograph and said *How scary.* Then he opened the door of the glass display cabinet and put it inside, locking the door. *You do know, don't you,* he asked me, continuing to stare at the photograph, *how many people this man killed?* But then he said nothing more and didn't wait for an answer, he slipped his arm under mine and said *What a great smell,* as he led me into the dining room. Then on the day of the dead he would accompany my mother to the cemetery, but he would wait for her outside, standing beside the car while she changed the water and the flowers on Mario's grave.

One evening my father and I went out to eat alone. I waited for him in the street beneath the house, I rang the intercom, leaving the engine running, and I got back in the car straight away. My father sat in the passenger seat, he gave my leg a pat with his hand. Every time he sat in that seat you could see he missed having the wheel in front of him, and he would hang on to the handle with both hands. It was the first time the two of us had gone out to dinner, we sat in front of each other a little nervously. He suddenly struck me as more fragile, shielded by the glass I was filling for him. And so the evening passed without either of us saying what we had thought. Sara was not even mentioned, she came in and went out without letting herself be seen, nothing apart from him asking me *Are you sure you're alright?* and my reply *Things will get better, you'll see.* We removed anything we had in common from our conversation, leaving him to talk about when he was a boy, all the things he could never have told me before, but could now, because I was no longer myself and my mother wasn't there. In the meantime our voices got louder, the waiter went back and forth. It turned ten o'clock, then eleven and our faces were flushed. Little by little, the restaurant had almost completely emptied. The owner stood at the door shaking hands with the customers, saying *See you next time.* At midnight the bell in the steeple rang out, my father suddenly became my father again, he raised his hand to ask for the bill, he said *Mamma will be wondering if I've been kidnapped.* When I dropped him at the door to their building, before getting out, he said *Look after yourself*, and then hauled himself out clinging to the door. He slapped the bonnet with his hand, but I waited for the door to close before leaving.

28

WITHOUT TELLING ME WHERE OR HOW SHE HAD FOUND THEM, my mother told me one day that she had other photographs. In fact they weren't photographs but rolls of film that had not been developed yet. She left them on the table, wrapped up like eggs in an old newspaper. I found her in the kitchen, sitting in the chair she used every time something happened, it was the fourth chair, the surplus one in our family of three. It was the same as all the others, but had a cushion on it, the wicker seat having caved in when my father had stood on it one day many years before. Since then it had always stayed like that, and no-one had had the patience to fix it properly, with only that cushion on it to mark the difference. Every so often, however, someone would sit on it by mistake, some friend of my mother's who still didn't know the secret hidden beneath the cushion. So if my mother wasn't paying attention for a moment her friend would end up with her backside in the hole, they all chose that chair precisely because of the cushion. First my mother would hear a smothered yelp, and then she would see her friend stuck inside the wicker, her eyes wide open in fright, my mother unable to stop laughing. She would say *I'm sorry, there's nothing to laugh about.* Then she would help her friend out of the hole, some with a sulky look, and my mother would smack the cushion with her hand, as if it weren't a chair but a dog that had bitten someone. She would sit on that chair every time she was upset, following a row with my father or a worry. I had found here there when Mario had died. She was sitting on it in silence, her elbows on the table so as not to slip down into the hole, her face focused on that effort, as if sitting on eggs, as if that chair were the place in the house where my mother brooded on her suffering.

*

When my mother gave me the rolls of film with the photographs of Mario inside, she was sitting there. Normally, she used to wait for me on the landing in front of the flat, she would watch me come up, a habit that started when I was a little boy, a reward from her for having climbed all those flights of stairs. But that day there was no-one on the landing, the door of the house was left ajar, the clothes-stand in the shadows like a lurking man with a hat stolen from my father's head. My mother was waiting for me in the kitchen, that packet on the table and her face crumpled with melancholy, as if inside that yellowing paper there was a swallow that had been found dead on the balcony. She didn't even get up when she saw me arrive, all she said was *Ciao Pietro*. For me it was enough to see where she was sitting, and then that upside down smile she always gave when she wanted to say the opposite. She took the packet and gave me it, she said *They're photos of Mario*. I took it with both hands, the way you take the body of a dead swallow, I removed the elastic band and the newspaper, *Where did you get them?* I asked, showing my mother the two rolls, one in each hand. But she brushed off the question with her hand, *Now what shall we do with them?* she asked. I looked at her, put the two rolls on the table, and offered her my hand as if inviting her to dance. She came away from that chair with a sigh, her face relaxed, and then she gave me a kiss and said *Hello, my son*, using the possessive as a way to say life was still beautiful, after it had been saved.

We developed the photographs when my father arrived, an hour later, the enlarger, the lamp, and the liquids retrieved from a big box in the cellar. When my father found out they were photographs of Mario he said he didn't agree, but then my mother said *Please, do it for me*. Suddenly it was dark, on that summer afternoon, with the three of us locked away in the bathroom, the blinds pulled down, the red light making our faces even more frightened. No-one dared to speak, my father pointed at things to us in silence and in silence we did them, as if words might ruin the entire procedure, as if they were light that would have burned the photographs. So Mario came out of the acid bath, each roll twelve photographs, steeping the paper in the liquid twenty-four times. My father had put on a lab coat because he didn't want to get stained and all three of us were bent over the edge of the bath, kneeling, silent in that reddish darkness, our faces watching.

Twenty-four times, with every sheet that my father immersed, we stayed there waiting to see if something would come out of the white. My father would shake the paper in the liquid with small plastic tweezers. My mother would shed a fat tear for every person who emerged into the light. And twenty-four times in a row Mario came out of the water, and out of the paper that was white before, he would appear bit by bit, my father pulling him out before he burned. They were all shots of a wooden bench, land around it, a tree behind. My mother said quietly *The clinic*, and brought her hand up to her mouth. I saw her close her eyes, take a breath, then open them again to look. Mario emerged this way, a little at a time, a phantom rising out of the dark, his body and his face that could only be glimpsed at first coming to the surface. In each of the photographs Mario was sitting with a different person. At the last photograph my father merely said *All done*, and he took my mother's head, brought it to his chest, and gathered her into his embrace. Shortly afterwards the photographs were hanging from a string, suspended like ghosts above the kitchen table, each with a clothes peg, all twenty-four on the bench with Mario. They were men and women, eyes on the lens, dressed up for the photograph, slippers on their feet.

29

ONE DAY WHEN HE CAME TO PICK ME UP AT SCHOOL WITH
my mother, many years before, Mario had asked me *Will you
promise to come and see me?* He had asked me this standing still
outside the door to our building. He was often like that, he
wouldn't say a word all afternoon yet at the last moment he would
ask a question to add an extension to the time allowed him. My
mother offered me her hand, the key already in the door, then she
would open it by leaning her back against it, and her last words
before turning and vanishing inside were always *Bye-bye*. It was in
that last moment that Mario would say something, driven by the
instinct to speak before he had found a word to say, making a start
just by opening his mouth. So we would stand there, my mother
already entirely inside the entrance hall, Mario outside on the
pavement, and me in that middle zone, I was already no longer
with Mario, but had not yet returned to my father, who was waiting for us upstairs at home. But sometimes Mario didn't say
anything, he couldn't find the word to make us stay. He would shut
his mouth again, and I would see his tongue vanish, teeth resting
against teeth – and he would take all his words away with him as
he turned.

One day when it was raining outside he asked me to promise to go
to see him. Faced with that question I hadn't known what to say,
I looked up at my mother just as she was looking down at me,
raising my chin and saying *Your grandfather asked you a question*.
So then I had said *Yes*, staring at the ground, Mario becoming my
grandfather again for the space of a question. But it was a yes that
nobody had heard, it had been carried off by the rain, which was
heavier, lashing the street. So Mario took a step closer to the door,

he arrived in front of me, bent his legs to come to get that yes, putting his ear to my mouth. I said *Promise* inside it, but once more I hadn't looked at him. He straightened up, nodded, content, and going back under the rain, on the pavement, he had said *Thanks,* but looking only at my mother. I, too, had looked at her, she had cleared her throat and told him *Don't mention it* and then *I'm sorry*, and it was clear that that *Don't mention it* and that *I'm sorry* regarded two different things. Then she had added *Anyway it was his decision, it's worth more.* As she said this she drew me towards her. Mario had smiled and said *We'll see*, which was a way not to harbour any illusions and not to have to blame anyone. And walking off with his back to us, going away in the rain, he had raised one arm above his head, he kept it there for a while, it seemed like an absolution.

I kept that promise more than twenty years later, by the time he was no longer in the clinic. My mother and I went one afternoon, when she got into the car she said *All I'm going to do is let you see it from the outside.* Then for the entire trip she said nothing, she looked outside, rummaged in her bag. She sat beside me in silence, and said *That way*, pointing to the left or right with her finger. Every so often I tried to say something to her, about the heat, a road I had never taken before, but she didn't reply, her bag open on her knees, and my words falling inside it, scattered among her wallet, keys and handkerchiefs. Then she would ask me *Did you say something, Pietro?* I would answer *Nothing important.* At a certain point I heard her say *Oh God*, bringing one hand up to her mouth, resting the other on my leg, her fingers digging into my thigh. She gestured to me to stop, I parked half up on the pavement, we got out of the car. And on the other side of the road there was a row of very tall buildings, each almost identical, only floors and windows, and in the middle of that line of glass and cement there was a hole, you could see the sky. It was like a tooth that had fallen out, and my mother pointed at it saying *I don't understand, it was there a month ago.* Both of us stood there with our hands on the wire netting looking at the crater, mountains of rubble, two excavators working, iron bars scattered all over. My mother pointed to the background, it was a lawn, she said *That's where the photos were taken.* But now there were only heaps and piles, a workman eating a sandwich with his helmet still on. She looked down and kept on saying *I don't understand.* When she got back in the car, she had a strange smile. With her face against the window she said with a sigh *It was destiny.* Then we left, and she looked outside the window, I heard her singing softly, a faint melody coming from her mouth, something that was for her alone, *Tell me for whom I weep, for what I shall pray tomorrow, if you leave me alone, for mercy's sake, for pity's sake if there is silence in your heart.*

<h1 style="text-align:center">30</h1>

AFTER MARIO'S DEATH MY MOTHER BEGAN TO USE HIS DIARY, to jot down notes in it, to mark things she didn't want to overlook. At first she hid it among the recipe books in the kitchen like a lover in the wardrobe. When I asked her what it was and tried to take it, she moved to put herself between me and the cupboard, she defended it with her body, and said that it was only a notebook in which she wrote down recipes. But while she was saying this she gathered her hair up into a ponytail, the elastic band hanging from her lips, and her eyes lowered just enough so as not to have to look at me. But one day she left the diary on the kitchen table, unguarded, while she was in the bathroom and my father had gone out to buy bread because I had said I was staying for dinner. I heard the shower jet and she asked me if I would put a pan of water on to boil. So I found the diary there, open on the table, for all to see, a pencil in the middle, the marks of her teeth sunk deep into its wood. And inside there were these lines that overlapped, Mario's words in capitals, in a different pen every time, and her pencil that had brushed lightly over the top. My mother's words were there with modesty, ready to vanish and be carried off with a resolute swipe of the rubber, a few specks and a blow on the paper.

Mario had written very little with each day that passed. The first thing he always wrote was his weight, noted down next to the date. They were sets of two numbers side by side – those of the days that increased, and those of the body that steadily decreased, from 81 to 72, as if a little hole had suddenly opened up, through which he had gradually begun to slip away. Beneath the weight of his body, Mario noted if he had gone for a walk, if someone had come to visit him, and the things they had given him to eat for lunch or dinner. At the beginning he only wrote *Went out* and *Didn't go out*. At first the *Didn't go outs* were rare, and a reason was always written alongside. *A fever, his legs, cold, pins and needles in his head, rain, his feet, no desire.* Then as time passed they increased in number, a couple of times a week and suddenly the diary was full of them, like snow fallen during the night. *Didn't go out, Didn't go out, Didn't go out, Didn't go out, Didn't go out*, without even a reason noted. In the meantime, only the evidence of the drop in weight, marked by the rhythm of the kilos he was losing, the number getting smaller every week. My mother seldom appeared, with only her initial and a few notes in brackets, *G came (short hair), G came (artichokes), G came (briefly), G came (sore throat)*. Some days there was only a G, with nothing beside it, and that solitary letter seemed like an ear appeared on the page, as if that were the point from which the paper listened. In the end there was no longer anything, on the last days the handwriting wasn't even his, maybe that of the doctor or a nurse, only his weight noted in a composed hand, the numbers certain, and afterwards *Didn't go out* and *The daughter*. Then only blank pages, and all the diary still to complete. As I leafed through it, the sound of the shower ceased, my mother set to singing, and the hairdryer began to blow. I went back to the beginning of the diary, now she was using it for notes, things to buy in the supermarket, columns for the monthly expenses, and then recipes, sometimes copied, others cut out of some newspaper and glued in place. In this way my mother lived in Mario's space every day, as if offering him her arm to walk at his side.

Then my mother came out of the bathroom, talking loudly to let me know she was coming. I closed the diary, she took it and put it back among the recipe books, above the sideboard, without any need to say or ask anything. She sat down beside me, ran a hand over my cheek, and said *Have you seen Sara?* as if a trace of her had been left on my face. So I told her about our walk along the riverbank, and about the baby she was expecting. At first, she said nothing, then *She came to see us one evening.* She looked at me and added *What would you have done in my place?* which was both an excuse and a rebuke. And my father, who was coming into the kitchen, heard my mother talking, and saw us there, our faces close, and stopped in the doorway. My mother said *She's still very upset, she was crying.* Then she said *The baby's father is only a youngster, she met him at the gym.* Then she glanced at my father motionless in the kitchen doorway, and looked for any kind of reaction in my face. But all I said was *Of course*, and my mother said *Anyway that's the way it went*, putting an end to the conversation, adding a sigh too. And when my father left, my mother lowered her voice and asked me *Have you ever seen an ultrasound scan?*

31

I LOOKED FOR TRACES OF SARA IN MY MOTHER'S FACE every time we saw each other. Even after she had left, Sara continued to call her now and then, of an evening. My mother at first would reply curtly, only a hasty *Yes*, and then she had started to say *Hi, how are you?* and she would sit down. At the beginning, she would tell me, like a confession every time. *Sara called*, she would say all in a rush while offering her gaze to me. All I said was *Oh*, and then I wouldn't speak, with my eyes I slipped my hands into her eyes, I would rummage about in them, among her things I looked for Sara's, the words she had left there. Silent, my mother would stand in front of me, her eyelids raised all the way, as if lifting her hands in the air. She didn't defend herself, she felt my hands entering inside her, she felt me poking about, a sound of sand and keys, and yet she would let me finish. But I never found anything, and what I took out after rummaging about were never things about Sara but only my fears. And I would accuse my mother of not telling me the truth and she would say *But how could I?* So then she stopped telling me that she was seeing Sara, but I would find traces of her just the same, I would collect them, take them with me. And every so often in my parents' house there were two coffee cups upturned above the sink, which was something Sara did, whereas my mother would wash, dry and put away in the glass cabinet. And one day on the balcony the plastic chairs were folded up against the wall at the far end, and once there was also an open deckchair, its legs spread out, and in the bookcase in the dining room there was an empty space in the middle, where the books on motherhood were kept, the things you need to know before you have a child.

*

Sara and my mother continued to keep in touch and to see each other, not a lot, but without ever breaking off. My mother had asked me if this bothered me, but she couldn't manage to elude Sara's requests for help. I told her there wasn't a problem, just that I didn't want to know anything about her any longer, nor about the baby boy or girl, whichever it was, and far less about the father. Yet there were always those scattered traces, Sara's perfume left on my mother. And I gathered it every time I gave her a hug, together with a sense of irritation, defeat and melancholy. There were also verbal traces of her, words that my mother had never used and that now suddenly found themselves in her mouth. I recognized where they had come from. My mother without even knowing it, day after day, became the noticeboard on which Sara left me messages. Once I had even seen them coming out of a supermarket together, Sara pushing the trolley, my mother walking at her side, and then the bags had disappeared inside the boot. I was in the car, going in the opposite direction, the trees between us. I tried see Sara's belly. Then the traffic light came, there was a queue and I remained at a halt, but they hadn't seen me. Sara was talking to my mother in an agitated way, her face continually turned towards her, even as she was putting the shopping bags in the boot and closing it. My mother was smiling at her kindly, answering her with a few words. She even ran a hand down her cheek, and Sara stopped her by putting her hand over my mother's. The last caress Sara had received from her mother was when she was eight, then she died, leaving her with her father. Finally the traffic light turned green, I moved off and later on I found those shopping bags in my parents' kitchen. They stood there, next to the stove, still unpacked, with the name of the supermarket on them, bulging with things. So I asked my mother why that supermarket, I didn't know there was one nearby. She didn't turn round, she began to empty the bags, her back to me. She put the vegetables in the fridge, then the cheese, the eggs, and she removed things that had gone off. Huffing, she tossed them in the bin, saying *It's not possible, it's always the same.* And when I asked her again *Why that supermarket?* all she said was *No, it's not close*, and she went back with her face in the fridge.

One day Sara and I almost met, but it turned out to be only a fleeting glimpse and a glance. I hadn't told my mother that I was going to have dinner with them, it was almost eight when I arrived, the lift was occupied and I went up the stairs, the ice cream in my hand. As I was going up I heard the lift start, the release from the floor, the cables running upwards, in the middle of the stairwell, and the cage coming down. I saw it descending above me, a square of brown wood ruined by use, nothing to do with the rest of the lift, like a shoe seen from below. Then the cage passed beside me, and I saw that the person inside was Sara. She was looking in the opposite direction, but she turned almost by chance, as if to obey an instinct. So our gazes met, hers came down from above and arrived in front of me, and she raised her head towards me then disappeared under the ceiling of the lift. Both of us had stood there, motionless, her hand raised in greeting, left in the air as if it were an oath, or a promise. I didn't move, I heard the lift arrive on the ground floor, the door of the cage opening and then closing, and her heels that lingered a while before walking towards the door to the street.

32

MY FATHER HAD CALLED ME ONE EVENING, HE SAID YOUR *mother is worrying me.* He had gone out of the house especially to call me. He telephoned as he went down the stairs, I heard his breathing together with his words, a hint of panting, his shoes marking the rhythm of his descent. He told me *Every night she gets up and wanders round the house, I really don't know how to get her to sleep.* He said this with the voice of someone who is seeking a remedy more than consolation. The stairs in the meantime had come to an end, I heard the echo vanish and the air opened out above him. And so my father began to speak louder, his voice clearer, the cars in the background, every now and then he said *Good evening* to someone. A dog was barking furiously, you could hear its nails scrabbling vainly on the cement, its mistress yelling *You never learn anything.* After a while the dog stopped, the lady said to it *You see, you can be good when you want to.* There was a helicopter flying up there, the sound moved away, was about to disappear, but then came close again. My father raised his head, I heard his words stretching, his neck straining towards the sky as he told me *Your mother can't resign herself to the fact that the dead are dead.*

So my mother couldn't sleep at night. She would wake up just after four, throw the sheet aside, step out of bed and go off to the kitchen barefoot. At first my father would get up when he saw the light and he would find her cooking at the stove. He would try to persuade her to come back to bed, but she said she wasn't sleepy, she had things on her mind, cooking was the only thing that made her feel well. So he would go back to bed, turn over, and yet he constantly checked to see if she was there. She would come back to bed when it was already almost morning, she would raise one of my father's arms stretched out there beside her and lie with her head on his chest. On the telephone he said to me that every time it seemed to him that a waitress had got into his bed. In the morning he would find all the dishes washed and dried, and on the worktop the results of a night divided into plastic containers. Some were for the two of them, some were for me, some others were intended for Olmo. My mother would get up later. My father would see her come into the kitchen, her eyes not yet completely open, and every time she would say to him *You didn't wake me*. Then she would put the containers in the freezer, and when she came out of the bathroom washed and dressed they didn't talk any more about what had happened that night. At first this happened every now and then, my father got worried and yet calmed down again the following day, he sought her in bed with his arm and would find her there beside him, the breathing of a sleeping body. Then insomnia had taken her hostage, it no longer gave her a moment's peace, it became the sentence of every night, and my father stopped getting up. From the other end of the telephone he said he no longer knew what to do, Mario's death had sent her off the rails. Then I heard him laugh, there below the house, in front of the rubbish skips, he was laughing so much he could hardly speak, he said *At least I've never eaten so well*. His words held a touch of melancholy, but in actual fact every day they were both getting a bit fatter. My mother's grief made you put on weight.

I talked to her about this one afternoon when my father wasn't there. We went out for a walk, she liked to be seen with me. She held my arm tight, sometimes she would rest her head on my shoulder. The walk was always the same, across the road, skirting the park for a bit, back again, and returning to the door passing beneath Olmo's house, twenty minutes at most. I saw her yawn twice, putting her hand up, and so I asked her if she slept at night, she replied *Son, at night all I have are ugly thoughts, I cook until morning*. Suddenly, she stopped, turned towards me, and pulled me towards her so I might embrace her. Then she said *It's the curse of Mario, waking up in the night*. She put her arm under mine again and we started walking once more, every now and then a yell would come from alongside us, in the park, a football match and young boys running after the ball. There was a period when Mario had come back home for a while, to live with her and her mother. Her mother had told her she had to understand now that she was nine or ten. To see that man with lunatic eyes frightened her, he had arrived from outside their home and got into her mother's bed and she had moved to the sofa. Late in the evening the bed would creak, my mother would hear it knocking against the wall, softly at first then louder and louder, and finally it would stop, and it would make her weep. And during the night Mario would get up, once she had seen him naked on the balcony, his legs against his chest, those bones with only skin over them. Now and then her mother would get up with him, in the middle of the night, she would run her hand over his head, blow warm breath on his neck. In the mornings he would sleep almost until lunchtime, you couldn't make any noise, her mother told her that it was the dead who kept him awake, it was the war that outside was over but inside they were still shooting.

We passed below Olmo's house, our walk almost over. She wanted to stop for a breather. I tried to drag her away, even though I knew that Olmo was sleeping at that hour and it was unlikely we would have met him. We had passed in front of the house many times, before then, and she had never wanted to stop. Now she was there craning her neck out towards the intercom, she said *I wonder who lives in our house now?* Then she went closer, pointed her finger against the nameplate, there was written O.C., she said *Shall we ring?* I said *No*, with a hint of vehemence. My mother stiffened, *What's got into you?* she asked me. We moved on, three blocks and we came to her door. In the lift, looking out, she said *Let's hope you don't catch it too, you can't even cook.*

33

THE YEARS THAT MARIO HAD RETURNED HOME STARTED ONE
Sunday morning. He had arrived at ten, this man my mother
still didn't know. She had opened and on the other side of the doorway there he was, his face bitten away, standing in front of her. *Ciao
Giovanna* he said. She had run back inside together with my grandmother, just behind her legs, all my grandmother said was *Mario*
and invited him in. Mario took a seat in the kitchen, my grandmother speaking to him with few words. Above all she looked at
him, he kept his eyes lowered, she had her hands linked on her legs,
below the table. Mario had returned from Russia when the war had
already been over for two years, first imprisonment and then the
return, his brain a mess. There was a place in which they gathered
all those reduced to that state. My grandmother had gone to pick him
up, with Mario's mother, my mother sleeping in her arms. And they
had gone up to him, Mario's beard, his eyes still in Russia, his empty
clothes, between his shoulders and head only his Adam's apple pro-
truding from his neck. He let himself be embraced, his gaze beyond
his wife and mother, their arms tightening the jacket over his bones.
Then they had helped him settle in the room that had been assigned
to him, three beds and three metal cupboards, mother-in-law and
daughter-in-law vying for the intimacy of putting his pyjamas on,
my mother still a small child, her eyes closed to keep her out of it.

Now she was there looking at them, sitting on the sofa, her mother
talking to that man in a different voice. It was little more than a
breath, a voice that came from a place she had never been to, the
extraneousness of that man all in her mother's voice, the voice of
another person. For the entire time that he remained sitting in the
kitchen, she had not looked at her daughter. She didn't look at

Mario much either, her hands had never moved, they too seemed like those of another person. And she hadn't even touched him either. My mother could see her legs under the table, their knees a few centimetres apart. Once she brushed his knees, but he moved his away, then brought them closer again. All curled up in a corner of the sofa, she could see Mario from behind. He was so close that if she had stretched out her arm she could have touched him. She had looked at the back of his neck, and that hole where the hair was missing, and below that she saw his spinal column emerge from the neck and run downwards, a long scar that crossed that thing she still could not know, a father's back.

Then when Mario went to take a shower, my grandmother's voice returned, and yet there was no need to tell my mother who that man was. From the sofa she saw Mario behind the frosted glass, getting skinnier with every garment he removed, first his jacket then his shirt, he was left like a rope stretched from floor to ceiling. My grandmother had opened the bathroom door, she slipped inside and came out with Mario's clothes held in her arms like a newborn baby. She laid them on the chair where he had been sitting, over the back of the chair. A sock detached itself from the pile and fell, a slow descent before collapsing on the floor. My mother stared at them for a long time, the corpse of the sock on the floor and those clothes, Mario's remains, the temptation to feel their consistency, to sniff them. Above all she wanted to touch his trousers, they were wide open where his body had been before, the zip and that leather belt with extra holes added, he had made them by hand himself, they looked like wounds.

In the meantime the shower was on, the water had run for at least half an hour. My mother had sought my grandmother several times with her gaze, with a question, why didn't she go into the bathroom and scold him. She would yell at her after ten minutes, she would come and turn the water off. But her mother said nothing, she pretended nothing was going on, she gave her a kiss leaning over the sofa, picking the sock up from the floor. Then she saw her bend over a blue basin and put all the clothes in it, Mario's things together with their jerseys, socks, and skirts, and this seemed like a violent thing to my mother, this was the first time they were staying together. And my grandmother put her hands in the clothes, kneading them into a single mass of sleeves and legs. Three hours later the clothes were hanging up, a single clothes peg held Mario's vest and my mother's nightdress together, and then another clothes peg with my grandmother's jersey. And there they were, attached to the cord, flapping in the wind.

34

THEN MARIO WOULD DISAPPEAR EVERY SO OFTEN, MY MOTHER and my grandmother wouldn't find him at home. After a while they would get frightened, once they even called the police. It almost always happened at night, sometimes late afternoon. When Mario went out he never said anything, he didn't say goodbye, all you heard was the door closing, the lock clicking, sometimes not even that. Simply he wasn't at home anymore, my grandmother would talk to him and when she looked for him all she found was his chair, pulled slightly away from the table. My mother was always the last to notice, she never stayed around Mario. If he was resting she would do her homework. If Mario sat down at the table she would go off to read on the bed. So when he went out, my mother didn't say anything, she didn't ask and she didn't say, merely going from room to room, timorously putting one foot inside, hoping not to find him anywhere, to be sure of that. Then my grandmother would hear her singing, sometimes lying stretched out on the bed, and every now and then she would whistle as she went around the house. It was a melody of a few notes that she would repeat, some strident passages, her lips not placed right, as if with that sound she wanted to purify the space. Sometimes Mario would return and no-one had realized he had gone out, my mother and my grandmother thought he was resting in bed. But then the intercom would buzz, my mother always wanted to be the one to ask. His weary voice came from below, his hoarseness, all he said was *It's Mario*, and my nonplussed mother opened for him. And shortly afterwards that long and bony body would come into the house and lie down in the other room to rest.

Sometimes he didn't return and evening would come. My grandmother set the table, the lamp lit on the table, and all around and outside it was dark. The table would stay like that for a few hours, three plates and three glasses, and that cone of light shining down. My mother used to start complaining, she would go in and out of the kitchen, asking how long it was until dinner. She would sit on the floor, her back against the wall. But she never asked where Mario was, she never mentioned his name. My grandmother would tell her to wait, dinner wasn't ready yet, it had to finish cooking. She tried to take her mind off it, help her to choose wool, the colours for a large blanket to prepare for the winter, and a jumper all for Giovanna, one for her friends to see. So for a while my mother would stop complaining, she would try on the colours, unwind the wool, the rooms becoming coloured cobwebs. But then my mother would get bored, the light still on the table and the darkest darkness all around. So she would end up on the sofa, sitting there motionless staring at the three plates and the three glasses. My grandmother would start to go out onto the balcony, leaning over, looking down. Every time she came back in she was a bit edgier. Somewhere, at a point near or far, there was Mario, either closed up at home all day or on one of his sudden escapes. In the end my grandmother would stay out on the balcony, she didn't even come back in, and my mother, the little girl, would fall asleep on the sofa, her arms wrapped around herself.

At times they had even gone to look for him in the city, my grandmother didn't know what to do with her daughter, frightened as she was of leaving her alone. She would dress her hastily, unceremoniously, my mother already wholly inside sleep, her head flopping, and my grandmother would have to take it and slip it through the hole in her jumper. After a while they were on the street, the few lampposts of the neighbourhood, going in and out of the zones of light, my grandmother breathless and my mother supported by a firm arm. Sometimes they would roam around the district all night, going back and forth along the streets, looking inside the street doors, crossing the park. They looked for Mario on the benches, at the feet of the monuments. Every now and then my grandmother would ask my mother to shout *Dad*, and she did so, but without conviction, a faint voice that came from her mouth and ended shortly afterwards. But they almost never found him and once dawn was breaking, my grandmother had gone back home, she met a man coming out of the street door, he was going to work. They said hello, he was beginning the day while she hadn't finished the previous one. They went up and Mario was sitting on the floor, his back against the door, all he said was *I'm sorry*. Another time they had found him at the tram stop, too late for one to pass. He had seen them coming, he had said hello, and they had sat down beside him. My grandmother began weeping as if she were never going to stop. My mother got up, hugged her, and asked her *Why are you crying?* Then she turned towards Mario, saying *You made her cry.*

35

A NEW BED HAD ARRIVED IN THE HOUSE, MARIO HAD ASSEM-
bled it one morning when it was hot. They had brought it up
enclosed in two boxes. He had carried them up the stairs one after
another. Then my grandmother had gone out, leaving Mario and
my mother alone in the house. He had taken his shirt off and stayed
like that, in his vest and his white skin stretched over his bones. He
put the two boxes on the floor, he bent over them, and asked my
mother to bring him a knife or some scissors to remove the sticky
tape from the cardboard. She went out of the room and shortly
afterwards she came back with a big kitchen knife, she stood in
front of him for a bit, the knife almost as long as her forearm. She
looked at him without moving, the point aimed at Mario, until he
held out his hand. He said *Thank you, Giovanna* and took the
knife from her, she let him take it, her arm fell back down along her
side. Mario opened the boxes, spread all the pieces on the floor, the
long boards, the short ones, the wire mattress and the mattress
itself propped up against the wall. Every so often he would look up
at his daughter. She was still there in the corner, her mouth twisted
into a grimace, filled with rancour towards him and her mother,
too, because she had gone away. She stayed to watch Mario working, his knees on the floor. A drop of sweat ran down between his
shoulder blades and slipped under his vest. For an hour he didn't
say another word, he just tightened the screws, joined the boards
up, the screwdriver on the floor, and the hammer hitting hard, over
and over. The floor shook, my mother felt it vibrating beneath her
feet, as he built her cross.

My mother never sat on that bed, she left it free of everything, not
even a doll placed on top of it. Moreover, in the evenings she would

always wait until the last moment, and my grandmother at a certain point would raise her voice peremptorily, *Brush your teeth and get to bed.* Mario was always the first to go, sometimes even before dinner, often with a headache. My grandmother used to say, when night fell, that inside his head in Russia they would begin to shoot. She would put some ice inside a floral patterned pillow case, and he would close his eyes and feel the cold entering his cranium. Then there were periods in which Mario had begun to work, or at least he tried to. For a few months he would enter and leave the house with a full bag, inside it his lunch and his overalls. My grandmother would prepare it for him before joining him in bed. In the evenings he would come back, wearing clothes he had never worn before, he would talk, gesticulating, until late, and sometimes he would laugh. It was a laugh that welled up slowly, as if emerging from inside a cave, my mother who would see it come out of his mouth and fill the kitchen, and he too was amazed to hear it rise up. He talked about his colleagues, the factory and the canteen, and in those days the house slowly spread outwards, making room for him little by little. My grandmother would sit there at the table, but holding her breath. She would look at Mario, and my mother, the little girl, would stare at him and then burst out laughing, his eyes with that completely new light, and she felt like praying for that thing never to end.

It had been enough for Mario to make my mother laugh a few times for her to decide to trust him. At first, her mouth put up a little resistance, then her lips had surrendered, leaving the field open to her teeth, and he saw her laugh and at that point she could no longer hide. So, in a short time, since Mario had started working, that silent man had vanished and this amusing fellow had come into the house. Sometimes in the evenings he would sing love songs with my grandmother, he gave her the tempo with his head, raised one arm towards the sky to make the song fly high. My mother would look at them and smile. After dinner every now and then he would call her into his arms, she would climb up on him without being asked twice. He would hold her close, take deep breaths and stick out his chest, and my mother would rise up and down with him. For a while they had even gone out together alone, on Sunday mornings, both dressed up, Mario even with a tie. My grandmother would first look him in the face then bend down to rearrange my mother's blouse. She would ask her if everything was all right, if she really felt like going out with him. Then, looking out from the balcony, she would follow them for a stretch of road, the first times my mother, the little girl, would constantly turn to wave to her, looking for her in the facade of the building. Then after a while she gave up turning, she went off like that, looking the other way, held inside her father's hand. My grandmother would wait for them at home, prepare lunch, taste to check the saltiness of the food, set the table for three. She would dismiss her worries, force herself not to keep an eye on the time. And when the intercom sounded she would run to it, asking *Who is it?* only to listen to the tone of the voices, hoping for gaiety in them, and then the wait on the stairs, hoping to hear my mother laughing with Mario, that laugh that would slip into the house, as my grandmother said *Now wash your hands, you two.*

But then came those cracks in his face, his head that ached, and he started going to bed early once more. So more and more often my mother and grandmother found themselves eating dinner alone, his napkin folded beside his plate, with him in the other room with the light off, and for the first time eating together meant that someone was missing. Mario began to stay off work, first only a few mornings, then he didn't go at all, the effort of taking off his pyjamas, and the beard that grew day after day, giving him another face, the same face he had had on his return from Russia. And so, little by little, my mother, the small girl, began to get scared. She didn't recognize this father of hers who had suddenly stopped talking. One evening, she tried to climb up onto his knees, after dinner, and he had brushed her off, a movement of his arm. It was a clumsy gesture, his left hand rose, the little girl fell to the floor, bumping against the corner of the table. There was a great cry, and blood, all three of them shouting, each with a pain all of their own, and the scar that my mother has next to her eyebrow to this day.

36

ONE DAY SARA ASKED MY MOTHER TO TELL HER ABOUT MARIO. The first and last time my mother had pronounced his name to her had been on the telephone – Sara with her suitcases all ready had transcribed his death on a note and had left it for me on the kitchen table. Then one day, as she accompanied my mother home, Sara had suddenly asked her *Will you tell me about Mario?* and my mother stopped, the key already in the door. She looked for herself in the glass, and in it she also saw Sara's face, reflected at the back of her neck. Then she removed the key, turned round, and said *Let's go for a walk.* So they crossed the road, went into the park. My mother talked for two hours and Sara listened. My mother stared straight ahead of herself as she talked, as if she were alone. And for the whole time they followed the same route, down towards the river and back again. Sara said nothing. All she did was walk beside my mother, a few centimetres behind. They met one of Sara's friends, they stopped, Sara said to her *What are you doing here?* She introduced my mother, *This is Pietro's mum.* With a hint of disingenuousness, the friend looked at the baggy sweater Sara was wearing and asked her with a smile *Are you hiding something from me?* Sara blushed, my mother looked down, and the friend said *How lovely*, and added *And you, Signora, should get ready too.*

So they sat down on a bench by the riverside, the sun was already low. Bicycles passed by, and pushchairs with mothers behind them, and the panting of the runners, and in front, on the river, there was a man teaching his son how to row. Then my mother began to talk again, to tell Sara about how Mario had become a secret thing, hidden under the ground, and about how when Mario had died she had gone to see him alone, on the bus, after that telephone call with her. In the funeral chamber she had found no-one, and looking at her father's body she thought she had made a mistake. And so she sat down beside the coffin and wept, and thought she would have made a mistake in any case, and that was the saddest thought. And someone had shaved Mario and combed his hair back, and when a candle had gone out a girl came in and replaced it, lighting a new one that would last longer. My mother talked about Mario, sitting in front of the river, and she sat there motionless, a grief that was almost a form of concentration. She was looking ahead, with Sara close by, her hands together on her lap, and her feet one on top of the other on the ground. In the meantime they had increased the volume of the music in the bar, and there were lots of people sitting, four or five youths leaning on the parapet looking out. There in front, on the river, the man was still teaching his son to row, a little boat with the name of the park and a number written on it in white. And every so often the man would yell *Damn it all*, and his son, a boy in a sweaty T-shirt, would repeat snivelling *I can't do it.*

For all that time Sara had wept in silence, without even sniffing. She ran her hand over her cheek, collecting the tears that ran down. And then when my mother finished and saw her eyes still moist,

Sara had tried to hide them by attempting to smile. So my mother, there on the bench in front of the river, said to her *I'm sorry, I didn't want to make you sad*. Then she gave her a hug and Sara at first had hidden her face inside the embrace, but shortly afterwards she pulled away and said *Let's go because it's getting late*. In the park there were almost no pushchairs any longer, but there were more and more people running in small groups, puffing in the middle of their sentences as they passed by, and in the meantime the sun had set. When they said goodbye, my mother said *Sorry, I never talk about my father*. Sara replied *It was a pleasure for me*. And when, a little while afterwards, my mother went out onto the balcony with my father, Sara's car was still parked outside the door to the building. They sat down outside, my mother had taken off her shoes. Further below, beneath the roof of the black car, Sara was there, her head thrown back, her eyes half shut, and they were the eyes of a daughter weeping for a father who had lost his way. Sealed inside the car Sara was thinking about Mario and yet she was also thinking about her own father, who since her mother had died could no longer do anything. All he had done was observe Sara growing up, asking her for help, and one day he had said to her *I wasn't able to do it*. And then when my parents looked out over the balcony again, Sara had gone, leaving an empty rectangle between two cars.

37

AND SO THE DIALOGUE BETWEEN MY MOTHER AND OLMO went on as it had begun. I served as a bridge between the two of them. She carried on cooking for him, and he warmed the things up in the oven. He had learned to use it by himself. In exchange, he talked to me about Russia, showed me the photographs, and I would report back to my mother. But the photographs he showed me were always taken from books, we would leaf through them of an evening, and he would show me this caravan of people walking in the middle of the snow, the white of the steppe matching that of the paper. He talked to me about the shoes they had given them, the clothes that were no good for those temperatures, and about how the soldiers would stop along the road, and how sleep would take hold of them. And when sleep opened the door then the icy cold would come in, and, together with the cold, death would also slip in. He always talked to me about the return, as if they had never really left but only turned back, walking through the snow. If I asked him what had happened when they were in Russia he would say *I'll tell you another time*, and go back to talking to me about the long road they had travelled, that that was the terrible thing, and that was why they had written books about it. Then at home I would read those books, line by line, looking at the dozens of photographs they contained, that multitude amid the white, the sunken faces, the eyes that were no longer there, everyone with holes on both sides of the nose, the war that seemed only a war against the cold. And the things that were written in those books were the things Olmo had said to me, sometimes even the same sentences, the same episodes, which weren't his, but had become so by dint of retelling them, a woman who had saved him and given him something to drink, a poor dog that they had eaten because they were hungry, and it wasn't bad either. And even the Nikolaevka bridge, about which he had told me dozens of times, the most important battle, the dead and wounded, the courage, the fear, and as usual the cold. He had never been at Nikolaevka. But Olmo didn't want to remain outside history, and so he took the history of others for himself.

One evening, a photograph and a postcard slipped out of one of the books Olmo had lent me. On the postcard there was printed *We shall conquer*, it was one of those the army handed out, the men used to send them home with greetings, with a signature and a date. In the photograph there was something that looked like a football goal, and a boy hanging from the crossbar. Below, another three soldiers were laughing, in different uniforms. Two were looking straight at the lens, the third was looking in another direction. It was an ordinary goal, in the middle of something that looked like a square. In the background a building loomed, there were some windows open and a few people were looking out. One had his hand outstretched as if he wanted to wave, or stop the execution. The Russian's body hung almost from the point where the crossbar and vertical post met, his neck broken, his face rammed forwards, drooping, his chin resting on his chest. The soldier was wearing a hat, it looked like a walking hat. The beards of the other soldiers below were not long. It was winter, there was snow, and their faces were ordinary faces, one was wearing glasses, he was the one pointing at the man hanging there beside him.

38

WHEN I SAW THE PHOTOGRAPH WITH THE HANGED MAN I sat down, as if I had been struck in the back. I looked at the rope taut around the neck, the boy's closed eyes, and then at all the distance between the ends of his feet and the ground, I felt my stomach knot, I ran to the bathroom, I opened my mouth wide, two dry heaves and only a thread of saliva that plunged down into the toilet. When I came out of the bathroom I had a white face and that body in my hand, because for me that body was much more than a pilloried Russian soldier. That hanged body was also a secret between me and Sara, from a different war. It was a secret hidden so well that in the end we had forgotten about it. To conceal it, to confine it in a past to be buried, for a long time had been the only way to carry on thinking of a future together. But now it returned like this, with all the violence of a sudden apparition, surrendered to the force of gravity, in a black-and-white photograph from 1943, a boy executed in the middle of a square.

For days, Olmo continued to show me photographs of men frozen to death, and I had that photograph in my pocket and didn't have the courage to talk to him about it. Olmo also had his own little home cinema, in the bedroom. Sometimes he would take it out when I arrived. It was a slide projector, beside it three trays full of photographs with which he fed it, the darkness inside the room and by way of a screen the back of a map of Russia. Sometimes he even invited the neighbours, but only the woman would always come, she used to say *Sandro is on shift*, which was a way of saying that he was at home in front of the television, partly to sleep and partly to wait for the time to go back to work. So only she and I sat on the bed, to watch the umpteenth repeat of the men who died of cold. We would sit there, close together on the bed, a rift in the mattress, creases on the blanket, our knees together in front. First Olmo would switch off the light, then stand beside the projector, the darkness all around and that circle of light on the wall. One after another, he took the trays, put them in place, and reviewed the photographs. Between each one and the next a window of white was thrown open. I looked at him, a half smile on his face, his cheeks flushed with the warmth, the glow of the projector lighting up a bit of his face. To see him there, standing at attention, he looked like a captain at the helm, with us seated close together in silence, our legs touching. I could feel her warmth, see her varnished nails.

And he stood beside us navigating a passage through the snow of January '43, a ship in the middle of the steppe. *Look*, he would say, thrusting his arm forwards, pointing at all those bodies in the sea.

So we would look at all those photographs that were always the same, that sea of mules and soldiers, the sledges bearing kitbags and outstretched bodies, a soldier lying in the white, his body fallen forwards like a cross that had been hacked down, his arms spread out on both sides, his face sunk in the snow. They went by, one after another, that sudden light and then another slide, our faces in the darkness, with my neighbour getting up, going out for a while and then coming back, her boyfriend constantly calling her on the mobile, and the mattress sagging every time she stood up. The slides we looked at were the photographs in the books, Olmo had taken them from the books and photographed them, some still had a caption. Some came round several times, that long snake of dark bodies dragging itself along in the whiteness as far as the background, a soldier offering a blanket to another soldier, and Olmo repeating *What martyrs we were, only the Lord saved us.* Then in one photograph there was a group of soldiers gathered round another serviceman whose hands were raised above the others. It was the chaplain who served Mass in the middle of the snow, with the soldiers looking at him. *It's a good job there were the chaplains to give us the strength to fight, they were the ones who kept the army on its feet* Olmo said. *To pray, fight and walk, hoping in mercy.* And then the projection ended, Olmo switched the light on, the projector fan carried on blowing and we looked at one another, rubbing our eyes.

Then one day I took out that photograph. I didn't say anything to him, I just handed it to him, he took it, looked in his pocket for his reading glasses and put them on his nose instead of the others.

Every now and then I would take Olmo for a spin, I would wait for him under his flat, the engine running. I would attach his seat belt leaning my chest over towards him, my breath cut every time, his breath under my hands. Then we would hit the ring road, sometimes we would spend hours in the car, talking to each other, looking outside the window, listening to music. Other times we would park, walk a few hundred metres and sit on a bench, then take another walk and head for another bench. One of the places we often went to was the park where Mario used to take me on the bus, and we walked as far as the fountain, the benches all around, people talking, reading, taking some sun. A duck was still swimming in the fountain, even though it wasn't the same one as before but another which resembled it. The children were still calling it and energetically tossing it biscuits. I had a photograph in which I was one of those children, my jeans rolled up above my shoes, my arm thrust forwards, my mouth open in a yell. Olmo and I would stay there as long as the sun shone. I even bought him a pair of dark glasses, maybe a bit big for his face. And so one day, sitting on one of those benches, I took that photograph with the hanged Russian soldier from my pocket, I handed it to him without adding anything else. He put his hand in his shirt pocket, put on his glasses, looked at it and took them off. Then he got up, I watched him walk around the fountain, sit down again, stare at the water, lower his face. I asked him *Which one are you?* showing him the gallows with the three soldiers laughing beneath it. *The one who took the photo* he replied.

39

OLMO DIDN'T WANT TO TALK ABOUT THAT PHOTOGRAPH,
yet at nights it continued to slip into my sleep. In every dream there
was Sara showing it to me, talking to me, but I couldn't hear. Olmo
had confessed to me that he had taken it, yet when I asked him to
tell me more, all he told me was that seventy years are too many to
remember. But I tried all the same, and so every so often I would
take the photograph of that boy from my pocket and put it on
the table. Every time I did this Olmo would gape, opening his eyes
wide to let all the photograph pass through them, first the Russian
boy and then the three Italian soldiers. Then he would squeeze his
eyes as if to swallow them. And having sucked them inwards,
his eyes would usually go away, and dark craters would appear
instead in the middle of his face. But he didn't say anything and the
photograph remained on the table, the soldiers with their smiles
and that boy there above, with his feet so far from the ground.
They had their hands in their pockets, as if the photographer had
captured them for posterity as they took a stroll. The boy's body
hung behind them like a part of the scenery, the square, a dog in the
corner, the building and the people looking out, all together to
make up a souvenir of Russia. They stood in front of him and it
was as if he weren't there, the everyday smiles, as if posed, to be
sent home to stave off their nostalgia. Olmo was the person who
had taken all there was to see and he had put it in the shot, the dog,
the boy and the tree nearby. Then he had stood behind the camera,
pressed the button, and had remained outside that souvenir photograph forever. So he didn't tell me anything more, and if I insisted
he would cough, his whole face going red and his voice lowering,
saying there are things that with time one gets rid of. And that thing
had gone away, eaten by the shutter of the camera.

*

All of a sudden Olmo didn't want to see me anymore. If I called he was busy or didn't reply. I contacted his neighbours, they said he was fine, they assured me he would call back, but then he didn't. Only once did he see me, but only for a short time. He came down and we chatted on the pavement. He told me that he hadn't been feeling well recently, he needed to be on his own. I asked him if the photograph had anything to do with it and he turned to look in the other direction, then he said yes. He told me *The dead should be left in peace*, and he said it as if he were the one who was dead and not the boy in the photograph. He shook my hand and went away. I was left on the pavement, Olmo facing the lift, his back to me, then he stepped inside, the doors closed and the luminous numbers accompanied him floor by floor. So I went off, without turning round, the car, one street after another, arriving, parking, switching off the lights, making the burglar alarm flash, reaching the street door. Under my door there was a note, it said *Where are you?* There was a drawing on the note, a very large sun begun with yellow and finished with black. It looked like an eclipse. At the foot of the sheet there was the signature of the little boy upstairs, name and surname, because I had told him that a work of art is a work of art only if the artist signs it with name and surname. I picked up the sheet and put it inside the folder where I kept all his things. He was a specialist in the sun, I had one of his drawings in which there were four of them.

I, too, got a sheet of paper, our agreement was that the response to one drawing was another drawing. I had disappeared for a while, even though I often heard him running about above my head in the evenings. But as the summer was drawing to an end he didn't stay out on the balcony very much, his homework kept him busy at the table. Even though we would sometimes greet each other, raising our hands, him standing behind the window as I passed by below. I would shout *Hi*, he would tap his hand against the window. In the end he had decided to come and see me, leaving that eclipse under the door and that question. So I, too, drew a sun on a sheet of paper, and below it I wrote *Here*. Then I went up the stairs two at a time and slipped the sheet under his door. I knocked and hurried back downstairs so as not to be seen. I heard the door open, and his grandmother calling him, then in a lower voice and laughing she said *You have mail*. A few minutes later I heard the door opening again, footsteps on the stairs, and the rustling of a sheet under my door, and then him laughing to himself as he went back upstairs. I took the sheet and unfolded it, on it was written. *Luckily*.

40

OLMO SHOWED UP AGAIN AFTER A WEEK, A STAMPED envelope in the letterbox. At first, my mother would ask about him, worrying that he was alone. But then she stopped and didn't mention his name, focusing only on her box in the broom cupboard in which she collected things she had found and bought on offer, waiting for the moment to be able to deliver them. Every time I went to visit them I would check and see the level of its contents rise. The box stood there in the dark like a prisoner, only seeing someone open the door, the light coming in, and then the darkness closing everything again. But my mother never said anything about that box, a container like any other for differentiated refuse. She hadn't said or asked anything about Olmo also because of that photograph I had brought her, the hanged soldier, the rope, the broken neck, and underneath those young men posing for a souvenir photograph. When she saw it she put her hands over her face, her eyes between her half-open fingers. She turned it over pressing her hand on top of it, the murdered boy and the soldiers all squashed against the wood of the table. Then that wail had come out, a lament from far away, as if it had climbed up through time to end up in my mother, to come out of her mouth like that and rise upwards. When she took her hands from her face her eyes were like those of another. And with those eyes she looked at one of the photographs of Mario scattered around the house in their frames and then she closed them, squeezing them tight.

In reality, I opened Olmo's envelope a few days after having received it. I hadn't even realized that it was from him. For a while it remained with the others on the floor, in the place where Sara's sofa had been. Since she had gone, all the things that had no place went into that hole, like the remains of food chewed in the mouth, all wedged in the place of the absent tooth. That was where I left boxes to be thrown away, old newspapers, mineral water crates, and it was there where I collected all the post that arrived and that I didn't feel like opening. The envelope lay there and it scared me, the fines, the bills, I would see the pile grow like a tumour, take up space for itself, waking me up at nights and making me sweat at the idea of all those things I still had to pay. So it was precisely at night that I would get up, sit down at the table and one after another start to open the envelopes, a sigh of relief for every piece of correspondence that wasn't nasty, the sheets laid one on top of the other and the envelopes crumpled up on the floor. On the envelope Olmo had sent me there was no sender's name, only my name, surname and address. I opened it early one morning, before dawn, the trams had just begun to pass by. Every time, the floor would vibrate, tickling my feet. In the meantime in the garden there was still the scaffolding for the neighbours' windows. It stood there in the middle, in that darkness that was now lightening, like the skeleton of some animal extinct for a few millennia and rediscovered there, in the courtyard of a building in the city centre. One day I came back home and saw the two workmen climbing up on the skeleton, their feet braced against its vertebrae. They greeted me, cigarette ends scattered around my garden. I stayed with them for a while, watching them fitting the big windows in the holes they had opened up. And when the first window was securely fixed, one of the two men opened it from inside the house, looked out and asked me *How does it look to you?*

Inside Olmo's envelope there was a note, all it said was *I must talk to you*. It was written in a shaky hand, full of hesitation, each of the letters a different size. And so I called him straight away, he replied before I even heard the telephone ring. *We have to see each other* he said, without saying hello or asking me how I was. He said it like that, in a single exhalation of breath, as if he had been holding it loaded in his mouth for days. I told him he had made me worry, vanishing that way, sending no news. I was glad though, I would go to pick him up in the afternoon of the next day. When I was about to hang up he said *One last thing*. I said *What? Have you been to Russia?* he asked. *No. Good, good,* he said, and afterwards he added *You'll like it, you'll see.*

41

IN THE MEANTIME SARA HAD KEPT HER DISTANCE, SHE would call my mother every now and then to ask her if she needed anything. But they were sporadic calls, a few minutes without ever mentioning me, circling around my name, and then they would hang up. One morning she telephoned when I was also there, in my parents' house. My mother answered and then went out onto the balcony, I heard her say *It can happen, don't worry,* and ended the call saying *Look after yourself, I'll call you later.* When she came back in she put the telephone on the table, picking up our conversation from where we had left off. But I had heard Sara's voice, when my mother had answered, even though my mother had kept her hand pressed over the mobile. Sara had said *Hi Giò,* shortening her name, my mother had instinctively looked at me, then said *Good morning* before going outside. When she came back in we both knew, but kept quiet about that detail as we talked. For fifteen minutes there were two conversations underway, which carried on in unison, mouths that talked about the shopping and going to the post office, and eyes just above them that spoke of Sara. Then I went out, to give her the time to call back. I told her I had two or three things to do, and I would drop in later. My mother accompanied me to the door, she stayed there for a bit, talking to me on the landing, she wasn't about to let me go. She stood there, with the door open, her mouth saying *Would you prefer it if we went to the post office right away?* her eyes above asking me *Would you really mind if I called Sara?*

Sara had telephoned because on waking up she had found a bloodstain on the sheet, she had been frightened. So when I went out my mother called her back and reassured her. And two days later Sara telephoned to say that luckily everything was in order in there, and my mother told her she shouldn't have been frightened. She also advised her to stroke her belly before going to sleep, to run her fingers over it lightly. My mother had done this with me. With her fingertips she had written words that her belly then absorbed, they had entered her flesh, the first words I had learned. My mother also advised her to sing, *It's like listening to singing in a church* she said. Then for a week Sara disappeared, she always showed up again with those quick telephone calls, with a medical test she had picked up from the hospital. She would read the results over the telephone while walking along the street. Her ankles, according to her, had swollen even though it was a bit soon. Sara began and ended all her telephone calls by apologizing to my mother, she would say *Sorry if I ask you*, and all my mother would reply was *Come, come, these aren't problems*. Then she would explain, give advice, say to her *Call me again for anything*, and Sara would repeat *Sorry, I promise to learn quickly to do things by myself*.

Once she called the house and my father answered, he told her that my mother was at the hairdressers, if she wished she could call her on the mobile. So Sara caught her between her shampoo and set and they talked. And that evening my father told her he had felt uncomfortable. My mother had just come home, just the time to take off her shoes, to say hello and receive no reply. She found my father in the bathroom, shaving foam on his face, in front of the mirror. He was touching his cheek with one hand, with the other he ran the razor over his face. My father spoke to her while continuing to look at himself, the razor removing the foam and the beard together, and he said *I felt a bit embarrassed*. They had both been a little intimidated on the telephone, Sara had apologized a thousand times, then my father had tried to make conversation, he got all the words wrong, Sara struck him as being angry. My mother laughed, there in the bathroom she laid her hand on his back. Then she sat down on the edge of the bathtub, behind the sink, she vanished from the mirror, leaving only my father inside it. And she ran her hand through her hair, asking him *What does it look this time?*

42

OLMO TWICE ASKED ME TO LEAVE FOR RUSSIA, THE FIRST request was drowned out by an aircraft that was landing, the second time he yelled it while looking at the runway. *We can talk about in good time* I said. He pointed at all the planes coming in as if it were possible for me not to see them, the shadow growing on the runway, the wings stretching out, the wheels hitting the tarmac, and then braking. It wasn't the first time we had gone to the airport, but it was the first after his disappearance. For a long stretch of road we raced in the car alongside the runway, the aeroplanes beside us preparing for take-off. We saw them loom above us, enormous and ready to fly, we were suddenly so small and slow, their shadow swallowing ours almost without opening its mouth. Every time, Olmo gestured at the shadow of the aeroplane on the grass, the shadow bigger than us, and said *It's eating us, eating us, eating us . . . eaten.* But then the plane proceeded on its way and a bit at a time we would emerge from behind it, and detach ourselves from it, delivered in that way onto the road and left to our slow race.

That day we went into the restaurant, a place in which the sound of the aeroplanes sneaked in only when the doors were opened, and remained outside when they were closed again. The restaurant overlooked the runway. A man we had asked for a less windy spot had shown the place to us. And there we ate like almost all those present, side by side watching take-offs and landings, the children pointing out every arrival and every departure, and the parents nodding without looking up from their plates. The waiters had a little aeroplane sewn onto their lapels, and there wasn't one dish on the menu that didn't have a Boeing, a fuselage, or a hostess in its name. Near the entrance there was a glass display case containing model planes of every size and colour, and photographs, the cook and her husband arm in arm with pilots who had just dropped in there for a bite to eat. Having drunk his coffee, Olmo pushed the cup aside and placed his retired insurance agent's briefcase on the table. He took out a notebook, opened up one of the maps he had shown me many times and laid that photograph on it, the one of the hanged boy. *Inside the notebook there are others*, he said, *but look at them when you get home.* Then he began to run his index finger over the map, brushing it slowly with his fingertip, his nails freshly cut. He moved his finger with care, as if it had eyes and he were using them to look for something hidden among the names of the cities written in large letters, the smaller towns and the slender curved lines of the rivers. Then he stopped on Rossoš, as he always did. He had brushed over it so many times the name was almost illegible, he had worn it out, a trench dug there in the middle of the white sheet. He looked up from the map and said *I'd like to go there.* And he spread out his arms, started laughing and laid his hand on my shoulder. *What can you do?* I merely gave a sigh, two aeroplanes had taken off in the meanwhile, a little boy beating against the window, banging his hand on it and calling to them. Then I said to Olmo that I would go there. And he raised one arm, looking for the waiter, the waiter arrived the way a steward arrives. *A vodka for the young man*, Olmo said, then he added *And one for me*, his hand open on the map.

Before leaving the restaurant Olmo asked the waiter if he thought planes for Moscow left from that airport. *Of course*, the man said. He said it as if they made those aeroplanes for Russia in the kitchen, a house speciality. Then he took a book and started to leaf through it, *Two flights every day, the first at eleven in the morning, the last at 10.25 in the evening. Would the gentlemen like another drink?* Olmo waved his hand, *For goodness sake no.* Then the waiter put the book back under the till and disappeared behind a door, as if going into the cabin, *Flight assistants prepare for take-off.* And a few hours later, after leaving Olmo, I was driving towards home, I saw a plane pass overhead, I followed its flashing lights for a stretch of sky. I looked at the time and it was half past ten, maybe that was the flight for Moscow. Inside the aeroplane someone would have taken off his shoes, stretched out his feet below the seat in front, trying to sleep. And maybe that someone, I thought later as I slipped into sleep, was Mario, or perhaps it was me going to look for him, and there was my mother, passing by in the car thirty thousand feet below, and she mistook us for a shooting star.

43

WHEN I TOLD MY MOTHER I WAS GOING TO LEAVE, SHE WAS frightened at first. I heard her silence on the other end of the line, her voice cowering inside her ribcage. In the background I could hear the television, I knew my father was watching it, his laughter bursting out a moment after that of the others. The less my mother said, the more I pressed the handset to my ear. She asked me *Why?* Then she told me to wait, because she had to go to the bathroom for a minute, she asked my father if he wanted to speak to me. So he arrived, I could still hear him laughing between the television and the telephone, the tail end of his laughter trailing off in my ear. He spoke to me and yet I sensed his eyes on the television, my words fell into a void, dying away before they reached him. I told him about Russia and he made no comment. Then there was another burst of laughter, he said *Sorry, sorry, wait a second.* He put the receiver down, shortly afterwards the television was switched off, he shifted a chair to come back to me. So I told him again about my decision, and he too asked me *Why?* But it was a completely different why, something in which he wasn't involved. Then I heard my mother coming, asking him to set the table, taking the telephone back from him, *Here I am.* All she asked me was if I was sure about making such a long journey, going so far away. I told her I was, that it was for Mario, and for Olmo, and that photograph that had frightened me. Yet I didn't tell her about the other reason behind it, the spectre that had first united and then divided Sara and me, a spectre that the photograph had called up once more. She told me that when Mario had done it, gone down there, she was only four days old. They had told her that he had taken her in his arms only once, but that he knew how to do it, an instinct, he knew how to put his hand behind the neck, hold her head in his palm, spreading out his fingers. And when he returned he no longer knew how to do anything, he was afraid of everything. Then I heard her swallow, a daughter faced with a father who knew only fear, and she asked me *What are you going to make to eat?*

After that, my mother started to think of my departure every minute of the day. She called me constantly, to know the details, how many days I would stay there, the places, the temperature. In the end she dealt with everything, the passport, the papers for the visa. One day she went to Milan to get the passport stamped – she who had only ever taken a few trains. She called me from inside the Russian consulate to ask me for some information, she spoke quietly. Laughing, she said *I'm on Russian soil.* I asked her *What time is it there?* She said *There's two hours' difference but you can't see that.* In the background I could hear the footsteps of someone walking, each step with an echo. My mother lowered her voice as the footsteps gradually came closer, and spoke louder when they went away. And when my mother left she called me, talking loudly, excited, a voice that broke loose from every part of her. She told me that they hadn't asked many questions, luckily, and that there was a kind gentleman, he had said *Have a nice trip* to her as he banged the stamp down onto the paper. As she spoke, every so often she would ask me the way, you could sense she was afraid of getting lost. She said *I have your passport in my bag, the photograph is really nice.* I imagined her walking in Milan, the pressure of her arm holding her bag tightly, and inside it, among the handkerchiefs and the umbrella, that passport she was protecting as if it weren't mine but Mario's, many years before. I went to pick her up from the train, and when she got into the car, in front of the station, she said *It seems to me like two years have gone by and yet I left only this morning.*

And in the notebook Olmo had given me at the airport I found a Russian telephone number, with an illegible name beside it. Olmo couldn't recall who it was. It was a number like any other, but with a Russian dialling code. He made great efforts to remember, then got irritated, he couldn't remember anything anymore. And one evening we tried calling, after a meal at my place. Half way through dinner the boy from the floor above appeared, he had rung. He came running into the house and when he saw Olmo he stopped talking and came to a halt. He sat down on a chair next to me, and lowered his face. He raised it only to tell me or ask me something, but he always kept Olmo out of his gaze. Then when I told him we were going to make a telephone call to Russia he looked at Olmo and asked me *For him?* So we showed him where Russia was, then we went over to the telephone. I asked him to dial the number by pressing the buttons with his finger. One after another, I dictated them to him, 007 47342 12438, and with the speakerphone on we heard the ringtones start. He followed them on the map, the entire journey they had to make to get there. Olmo didn't even seem to be breathing, and then a voice replied, a man's voice, and Olmo got frightened, he slammed the telephone down.

44

OLMO HAD BEGUN TO LAY HIS MEMORIES ASIDE THE WAY people lay things aside for a son who drops in every so often. He gathered them little by little as they came to mind, and then he collected them in an attempt to make a complete one. He tried to put together a Russia that would suit me too, yet something always happened, the way the wind suddenly makes papers fly. The nearer my departure came the more his confusion grew, as if he heard a buzzing from somewhere but didn't understand its source. On certain evenings I would find him with his face tormented by effort, his eyes would narrow and he would say *I don't understand anything any longer.* He got all the place names muddled, and people too, and by putting together the summer of those days with the Russian winter that froze in his head, he could no longer find anything. He had tried to draw a map, day after day he would do it again, then throw the lot away. On that sheet he would spread out on the table there were always tanks lined up, and landing strips carved out of the meadows for the war planes, landing in the middle of snow and bullets. And there was the headquarters, the sick-bay, the commissary for the soldiers, the road that led down to the river, this long river that took up half of the page, bigger than the entire country. It ran down to the furthest extremity of the page, it seemed to overflow onto the table. But then Olmo would suddenly tear everything up and bang his fist down, he felt like crying out of irritation and frustration. Once he got angry because he had put the square in Russou in two places at the same time, and in reality the school he remembered wasn't there, but in another town, in Italy. It was an erroneous memory that ended up there in the middle, a building transferred thousands of kilometres, slipping across Europe to fall onto a page.

He gave me the map the evening before my departure, *You'll see,
it'll come in handy* he said. After throwing away so many sheets of
paper, he had completed it in pencil, to be able to get it wrong and
make adjustments, erase and redo it all from square one. So now
there was a network of streets, some buildings, the river, the square
and tanks lined up everywhere. There was also a cross, at the far
end of the square, which was his way of showing me the gallows,
the hanged boy. But mainly there were all the rubbings-out he had
made, before arriving at that final version. You could see them
clearly, they were there, all carved into the sheet of paper, the
rubber had tried to take them away but hadn't succeeded. He had
removed things at a stroke, but the marks had remained. So on the
map he had drawn for me there were also all the things that had
only passed through, that had been in the town for a while and then
had gone away, taking their leave. And where the school had been
before, now there was a football pitch, and in the river there was
what looked like a drowned tank, and he had drawn a church and
rubbed it out twice, removing the cross. At first he had filled the
town with people, populating it with figures sketched with a shaky
hand, some bigger, some smaller, in the middle of the street. He had
also put some bicycles propped up against the trees alongside the
avenue, with wheels that were two circles with a line to join them
up, and the square was full of people, a few civilians and a few
soldiers, the soldiers had rifles that stuck up from behind their
shoulders, and from the windows of the school asterisks looked
out, and *SCHOOL* was written on the wall. But then Olmo had
removed them all in a single stroke of the rubber, the people overwhelmed by the relentless fury in his hand, sweeping away men,
women and children. Yet they were still there, they resisted, buried
in the paper and visible to the eye. Some had even survived in part,
because Olmo had rubbed everything out clumsily, and so the C of

SCHOOL was still there, in the square there was a piece of bicycle, and the page was full of rubber shavings, like shell cases left after an execution.

Before leaving, I bought Olmo a mobile, I told him it was important for me to be able to call him from Russia, I showed him how to answer, and how to plug it in to recharge it. He took it in his hand and his face broke into a smile, as if it were useful for his departure, and not to stay and wait for news. I saved my number in the memory, and also that of Giovanna, my mother. I told him, *If there's anything you need, just press here to call her, she already knows everything.* He said *O.K.*, his face concentrated in the effort of memorizing, with a hint of bewilderment too. And two hours later I called him to let him try it out. Three rings and he answered. *Yes* he said. He said it as if I were already in Russia, as if he were standing to attention, ready to come to my aid.

45

THE WAITER CAME TOWARDS ME AND SHOOK MY HAND, he said *Welcome back*, the aeroplane still in flight on his jacket. Then he also greeted my mother and pointed to a table at the back. He preceded us saying *I'll lead the way*. Then he opened the menus in front of us with the grace of a conjuror, a pack of cards that wasn't there before and then was. Outside it was already almost dark, the lights on the runway outlining the track for the aeroplanes about to take off. Some stayed there without moving, lights flashing on the wings marking the time of the wait. Rather than look outside, my mother talked to me, her fork hovering over her plate, she repeated the list of things not to be forgotten, the advice.

After having lost it for years, and having been kept at the door by Sara's presence at my side, she had now returned to this motherly concern. She was almost on the edge of her chair, turned towards me. Then she put a hand on my arm, lowered her voice and said *I told Sara you were leaving*. In the meantime the waiter came and went, with the relaxed composure of a steward, the dishes arriving from behind, like planes emerging from behind a mountain and landing on the tablecloth. And when the waiter brought us the bill he remained standing beside the table, and asked me if I was satisfied. *The second time is the one that counts* he said. Then he looked at my mother and asked her if she had enjoyed it, she said *Very much indeed*. Then he smiled, thanked her with a little bow and added *Your father, Madame, is a phenomenon, still drinking vodka at his age*. And he said to her *Will you say hello from me?* My mother replied *With pleasure, thank you*, but she was ill at ease.

At the airport I waved to her, my shoes still in my hand after the security checks. She was on the other side, in the midst of the relatives, all there to watch the others walk away, their backs turned, first emptying their pockets, taking off watches and belts, and stepping through the metal detector in their socks, their arms raised, leaving sweaty footprints on the floor. I saw her head off towards the exit, I lost her and then found her again in the swarm of people and suitcases coming and going through the door. I followed her until she disappeared beyond the door leading to the car park. She hadn't driven for years and now she was determined to take it up again. She hadn't wanted my father to accompany us, she had said *We're off, and I've left you something for dinner, in that pot on the stove*. When she told him this I was there too. He made no answer, but a hint of melancholy came into his eyes, *Do you still remember how a car works?* he asked her. But she didn't want to drive to the airport, she was ashamed for me to see her, she changed radio stations, looking for songs that she could sing. And when we arrived I looked for a parking spot that would be easy to get out of, a few metres in reverse and down the ramp.

Now she would have got into the car, she would have pulled the seat up, almost as far as the steering wheel, and she would have mentally repeated every action before doing it, *Press the clutch, select reverse, let out the clutch, accelerate, look in the mirror, brake, select first gear, go.* And in the meantime I would have waited for boarding, and maybe sipped a coffee during the wait, keeping an eye on the other passengers. And she would have slipped onto the ring road with humility and fear, clinging to the wheel with her hands, the only slow car in the midst of a flow of self-confident drivers. And finally they would have called the flight for Moscow and we would have formed a queue, the ticket inside the passport, the stamps on the visa, and inside the passport the photograph my mother liked so much, and words in Cyrillic. And we would have boarded the plane, each passenger in his seat, sharing the space in the overhead lockers, standing up to make way for the new arrivals. In the meantime my mother would have started to enjoy driving, and she would have gone into fourth and then fifth, she would have relaxed against the seat, and she would have even sung, in the end, and she would have wondered why she had spent all those years without driving. She would have gone into the house and apologized to my father, asking him to massage her feet, and he would have looked at her, and then he would have taken her feet in his hands, one after the other. And on the plane they would have switched off the lights, and perhaps in the restaurant someone might have watched us leave.

46

I SPENT THE WHOLE JOURNEY FROM MOSCOW AIRPORT TO the hotel reading and answering the messages received during the flight, the Russian night already heading towards dawn. I gave the taxi driver the slip of paper, the name of the hotel, the address, and he gave me the thumbs-up in token of agreement. *Italy?* he asked me. I gave him the thumbs-up, instinctively smiling in a different way, as you would expect an Italian to smile, lots of teeth and few worries. Among the messages that had arrived there was one from my father, it read *You've arrived safe and sound*. It was written like that, with no question mark, as if weren't a question but a statement, as if he had himself heard the windows shake and then the floor at home give a jolt. My mother and father wrote mobile messages together, both with reading glasses on, one head leaning against the other, together on the sofa. They would sit there, my father's fingertips pressing the buttons and my mother pointing at the letters with the tip of her finger, losing patience now and again, grumbling. Then when the message was sent, they would both take off their glasses, lean back exhausted against the cushions, the mobile abandoned a little further away. So these messages would reach me worn out, sometimes even blank, sent without words, like an aeroplane that had taken off without passengers, and the passengers still below, watching it go away. The message they had sent me kept arriving, goodness knows how many times they had pressed the button, to be certain that it had gone, and after that another time once more just to be sure. *You've arrived safe and sound, You've arrived safe and sound, You've arrived safe and sound*, I heard every message burst in my pocket like popcorn. And there was also one from Sara, *Welcome to Russia*.

*

There was traffic despite the hour, a road with four lanes, but I carried on looking only at the telephone display, reviewing the old messages too, rereading them. I took shelter in Italian the way you take shelter in a doorway, finding it ajar, going in, closing it firmly and leaning against it. Since I had arrived in Moscow I was left without words, the information on the signs in another alphabet and in people's mouths this abrupt language, with nothing to hang on to. At the airport I had looked around, seeking a way forward, my feet weren't moving anymore, paralysed on the spot where I stood, the moving walkway running empty in front of me, with all the people who had retrieved their luggage already gone. It was as if they had suddenly taken my words from me, collected them in furious haste and carted them off in the night. And it was as if once all the words had been taken away nothing else remained, the people and things had also suddenly vanished, every word a piece of the world that had dissolved, one puff and then air in the air, one blow and then nothing ahead. I was left motionless in the middle of that unexpected desert, nothing and nobody around, until I saw a sign saying *TAXI*, and an arrow, and other signs with an English translation underneath. I handed the taxi driver the slip of paper the agency had given me, the only chance I had was to have faith, to trust in him blindly. And so I took refuge in the messages on my mobile, my language and the things that came back to me on the screen, a pop and my father and mother, another pop and there was Sara, like rubbing the lamp and seeing them appear, sitting in the taxi with me, squeezing up to stay in there all together. I said my name out loud, without thinking, *Pietro*, I repeated it several times, the driver's eyes looking for me in the mirror, and I smiled the way you expect an Italian to smile when he talks to himself.

We arrived at the hotel without even entering the city, thirteen floors of windows and a neon sign, *NOVOTEL*, a Novotel the same as all the Novotels in the world. The rest was a cement square, the flashing lights of the casino all around, and the dawn beginning to unfold from behind the buildings. There was the nauseating smell of a van selling sandwiches. A woman was cleaning the hotplate and a man in front was yanking down the shutters, the van gradually became a coloured box from which the man and woman emerged. I saw them get into a long, ramshackle car, the woman in the driving seat. First the lights came on, then the engine, and they vanished behind the hotel, leaving the orphaned box in the square. I went up to my room, the eleventh floor, a very tall girl pressed the button in the lift, she accompanied me up, talking to me in English. She pitched on her heels when the lift stopped. She showed me my room, asked if the bathroom was to my liking, and the bed, and the window that looked out over Moscow. In the distance there was also a balcony, and a chair to sit in when the weather was fine. In front, there was a huge building, in all colours, railings all around it, lights trained on the facade. It seemed like a castle in an amusement park. I asked the girl what that building was. She told me it was the Kremlin. Then she started to laugh, and told me it was a fake Kremlin, a copy made for the tourists. She told me it had been built for those who were only passing through, a stopover in Moscow and then off again, to be able to take at least some photographs to show on their return home. Then she took her leave and wished me goodnight, even though by now it was almost day. The light fell softly on the buildings of Moscow like snowfall, illuminating them, and then the gardens, and the parked cars, and the mopeds tied to the poles, and that coloured Kremlin that looked like a birthday cake. And I would have blown on it, to put everything out, to make the night the girl had wished me come back, to sleep, my eyes were hurting.

47

I SAT UP IN BED WITH A START WHEN THE CHAMBERMAID
threw the curtains open. The light spread over my face and the
woman who had knocked down the door of dreams stood at the
foot of the bed with her hands on her hips. She was a small, edgy
woman, a white bonnet on her head, an apron round her waist
and two eyes that you almost couldn't see. For a few moments we
looked at each other in silence, my back to the wall and my knees
drawn up against my chest, and she with her obvious resentment.
First she looked at me, then at the clock on the wall, as if the
problem weren't so much my presence as the fact that I was still
sleeping at that hour. But she said nothing, she disappeared for a
moment and reappeared behind a hoover, and vacuumed all round
the bed. I followed her with my eyes, the embarrassment at being
naked under the sheets, and after having looked down on me, she
simply took to ignoring me. She came in and out of the room, I
could hear her shouting in the corridor, she dusted the television
as if washing someone's hair. I stayed sitting there, wondering
how I could get out of bed, the woman had opened the window, a
draught blew in, swept over me, and Moscow burst into the room.
Every so often another woman would come in, same apron, same
height, she also ignored me as if I were the bed and not a body lying
in it. They were yelling agitated phrases, which carried the words a
bit higher than the sound of the vacuum cleaner, and when the
machine was switched off the voices would deflate, like a cake
when the oven is opened too soon. Then the first woman laid a pile
of sheets on the bed, raised her eyes to look at me, then turned
round to let me get out, offering me her back as a screen. So I
slipped furtively out of bed, Moscow's air tickling my backside, the
floor cold under my feet, and went into the bathroom.

Later, I found the girl who had shown me to my room at the reception desk. She greeted me with a smile as she spoke, the badge on her breast said *Tatiana S.*, and behind her were four wall clocks, Moscow time, Tokyo time, New York and Paris. She was standing there, with her head among the clock faces, her round face between Tokyo and New York. I watched her as she spoke to other people, waiting for my turn, preparing the questions I had to ask. And I looked at that face in the middle of the clocks, as if she had a different time, which wasn't that of Tokyo, New York, or Paris and yet not even that of Moscow, but a time that was hers alone, faster or slower, further ahead or further behind that of other people's. When my turn came she asked me if I had managed to sleep, if the ambulance sirens had disturbed me. I looked at her with the expression of someone who thinks he hasn't understood. She explained that foreigners often complained about the ambulances, even though it was normal, in a metropolis, for lots of people fall ill, you need to save them. And in fact even now, as she was talking to me from behind the desk, from inside that different time of hers, you could hear the sirens wailing along the road, overlapping, coming closer and receding into the far distance. And the sound of the sirens was very different from the Italian one, as if illness and the fear of death were different over there. In any case I said no, they hadn't disturbed me, I hadn't even heard them. I had only got a scare when the cleaner had come in without knocking and opened the curtains. I didn't even remember where I was.

I told her I wanted to go to Rossoš, and could she give me a hand. She asked me when I wanted to leave, she gestured at me to wait and then disappeared for a few minutes. A few steps away from there the lift door opened. The cleaner who had woken me up came out, pushing a trolley with piles of ironed sheets on it. She came up to the reception, spoke to one of the other girls wearing a badge, her arm on the desk and one foot out of her clogs, using it to scratch her calf, before slipping it back in her clog. When she saw me she turned her face towards me and looked me up and down without stopping talking. Then she said something to the girl behind the desk and, on looking at me both of them burst out laughing. I laughed too, raised my hand in greeting, and blushed. In the meantime Tatiana returned, holding some sheets of paper with all the train times written down in a column, departures and arrivals, at least ten hours' journey, change train at Voronezh. Otherwise there was a coach, which was perhaps easier, Russia is even more beautiful when seen that way. And she took out a folder from under the desk, opened it and turned it towards me, her pen poised like a helicopter above Moscow. Then it descended, marked a cross and we were there, at the intersection of those two blue marks. We set off, the tip of the pen showing us the way, heading straight. And there was a park that never ended, with a little lake in the middle. We skirted it, and took a big avenue, then we left that for a side street, and suddenly there was the square, and there the pen slowed down and stopped. Then the coach arrived, a blue square stopped at a corner, the time to take on the passengers and we were off again.

48

WHEN MY MOTHER WAS A LITTLE GIRL SHE CAME HOME one day and Mario had gone. She had pressed the intercom and a woman had replied, and on tiptoe she had said *It's me*, and then the street door opened. When the lift got to the floor, the door to the stairs was wide open, the doormat folded in two, and women's voices were coming from inside the house. My mother stood in the doorway and inside she saw my grandmother and a woman, both with red rubber gloves on their hands, my grandmother had her hair gathered up into a ponytail. She remained in the doorway for a little before they noticed her. The woman took a rag out of a basin, wrung it out and threw it on the floor, pushing it with the scrubbing-brush. My mother looked inside without saying a word, the kitchen all topsy-turvy, the three chairs upturned on the table, the window open, the smell of ammonia. Then my grandmother noticed her, smiled, straightened up, left the cloth on the piece of furniture she was dusting, and said *What are you doing standing there in the doorway, come inside, walk where it's dry.* My mother crossed the kitchen the way you cross a stream on stepping stones, and my grandmother said to the woman *Here she is, my daughter.* *How big she is,* the other woman said. All my mother said by way of reply was *Ciao.*

On the balcony, upside down over the balustrade, the carpet was dangling into the emptiness, and there was that intense smell of ammonia throughout the house, it stung inside the nostrils. My mother was sneezing continuously, then her eyes began to water and she started coughing. The woman gave her a drink, she said *Little one,* patting her on the back, gently, lightly, and she quietened, her tears running down into the glass. And there was no longer anything of Mario in the house, the chair on which he used to lay his clothes was being aired on the balcony, and the door to his part of the wardrobe, where he kept his things, was wide open. The woman was hanging up my grandmother's winter clothes. She asked her confirmation by holding up the hangers with the clothes before putting them inside. Mario's shoes had also disappeared from the entrance, the only trace of him was his bathrobe in the bathroom, behind the door, alongside my mother's. For the entire time the woman was there, my grandmother had said virtually nothing, only given instructions, a few words, mainly gestures with her hands, constantly redoing her ponytail that would not stay in place. My mother, sitting on the bed, could see them on the other side of the door, the two of them pushing the sofa, taking the cover off, the woman cleaning the glass front of the cabinet, her reflection growing clearer and clearer. And my grandmother said nothing about the fact that Mario was no longer there, nor did my mother ask, even though she constantly sought her gaze, and my grandmother never returned it. But then she broke a fingernail, yelled *Damn!* too loud, and burst into tears. *It's only a nail, come here*, the woman said. She put a plaster around it, my mother came running when she heard the sobs, and my grandmother said *It's nothing*. Then they went into the bedroom, my grandmother asked my mother to help them. On the double bed the mattress was stripped, the sheets piled up near the window. The woman gave a carpet-beater to my mother too, all three had one, and she said *Now give it a good thump*. They all raised their arms and began to beat the bed, building up the strength and then striking, taking it out on the mattress. My mother felt the sweat run down her back.

All of a sudden Mario had vanished, his things, his smell and his presence in my grandmother's mouth. My mother asked for explanations a few times and, every time, my grandmother would leave the question like that, hanging in the air without an answer. Yet on certain evenings my mother would not content herself with this, and if she was tired she would stamp her feet on the floor, cry quietly at first then start shouting. Once she yelled in her mother's face *You kicked him out*. My grandmother asked her to repeat what she had said, and when my mother did, *You kicked him out*, my grandmother raised her arm and slapped her. It was a sharp slap, with an open hand, my mother didn't even cry, she only looked her straight in the eye. *Why?* she asked. My grandmother didn't say anything, she merely turned, went to the bathroom, stayed in there for half an hour and then the flush was heard. That evening my mother joined her in bed, she had a bellyache, and she slipped under the covers. My grandmother laid a hand on her cheek, she asked her if it still hurt. Then she pulled my mother to her, *Papa was very ill* she said in her ear. All my mother said was *Yes.* She fell asleep in her mother's arms, my grandmother took her back to her bed, the blanket tucked up to her chin. Initially, when Mario was no longer there, my grandmother had trouble sleeping, the thought of him, the fear, his violence over the last months, a punch at the metal cabinet on the balcony, the marks of his knuckles still on it. And then with time the fear went away, and all that was left was a great melancholy.

49

FIRST IT WAS DAYS, THEN MONTHS, AND AFTERWARDS YEARS. My mother went to school and back every day, my grandmother said goodbye when she went out, and when she came back she sat her down at table. As for Mario, they continued to say nothing, as if he were dead. When they were in a good mood, the memory of Mario didn't even surface, my mother would laugh, my grandmother too, and seeing her daughter laugh it seemed to her that she didn't need anything else. Yet, sometimes, at the peak of that good humour, precisely at the end of that laugh, all of a sudden there would come that thought that ruined everything. And there were also rainy days, when my grandmother looked outside and my mother, the child, would stare at her furtively. Over time even the third chair in the kitchen disappeared. My mother had used it to put her homework notebooks on, afterwards she put it in her room, close to the bed, saying *Anyway it's no use in the kitchen*. On top of it she put a table lamp, a stem with a shade, and the flex that ran down to a plug in the wall. Of an evening my mother would read in its light, and my grandmother would arrive, sit down on the bed and switch off the light. And when my mother would wake up every so often in the night, she would turn beneath the blankets and see the silhouette of the lamp in the darkness, to her it seemed like a tree seen from a distance, in the middle of the countryside, the trunk and the crown, the tree under which her father was buried.

The years went by this way, with my grandmother leaving my mother with the neighbours once a week. When she came back in the evenings she was always a bit gloomier, and at table all you could hear was the scraping of cutlery in the plates. One day she dressed my mother up nicely and, instead of leaving her with the woman next door, she took her with her, both of them sitting and waiting at the stop for the next tram to come. The journey lasted a little less than half an hour, my mother had a grip in her hair, polished shoes, and her legs were bare with a scratch on her knee. She didn't say a word for the entire trip, leaning against the window, the rain beating against it. My grandmother was sitting behind her, sometimes looking at the back of her neck, sometimes looking outside. The tram emptied bit by bit, first the bell to request the stops and then the voices of the passengers dying away in the street. The city thinned out and afterwards it ended, only meadows for kilometres, and when the tram came to the end of the line they were the only two who got off. They covered a stretch of road on foot, my grandmother took my mother's hand, and she moved away a bit to dodge the puddles. Then a car passed by and splashed them, my grandmother shouted *Watch where you're going*, trying in vain to wash the mud off my mother's skirt. When they arrived at the building, there was a barrier for the cars and a porter's lodge, my grandmother's arm grew tenser, her grip stronger, she gave Mario's surname to a man with glasses behind the window. *His daughter too* she added, the man got up from his seat, brought his face to the glass and saw my mother, the little girl, a bit further below. Then he sat down again without saying a word, he only stamped a sheet of paper, my grandmother took it, folded it and put it in her bag. They disappeared inside a tunnel, the echo of my grandmother's heels behind them.

When they emerged from the tunnel, one hour later, the sun was shining over the lawns, a little further away the tram was standing at the terminus. They came out quickly, the echo of my grandmother's heels and the two of them arriving behind it. They went past the lodge without saying goodbye, the barrier was up and a van was entering at that very moment. They started to run, my grandmother raised one arm to ask the tram driver to wait for them. My mother was crying, my grandmother was looking for her hand, but she didn't want to give it to her, she pulled it away. Then my grandmother stopped, she hugged my mother, the little girl began to cry loudly. My grandmother felt her trembling in her arms, and she was almost crying too, *Don't be like that* she said, and blew softly on her head. My mother was still trembling. *We won't come here again* my grandmother said. And fifty metres further away the tram doors closed and it began moving off.

All of a sudden Moscow ended, the ugliest buildings all lined up on its borders. When we left it was just after dawn, the sky was gradually lighting up. The fields immediately opened up after Moscow, a queue of cars already flooding the three-lane road at that hour. After a while we stopped, the outskirts stood there, watching us leave, thousands of windows and each window a satellite dish reaching out as if to seek the sun. Beside me there was an imposing woman, at least one metre eighty in height, broad shoulders like a man's, and eyes that looked like they had never said sorry. She had arrived shortly after me, and sat down, squashing me up against the window, a bag on her knees and feet so small they seemed to be stolen from someone else. I could feel her close up against me on one side, the window on the other, and beyond the window the fields. We travelled onwards this way, parallel stretches of cars on the road, and there were some that shot off and some that waited until the one in front had covered a few metres before moving. And from up there, from high up inside the coach, to see all those different cars, large ones and small, jalopies as well as ones fresh from the factory, and the lorries, and the coaches, and the motorcyclists, to see them all together on the march, covering a few paces and then stopping, it seemed like a new Ice Age, all the animals of the earth fleeing from the city.

The lady sitting beside me took a boiled egg from her bag, began to peel it, her feet tucked together, and collected the bits of shell in a handkerchief. Before eating the egg she turned, offered it to me in her hand, and with my hand I said no. She smiled, and almost all her teeth were gold, a sudden dazzlement. But she immediately closed her lips, as if it were a secret, going around the world with that light hidden inside her mouth, protecting it, watching over it like a vestal. After eating the egg she fell asleep leaning against me, the queue of cars had got underway again and Moscow was fading behind the big blocks. I felt her slip gradually on top of me, only her arm to begin with, then all her weight I looked at her head from above, without moving so as not to wake her, squashed up more and more against the window, her thick grey hair foreign to me. In sleep, she adjusted her position, seeking with her ear the most comfortable part of me, as if she wanted to look for the point

147

in which she could hear better, measure my heartbeat, hear the air blowing in my lungs. My eyes followed her centre parting, I would have liked to run my finger all along that spike of hair. The coach began to go faster, and outside only the fields and the odd tree now and then. I fell asleep, my forehead against the glass, and the lady continued listening to me, with that secret she held in her mouth, that light that didn't go out even when she slept.

We woke up all together when the coach came to a sharp stop in an unmetalled lay-by at the side of the road, the gravel crunching under its wheels, and the engine switching off, a final shudder like a shake. We had all been asleep until shortly before, all it took was to leave Moscow, to stretch out along the road, pick up speed and the voices dwindled one after another until they dissolved, evaporated inside the coach. Then that sudden braking, the manoeuvre, and everyone gradually emerged from slumber, slipping out of it as if from a hole, an arm to start with, after that the other arm, and then heads, shoulders, a torso, sitting up, looking around as if coming into the world for the first time. In front of us there was a wooden hut, three cars parked outside, a woman selling sweets laid out on a table, and all around fields as far as the eye could see, then they vanished in the misty background. My neighbour woke up with a start, frightened at finding herself on top of me, embarrassed by not knowing what to say. So she looked at me from inside that silent awkwardness, her eyes against mine, and opening her mouth, showing me her light, was the only way she could tell me she was sorry.

I was the only one to enter the hut, I sat down by a window whose glass was broken, held together by a strip of brown sticky tape set crosswise. There were a few plastic tables, a metal counter with a girl behind it and on the top an example of each of the few things available to eat sandwiches snacks, and soup. Above, in the middle of the room, a fan rotated slowly, a creak at every turn of the blades and an unsteady movement, as if it were steadily unscrewing itself. Apart from me there were only two youths at another table, both wearing pointed shoes, shirts open over their chests and beer bellies resting above their belts. But they went away almost immediately, they went past me, their shirts like wings open wide on both sides. I saw them fly as far as the door and then vanish. And while the girl was bringing the sandwich and beer I had pointed to on the counter, I took my mobile out of my pocket and dialled Olmo's number. It rang, but he didn't answer. I imagined him in the street, not hearing anything to begin with then suddenly noticing the ring-tone, starting to look for the mobile in his clothing, patting his hands over it as if to kill a fly. All the while, outside the window I could see my fellow travellers, some sitting on the edge of the pavement, others close by, all of them eating the things they had prepared before leaving. The driver was standing next to the coach, smoking, one foot on the step as if he were afraid it might go away by itself. Then I heard Olmo's voice on the telephone, he yelled *Who is it?* as if he were on the intercom and I were down in the street. And when he realized it was me he began shouting my name and asking *Where are you? In the middle of the steppe* I replied. He remained silent for a while, his steppe had suddenly showed itself before him in its entirety. And I didn't say anything either, sitting at the plastic table, the beer in front of me, the fan rotating above my head. I was on the other end of a telephone call, almost seventy years long, Olmo calling from 1943, with me in that unmetalled lay-by alongside the motorway seven decades later, unable to speak in order not to ruin everything. Then he asked me *Will you let me hear the steppe?* Outside, the driver was gesturing that it was time to leave, some passengers were already on board. I moved a little further away from the others, walked a few metres through the grass, I could feel it yielding under my feet. *That's a fine wind blowing* Olmo said, and I raised my arm in the air, in the middle of that 1943 wind, to let him hear its whistling.

So seeing Mario had become a matter for my grandmother. The years had gone by, my mother had grown and she no longer went to the neighbours to wait for her to return. She would stay at home, sitting at the table, an adolescent already. My grandmother, before going out, would fill a bag of things to take to Mario and then she would ask *What are you doing this afternoon?* Every time, my mother would raise her head, look at her standing in the doorway, her bag in hand. All she would say in reply was *Studying*, and put her pencil in her mouth, her embarrassment reduced to a gesture, her teeth bringing the pencil to the height of torment. Then my grandmother would go out, and instinctively she would stand still for a few more moments on the doormat, my mother sitting motionless at the table, on the other side of the door. Then my mother would hear my grandmother move on, footsteps growing fainter, floor after floor. My grandmother would go down with her thoughts still at home, every time the doubt that she was wrong not to insist, as Mario for years expected his daughter every time, while, instead, for my mother, day after day, he had merely become a duty to be avoided. And then in the evening my grandmother would ask her *Have you finished studying?* and she would say *Yes*, and my grandmother would fold up the bag in which she had put the things for Mario and place it in a drawer.

Since Mario no longer lived with them, my grandmother had emptied the bottom drawer of the chest, and in it she put everything she had bought for him during the week, ready to take it to him on Thursdays. Accompanying my grandmother to buy clothes was the only thing my mother still did for her father. Sometimes they would go to the market, more often to the shops. They would go in and start to look, reviewing all the trousers, jerseys, shirts. They would stay for hours in the shops, most of the time in the women's department, talking quietly and laughing, my mother growing all the while, and they would laugh more and more often at the same things. Then the assistant would come and ask if they needed any help. My grandmother would compose herself and call her daughter to order. My mother would blush, beside the pile of skirts they had tried on. Then my grandmother would clear her throat and say that, in reality, they were looking for menswear. She would say *It's for her father.* So they would move to another part of the shop. The assistant from the height of her heels said *Men are all the same, they never want to buy anything*, adding *Then they often complain about it.* So the assistant brought piles of different trousers and jerseys, laying everything on a table. My mother and my grandmother would examine them for a while. My grandmother would unfold them and hold them up, and my mother would say *For heaven's sake* or *This isn't bad*, and she would look after her father by giving shirts and trousers the thumbs-up or down. At times, my grandmother even asked her to try them on, even though my mother was short and Mario long and lanky. She said it was because of their eyes, both green, to see how that shirt looked on her, to check the colours were complementary. And my mother would come out of the changing room like that, barefoot, her nails covered in their first varnish, and those shirts more or less the same, grey or blue. She would stand there to be looked at, trying on and taking off clothes, waiting for the next item in her bra.

So over the years Mario had remained inside that drawer in the chest. He stayed closed up in there, once in a while it would be opened to put a new purchase inside or to take one out, a little light came in and afterwards the darkness returned. It was in front of him that my grandmother would undress every night before going to bed, she would look at herself in the mirror, one look every day, to check the passing of time, and after that she would slip between the sheets, the light switched off, the chest in the dark together with the bed. During the day the room would almost always remain empty, the chest by the window, and sometimes my grandmother would pass by, take a handkerchief from the top drawer and leave. From one day to the next, my mother had also begun to appear in front of the mirror. Seldom at first, an afternoon party with her school friends, to see how a red necklace went with a white blouse. Since then she had returned more and more often, she would look at herself continually, sometimes she would repeat the lesson making faces at herself. Afterwards there had been arguments, sharing the mirror with my grandmother, my mother wanted to be alone, my grandmother to look at herself, standing one step behind. Every day my mother was taller in the mirror, first there was only her face, then her neck, then her chest and her belly, and putting on earrings for a boy she had to meet. Time passed quickly, every Thursday she would stay at home alone, sometimes she was really alone, other times a boy she had met would come up, at first they were friends and then in front of the mirror one afternoon they had stripped off. After that boy in the mirror, others had passed in front of it too, a couple for a few weeks, some for months, one had remained for two years in a row. And once my grandmother had embraced my mother from behind, two faces next to each other, and my grandmother had asked her *Are you happy?* my mother had said *I don't know.*

50

ON THE LAST PART OF THE JOURNEY, THE WOMAN SITTING beside me talked to me incessantly for two hours. She had spent the entire break sitting in the coach, empty seats behind all the windows except hers. She only got off to have a pee, joining the queue with the others in front of the two plastic cabins for the chemical toilets. One after another they had gone inside, and those waiting outside stood there with faces crumpled by their recent awakening, few words, eyes lowered, one person yawning before all the others started in turn. The chemical toilets were in an isolated spot, two cabins rose up in the middle of the steppe, an expanse of green grass that went on until it lost itself among the fields. I had watched them from inside the hut, the coach parked in the lay-by and those two plastic boxes on the grass, the people going in and coming out as if from another dimension, satisfied, they would stop for a moment in the doorway looking at the panorama all around. I found the woman again in the coach, she stood up to let me pass, and then she squashed me against the window again. The driver closed the doors, and shortly afterwards we set off in a cloud of dust, the gravel scrunching under the coach. The woman selling sweets had bade us farewell by holding her arm up for the duration of the manoeuvre, then she let it drop back down on her legs. None of us had bought anything from her, but some people had sat beside her on the pavement to eat the things they had brought, exchange a few words, then they had got up and left. And when we were moving back onto the motorway I saw a man come out of the chemical toilet, take a couple of steps, turn back, close the door behind him, and disappear. He was elegantly dressed, I hadn't seen him go in. He came out and went back in like that, with the expression of someone who has just remembered something.

*

The woman started talking to me, pointing to the sheet I had spread out on my legs. It was one of the maps Olmo had drawn, all the rubbings-out visible, the rivers running shakily down the paper, with all the trembling of the hand that had poured them there. The drawing showed a plain, a few trees here and there, and all the rest was black dots amid the white. On the top, above everything, there was written *Valley of Death*, and those dots he had made were the dead who had fallen there, as if they had plunged down from the sky. The woman looked at the sheet, then she took it in her hands and pointed first at the drawing and then outside, far beyond the window, into the steppe. She brought her head closer to the window, moved next to me and screwed up her eyes, as if seeking, in the middle of the green that was all the same, the exact point in which all those black dots had fallen. Then she straightened up against the seat once more and said something to me that I didn't understand. I shook my head, cautiously, shrugging and smiling as if to apologize for understanding nothing. But she took almost no notice, she remained silent for a few moments and began talking to me again, without turning a hair, looking a bit at me and then looking outside, her pupils skipping over the fields. At first I tried to stop her, pointing to my mouth and ears to tell her that I could neither understand nor speak but, unconcerned, she carried on. So she talked to me for two hours, and without realizing it I was suddenly following her words. She talked and there was this beautiful light that appeared and disappeared in her mouth, like a lantern on a ship at night, constantly swallowed up and restored by the waves in the middle of the sea. And I managed to follow her, in this expanse without words anymore, docile, I went behind her. She talked to me and I would laugh when she laughed, and I was amazed at myself. I pressed her with my gaze, I encouraged her as she said incomprehensible things in an excited voice. I understood them all, I invented them differently, and they were the same.

In the meanwhile, outside, every kilometre was the same as the one before it, the endless fields, and a few little paths that crossed them. Those dirt tracks that branched out among the steppe were like secrets, they appeared only when someone was walking along them. Then all the pathways would emerge, my gaze following a woman on a bicycle, seeing her run along the line hidden in that green sheet, re-tracing it, strengthening it, drawing it another time, remembering the road already covered, a road that went back to conceal itself in the grass. And then losing the whole drawing, seeing the woman become smaller, disappearing into the background before finally she too became steppe. I would look outside and then at Olmo's drawing, the words *Valley of Death* and all those black dots scattered across the sheet like pepper. I took my camera out of my bag, pointed it at that expanse of green, yet I didn't press the button, I put the camera away. A hundred metres further on a little lake opened up on the right, and a black bird flew over it, its reflection making it double, a shrill cry, and then it left the lake, alone again above the fields.

51

THE AFTERNOON WAS DRAWING TO A CLOSE WHEN WE GOT to Rossoš. Meanwhile, the coach had filled up with the smell of our bodies exhausted by the heat, many hours sitting in the same position, creases in our clothes, and those very private body odours, pungent in the nose. An old lady had also felt ill during the journey. The woman next to her had shouted, then another one after her, and the driver turned and then braked sharply, parking at the side of the road. So we didn't move for almost an hour, the coach tilted towards the fields, the cars overtaking us, some blowing their horns, some stopping to take a look, rolling down the window, others again simply slowing down and moving off. They had the lady get off, the driver accompanied her bending over as he guided her along the aisle Then I saw them appear below, the two women who had given the alarm, walking alongside her, one of the two put her hand on the old lady's forehead and smiled at her. They took her shoes and had her lie down in the grass, her feet outstretched, the wind had lifted up her skirt, and she searched for her shoes with an outstretched arm. So half of the passengers stood against the windows, some took advantage to get out and have a smoke. The lady lay for a long time in the grass, the other two leaned over her, and all the others were looking at her from behind the windows as if she were there by chance, a woman's body plunged like a meteorite from space.

Before we entered the town, the woman sitting next to me pointed out the bell tower, stretching her arm over the seat in front, above the heads of two people. She said Rossoš, and broke out in a broad smile of satisfaction, as if she had built it all herself, a sunbeam struck her mouth, bursting against her gold teeth. So as soon as the town came into sight everyone started to get up all together, the women sprucing up their hair with their hands, the men tucking their shirts into their trousers. Suddenly they were all in the middle of the aisle trying to make room for themselves, taking their bags from the overhead racks, shoving the others away with their backsides, dropping everything, and the wives gesturing at their husbands to move, to let them see to things. The woman and I remained seated, looking out of the window. Every so often she would point outside and I would look where she wanted me to.

The sunlight slanted through the air, catching the windows of the buildings. We stopped at traffic lights for a while, a car further ahead had stalled, a girl was standing beside it, spreading her arms out to apologize to the other cars in the queue behind. Alongside us there was a little football pitch, a rectangle of ground, two goals without nets, and ten or so boys running about bare-chested. Every now and again the ball ended up outside the pitch, on the road, once it hit the side of the coach, the driver opened the window to look at the boy who came to retrieve it. Then we moved off again, shortly afterwards the coach slowed down, a square opened up to the left. And in the middle of it there was a statue of Lenin, very tall and dark. It cast a long shadow, extending over a row of benches in the far end of the square, all the old men sitting beneath it.

And half an hour later everyone had gone. The driver had opened the luggage compartment, and one after another people reached inside it, took their suitcases out and left. I watched them disperse, some towards the road from which we had arrived, others behind the immense building that dominated the square, to the back of the monument to Lenin, the Russian flag hoisted on a pole. The last to leave was the old lady who had felt ill, a man with a receding hairline had come to pick her up. She hooked her hand over his arm the way you hang an umbrella by its handle, her eyes fixed on those shoes that had finally returned to her feet. Then I didn't see them anymore. Only the woman with the gold teeth and I were left. I showed her a sheet of paper with the name of the hotel. She stretched her arm out forwards, pointing to a low building, beyond the road, a coloured sign. And in the meantime the sun had got a little lower, a group of young boys cut across the square on bicycles. And Lenin's shadow had moved, the benches were left bare, as if a blanket had suddenly been pulled away, an old man raised his arm, his palm against the sun.

My mother had been calling me for an hour without realizing it. I was lying on the bed in my underpants, the room almost entirely in darkness already, my mobile lighting up without ringing. I would say *Hello*, but she didn't answer. I raised my voice, repeated her name changing the tone of my voice, then I lost patience and hung up. After a while it rang and so I lay there waiting for it to stop. The light would pulsate intermittently, as if it weren't a telephone but a heart lying on the bedside table, every dark spell a contraction and immediately afterwards a dilatation, the room sprayed with a light that would suddenly appear, and then die down again once more. My mother often used to make these involuntary telephone calls, the mobile in her pocket or her bag, and the call would begin, one telephone seeking another telephone far away. I would answer, and if I didn't hear anything I would begin to call out to her, saying *Mamma*. At first I did this delicately, as if I were calling to wake her up in the morning, saying her name in a quiet whisper, trying to find the word that would work, the one that fitted the keyhole, pronouncing it and seeing a body opening up, shrugging off sleep. But I never found that word. So I began to shout *Mamma*, bringing the telephone nearer to my mouth, shouting *Can you hear me?* And afterwards I would try with her name, *Giovanna, can you hear me?* It was pointless, yet I continued, my voice yelling in her pocket, as if it had fallen inside it and was asking for help from there. Every time, I hoped that by raising the volume I would manage to get out, to climb up from the inside to the edge of the pocket, and from there to escape. But it was useless, and that gesticulation of my voice was like crying for help in the middle of nowhere.

Outside Rossoš there were only cars passing by. They came to me like a heavy sea below the window, the green and the red of the traffic lights making them move or stop. Every so often, one would enter the hotel car park and shortly afterwards head off again onto the road, in order to make a manoeuvre, change direction and disappear, attacking the tarmac with its wheels. I would see their headlights scour my room, the ceiling, the door, the wardrobe, my face, and then leave, jump through the window and slide downwards. Some cars would stop, the lights and the engine switched off all at once, the doors opening and slamming, and footsteps and voices and heels, someone laughing, the creaking of the hotel door. At times, soon afterwards, I would hear them walking in front of my door, along the corridor, the same shoes as before, the voices closer, the suppressed laughter. And then the key, the lock turning, and the voices that closed themselves behind the door. In the meantime, my mother carried on calling me without realizing it, the room flashing for an hour as if an ambulance had stopped there. In the end I answered and didn't say anything, neither *Hello* nor even one word, just pressing the button with the green handset icon. On the other end there was my mother, thousands of kilometres away. In the distance, faintly, I heard my father's voice that resounded lower and even more distant, only a word now and then, a sign he was listening, an invitation to continue. I understood that they had been to the cinema, she was saying *What a great sleep I had* and she asked him what happened at the end. But my father's voice was too faint to come to me, all I heard was the vibration and her complaining, saying *It's just not possible*, and then bursting out laughing. There was a long silence, a few words thrown off in the car, the reply coming a long time afterwards. There was the street, in the telephone, my mother and father had stopped talking, and he would cough now and then. And then I heard from outside the window, down in the street, a car passing by; instinctively I got off the bed and went to the window, I followed it as far as I could see.

*

Outside the window there was the square, the statue of Lenin in the middle, behind the monument stood the building and the Russian flag hoisted on its pole. To one side they had erected a stage, green cloth posters, the words in Cyrillic. I stood at the window, in my underpants, my bare feet on the floor, a man crossed the square in the semi-darkness. I saw him pass, the street lights lengthening his shadow, at each new light his shadow moved, leaping over him, first it would lead the way then it would follow him immediately afterwards. There were three lampposts on all sides, and on each side there was one that wasn't working. The man stopped, looked for something in his pocket, rummaging through his trousers and jacket. Then he carried on with shorter, faster steps than before, his shadow running ahead of him. In the end, he turned round, cut across the square again, passed below the statue, and emerged at the far end, his shadow trailing him. All that remained were the street lights, heads bent to cast light down below. And that was the square Olmo had drawn on the sheet, the cross in the background to mark the point of the hanged boy. It was there that he had taken the photograph. I took it out of my wallet and rested it against the glass. There were those young men in black and white, one hanging and the others below, and above them, beyond the window, there was the monument to Lenin, and the Russian flag behind, and a car drew up, a girl got out, she turned to wave goodbye.

52

I WOKE UP JUST AFTER DAWN HAD BROKEN, THE ROOM slowly beginning to expand with light. Outside, on the street, there was a queue of tractors, the noise of the engines, the big wheels, and drivers in jeans and dark glasses. They entered the square and parked, greeting one another with a nod of the head. Then they stood around, each driver beside his tractor, some didn't even get down, they lit up cigarettes, signalling to others to park behind them, pointing at empty spaces further away. At the same time, two men got up onto the stage, they hung a red banner up at the back and put two huge loudspeakers at either side. Every time they switched on the power the loudspeakers began to shriek, the drivers below complained, some blew their tractor horns in protest. The sun was rising fast, as if someone was hauling the sky downwards, pulling on a rope, clinging to it with all his weight.

Only with the light did I realize the colour of the room, whose walls were all pink. Bright pink had also been used for the wardrobe doors, the shower curtain and the towels. The evening before, when I arrived, a man dressed in Texan style had showed it to me. He was wearing a hat and had an unlit cigar in his mouth that he chewed on while he spoke to me in Russian, adding a few O.K.s every now and then. My room was midway down the corridor, previously he had opened one that was all green, then a red one, and finally mine, which in the darkness had struck me as the most sober. Every time he went in he would sit on the bed, inviting me to feel how soft it was. I sat down too, he made me bounce, the pair of us going up and down on the mattress. He also showed me all the bathrooms, drew aside the shower curtain, proudly pointing out the artillery of taps and hydromassage units. When I had picked the pink room he gave me the thumbs-up in approval, slapped me on the shoulder and winked. Then he gestured at me to wait and came back shortly afterwards with a bottle of vodka and two glasses, sat down at the table, poured some out for both of us and put a glass in my hand. And there we were, he agreeing with me hoarsely and tendentiously, his boots crossed and his leather bomber jacket open, and I was left wondering how I could get rid of him. I had to avoid returning his smile. Before going away, he left me a brochure of the hotel, shook my hand, and gestured at me to call him, his hand to his ear as if telephoning. He even took off his hat, an uncouth gentleman, and then he pulled the door shut behind him. The brochure had the prices in roubles, a photograph of a swimming pool, and naked girls clinging to a pole, golden stars on their nipples, smiles to seduce the guests and the camera lens. But then I switched off the light, got undressed and stretched out on the cool sheets, trying to wrap them around me as closely as possible, legs, arms and shoulders. That night I woke up a few times, the thumping sound of disco music from the floor below, loud voices and laughter beneath my window, in the car park, and still the vibration of the bass notes. Every time I turned over in bed, I saw the bottle of vodka and the two shot glasses left on the table. I looked at them in the darkness, just beyond the foot of the bed, and to see them from there, sunk in my pillow, they looked like a bell tower with two low houses beside it, a scarcely populated village at the other end of the room, as if in the middle of a valley, where everyone was asleep, and even the church clock had stopped.

Before I left the hotel I asked the girl at the reception desk to help me make a telephone call. She was petite, two narrow eyes that looked carved, and above them so much forehead that her face seemed upside down. She looked at me, and I felt like turning my own head upside down, as if searching for someone under a bed. The girl said she would willingly help me, it was her job. After she said it, she blushed because of the English appearing on her lips, the thoughts that had set off imposing and strong in her head, and had come down through her palate to emerge in such a sorry state, lame, unrecognizable. I had Olmo's notebook with me, I opened it, showed the girl the telephone number we had tried to call from

Italy. She looked at it, told me it was a Rossoš number and tried to call, but the line was engaged. In the meantime the Texan came along, his hat still on his head, giving the impression that he hadn't taken it off since the evening before. He said something to the girl, gave me a pat on the back, and went off stamping his boots, without turning round, removing his gaze, his jeans low over his backside. On the other side of the street the square was full of people and tractors. The loudspeakers were now working, a man was shouting into a microphone and gesticulating on the stage. There were dozens of tractors parked pretty much everywhere, the men who had first driven them were now inviting those who wished to try them out to climb aboard, a few mothers took photographs of their sons with their hands on the steering wheel. As I was watching, a man bought a tractor, the owner counted the money, they shook hands, then the man climbed onto it and got settled, bouncing on the seat. I saw him take to the road, the queue of cars suddenly began to move at walking pace behind him. The receptionist called me, beckoning at me to come. Covering the mouthpiece with one hand, she asked me what she had to say to him, he was on the line. I told her I needed to meet him, I had come from Italy. And while she was explaining in Russian what I had said to her, I looked outside: the square, the flag, the statue of Lenin and all those people, babies in pushchairs. One of Olmo's photographs had been taken in the same place, and instead of the tractors there were five tanks lined up. There was nobody in that black-and-white photograph he had shown me one evening. Only the deserted square and these enormous tortoises that walked across it, their cannono pointed ahead, all against the statue, Lenin in their sights.

53

THE FIRST TIME MARIO HAD ASKED TO SPEAK TO MY MOTHER she had refused. My grandmother, who was looking at her, repeated over the telephone *Do you want to speak to Giovanna?* Then there was a moment of silence, whispers and embarrassment, my grandmother covered the mouthpiece with her hand, and my mother whispered to her *I'm not in,* accompanying this with a vigorous shake of the head. My grandmother pressed her hand even tighter over the mouthpiece, as if she wished to silence the telephone rather than prevent him from hearing. She looked at my mother with a gaze that held both plea and reproof. Then she freed the mouthpiece, said *What a pity, Giovanna has gone into town,* and afterwards she added *You know, this boyfriend, he comes to pick her up in the car.* She lowered her eyes, stared down at her legs, wringing her skirt with her hands. My mother then left the room, went into the bathroom, and heard my grandmother say *Of course, she'll be happy, she'll call you back, you'll see.* Before turning on the water my mother waited for the telephone call to end, her face in the mirror, her ears listening entirely to the sounds outside the door. Then my grandmother hung up, she said *Bye, look after yourself,* and the receiver was put back down. My mother turned on the shower, the water pouring out like a defensive barrier. When she emerged from the bathroom, my grandmother was still there, her hands clasped together, with the lie she had just told still on her face. My mother sat down beside her, both guilty, my grandmother for having given her that man as a father, my mother for not having taken him.

Then my mother called him late one afternoon a few days later, she spoke with the door closed. My grandmother was left outside, the silhouette of her daughter on the other side of the frosted glass, a shadow that barely moved, she could not make out the words, all she heard was the tone of voice. At the beginning of the telephone call my grandmother moved quietly, partly to try to listen and partly so as not to disturb. But when the call didn't end, my grandmother began to cook, the door still closed, the darkness gradually swallowing my mother up on the other side of the glass door. My grandmother set the table, the tablecloth, the plates, the pan sitting on a chopping board. On passing by the door she heard my mother laughing, she stopped for a moment, and my mother laughed again, so hard she even got hiccups. My mother emerged from the darkness an hour later. My grandmother was sitting at table, in her place, on the tablecloth there were the crumbs of the bread she was eating. She raised her head at the sound of the door. Dinner was eaten in total silence, my grandmother not asking and my mother not saying, her eyes on the plate, those of my grandmother on her daughter's lowered head. Then they cleared the table together, *I'll wash up* my mother said. She filled the sink with suds, put the plates to soak and sank her hands into the water. She turned her back on my grandmother who carried on staring at her.

So my mother began going to visit Mario alone. The first time one afternoon, furtively taking the tram. Once more, many years later, covering the road without my grandmother, her face in the window, her handbag on her lap. She was wearing a skirt bought a short time before, and shoes with just a hint of heel. And she sat there looking at the city passing by the window, each building with different windows, and the plaster, the whites, the grey and the beige, the city that over the years had grown on the countryside, spreading kilometres of buildings and balconies on top of it. When the city ended there was still a few hundred metres of fields, the tram terminus, and the little building in the background, which my mother reached walking fast. Inside the porter's lodge a woman was sitting, sixty years old and a blue coat. My mother gave her some identification, and she gave her a paper in return after having given it a good thump with the stamp. My mother vanished in the tunnel, her low heels echoing, resolute steps, and then half an hour later the same steps re-emerged. And on her face there was an extra sadness, but the same resolve as before. She reached the tram, and waved her arm to ask for it to wait, before boarding, going back home, retracing the road in the opposite direction. Then that evening she told my grandmother, *I've been to see Papa*. And my grandmother stopped. *He must have been happy*, she said to her, then she started eating again. In this way, Mario had become a matter that concerned my mother too. She would go to see him alone and my grandmother let her do so. At times my mother gave only a hint of her intention, and my grandmother would watch her get dressed before leaving. From then on my mother went in and out of the little building, every time those resolute steps, taking a breath before going in, throwing herself into the tunnel. When my grandmother went to visit Mario she would see the traces, the things that her daughter left for him, the photographs on a cork board, pinned to it with thumb tacks, and sometimes there was even a bunch of flowers in a vase. There was a photograph of her with a friend, sitting on top of a big rock, shorts and walking boots, both with a sweatband on their foreheads, and another in which she was embracing a young man with thinning hair. That youngster was my father, my mother's head resting on his shoulder.

54

I SAW THE WOMAN WITH THE GOLD TEETH AGAIN; SHE WAS
sitting on a bench, arms crossed, and there was a little boy going up
and down on a swing. Her head was following his movement, tilting back and then falling forwards. The boy said nothing, he went
up and then plunged down without expression, his mouth closed,
his hair flying in the air, and his feet pointing at the woman and
then suddenly rising up against the buildings. When she saw me
coming, the woman raised one arm without really looking at me.
Then she placed a hand on the bench, beside her, she gestured at me
to sit down, and I sat down where her hand had been. Near the
swing there was a slide a few metres long, at the foot of the steps a
queue of children. One after another they climbed up, appeared on
the top, then let themselves go until they landed in a hole in the
sand. There was one boy, carroty hair and a starry spray of freckles
on his face, who stubbornly insisted on returning to where he
had come from, climbing back up the slide by hanging on to
both sides, blocking the flow of children coming down. The others
complained, a girl launched herself down, crashed into him, and
both ended up in the sand crying. The park was a playground of a
few square metres set in the middle of four condominiums made
of reinforced concrete. Some people were at the windows looking
down, but most of all there were parabolic antennas seeking the
signal in a precise point of the sky. When I sat down, the woman
said something to the boy, the light in her mouth at every word she
uttered, as if it were the Morse code with which they talked in the
family. He didn't say anything, he merely looked at her. Then he
stopped thrusting himself upwards, the rope grew slacker, the arc
of the swing became shorter every time he leaned backwards.

*

When the boy joined us he stopped in front of her and raised his arms in the air as if to be searched. She pointed to him and said *Kolja*, I pointed to myself and said *Pietro*. Then the woman tucked his T-shirt into his jeans without unbuttoning them, stuffing it in in two or three places and then looking at him. From the square, two hundred metres away, the music came in waves, the tractor fair right in the middle of the early afternoon, gusts of wind picked it up in pieces, bearing them like ashes throughout the town, and scattering them on things and on people. The children stopped, they heard them falling from above, they raised their heads, then started playing again as before, the wind changed, taking the music back to the square as if nothing had happened. We stayed there for a while, the boy sat down beside the woman, his gaze on the slide, and at a certain point she took the guide to Rossoš that was lying on my knees. It was open on the map at the end of the booklet. The girl in the hotel had marked where I had to go with a cross, and alongside she had written that telephone number. The woman took the book and turned it in her hands to orient it in the right direction, as if it weren't a map but a steering wheel, as if by turning it she made the whole town turn with us. Then as soon as she had finished moving Rossoš she put the map back before my eyes and showed me the route among the buildings, ran along it with her hand, turning immediately, the first right, then the left, crossing; and I got lost. I stopped her by laying a hand on her arm. She looked at me and smiled. She said something to the child, they got up, he put his hands in his pockets like a boy, and she beckoned me to follow them.

So we left there, the queue for the slide was moving along slowly, the little boy with the freckles had been dragged off by a very young girl who had put him in a pushchair too small for him. For a bit we walked alongside the railway lines, the countryside opening out on the right, and in the background you could no longer see the tracks. The boy followed us a few metres to the rear, then he would overtake us and run fast every time a train arrived from behind. The train would suddenly catch up with us, first the din, then the locomotive, and Kolja flashing by alongside us. Then the train got smaller, and even its tail dwindled into the distance and it was gone. Kolja stopped all of a sudden and turned round, resigned to staying there with us. He hid behind the parked cars and leaped out when we arrived, inexpressive even when playing. We stopped in front of a low house, a blue sheet-metal door, the windows overlooking the street, the curtains wound around the handles. The woman asked me for the book, pointed at the cross on the map, and those windows. There was a woman on the other side of the window. Then she gave me back the guide book, there was a dog ear on one page, the photograph of Lenin Square, another with women in traditional costume, and below them a group of Alpine troops on parade, waving the Italian flag.

55

BEFORE GOING AWAY, THE WOMAN WITH THE GOLD TEETH tried to explain the route back to my hotel. First she tried to show me it on the map, then she bent down, took a twig, and drew it in the sand at the side of the road. When Kolja saw her drawing it, he, too, hunkered down, his backside between her feet, his elbows on his knees, his face between his hands, that piece of Rossoš gradually growing under his eyes, the houses, the streets, even the traffic lights at the crossroads. Then she straightened up, looked at me and asked me a question. I didn't understand it. So then she pointed to the blue gas pipe that ran alongside the house. It carried on further, it delineated the outlines of the other houses and continued on its way, and on arriving at the end of the street it entered the straight, and from there it went round the entire town, each building in its blue frame, every house contained as if in a photograph. The woman showed it to me as if this was the best way not to get lost, keeping an eye on it until the hotel and from there letting it go its own way. I followed it with my gaze, in the direction she was showing me and then also in the opposite direction, running down towards the fields, the steppe, a single line that took in all of Russia, thousands of kilometres and that pipe that outlined them, town after town, field after field, I was to follow it faithfully, leaving the Minotaur inside the labyrinth.

The woman at the window opened it, looked out, and we all looked up except for Kolja, who was crouched down adding details to his city in the sand. Then the woman disappeared, the window was closed, the curtains were drawn once more: shortly afterwards the sheet-metal door opened. In the middle there was a tiny figure, the same one who had been at the window before, but now suddenly smaller. I stared at her in amazement, as if her height had allowed her to look out from there, and not the first floor of the house. She was standing there between the doors without saying anything. A vegetable patch peeping out from behind her, a man's bicycle propped up against a tree, and an old dog that emerged beside her. It looked at us, and wearily turned back, throwing itself down in a patch of shade. The woman opened her mouth to talk to us, the woman with the gold teeth stepped forwards and explained matters. Then we suddenly found ourselves in a living room, our six shoes left outside the door together with dozens of other shoes, one beside the other like cars in a car park. We stood against the wall without knowing what to say, everyone around a woman who was weeping, one after another they sat down beside her on the sofa, some gave her a kiss, others spoke to her in low voices, she would nod and then before any sound could come out of her mouth a tear would run down her face. The little table in front of the sofa was full of picture frames, in each one a photograph of the same man. And the woman who had opened the door came up to us, laid a hand on Kolja's head, and pushed him towards the weeping lady. The lady gave him a hug, and he let her do it, he even let her kiss him. And he looked at his grandmother, from inside the grief of others, and all I could do was clench my feet in my socks.

We left the house almost without breathing, as if slipping silently from beneath blankets. We brushed aside all that grief in order to go out, the people spread around the house to suffer, every chair a station of that mourning, as we crept out backwards, the weeping dying away. Even in the hall there were photographs of that man, hanging on the wall together with the widowed woman now weeping for him on the sofa. Near the door there was an exercise bicycle, at the end of the carpet, as if it had tried to escape but had collapsed in that moment, shot in the back as it tried to flee. Now the exercise bicycle stood there, stopped in that intention, people had hung their jackets on it, one tossed on top of the other. Part of the handlebar stuck out, and beneath it the tip of a pedal, on passing I covered it with the flap of an overcoat. As we were leaving, a man came out of the bathroom, a tall chap, and with him the sound of the flush. The man looked at me, I looked beyond the door, inside the bathroom, a little square mirror above the tap and below that a sink with two toothbrushes. Then he went back to join the others, his broad shoulders against the light from the living room and a hole in the heel of his sock. At the door there were all those shoes, and I had an urge to look for feet inside them, to associate them one by one with the people mourning the dead man in the other room, the violated intimacy of looking inside them, the soles deformed by walking, and I even thought of putting a foot inside, to feel the curves, the temperature, the hollows carved out by the toes. Since our arrival another pair had been added, the laces had spread over my shoes like a stranger's embrace.

We shut the sheet-metal door, the air outside and the warmth on our shoulders. Kolja went to see what was left of his metropolis of sand, a bicycle wheel had crossed over it. Then he took a stick and stuck it in the ground, a hasty burial for the entire city. Then we went away, I was still clutching my guide to Rossoš. For the whole time I had kept a finger inside the book so as not to lose the page for the map, my finger had gone numb. And there was that telephone number, the number that Olmo had jotted down goodness knows how long before in his notebook and that maybe had nothing to do with anything. At the junction we separated, they crossed and I proceeded along the route of the gas pipe. The woman took Kolja by the hand, waited for a lorry to pass and then they cut across the road, a queue of cars swallowed them up, and when the traffic moved on they were gone.

The girl from the reception was outside the hotel. She was sitting on the edge of the pavement, her head resting against the wall and her neck taut with the pleasure of feeling the sun on it. I sat down beside her, she told me her name was Olga, we shook hands. I told her about what had happened, that I had wound up in a house where they were mourning a dead man, I hadn't even understood who he was. She smiled without opening her eyes, I could just make out that she was laughing by the sight of her belly and bosom under her T-shirt. She told me that if I wanted she could go back there with me to help with the language. Then her telephone rang. She put it to her ear, said a few words, and paused a few times, savouring the sunshine. Then she put the mobile down, and there was a photograph of a little girl on the display screen, on her nose she had sunglasses that were too big for her, green frames and mirror lenses that covered her face. *Saška*, she said, pointing to her.

56

OLMO CALLED ME WHEN I WAS AT THE DOOR. OLGA WAS beside me, and in front of us the widow was leading the way through the garden. The dog let us pass without even raising its muzzle, exhausted beneath the tree and the bicycle, one paw over its eyes. There was a shelter, a little further on, and under it stood a moped covered by a black tarpaulin, the rear wheel flat with all the weight on it, and alongside a dirty jerrycan in which you could glimpse a little petrol. When she saw me on the other side of the door the widow said nothing, she merely pushed it open to let us in. Olga held out her hand, the widow smiled at her and they talked. The widow took a step backwards to look at her from top to toe, as if she had known her in another age and then a long time had gone by, and now she had found her again in a different size. Olga blushed, that look had obliged her to become a little girl again, for a moment, her clothes suddenly too large for her body, the T-shirt down to her knees, the shoes too big for her feet. Then the widow ran a hand down her cheek, making her blush flare up even more, as if she had blown over embers. But Olga eluded this with a gesture, slipping away from it, she showed the woman the photograph of her daughter on the mobile phone, and all of a sudden she became a mother once more. Afterwards, the widow looked at her in a different way, a look that also held a touch of slyness, Olga's body no longer immaculate but one defiled by sex.

*

When Olmo telephoned I gestured to Olga, asking her to be patient for the duration of the call. I sat down on the ground, my back against the tree trunk. Olmo's voice was a little anxious, he said he didn't know where I had ended up, he was afraid for me. I told him there was no reason to be afraid. And so he relaxed, his throat did too. He inhaled and said *Thank goodness*, emitting breath and words in a single puff. In the background I could hear his television, the volume so loud that it transformed every phrase into a shout. A man was talking to a woman, reassuringly, she replied to him in a broken voice. In the middle of that film, Olmo asked me where I was. I told him that finally I was in Rossoš, in the garden of a wooden house, a dog sleeping beside me. He kept quiet for a few seconds, giving himself the time to see me appear in the frame of one of his photographs. So I replied to him in black and white, from inside the years of his youth. In the meantime I saw Olga and the widow flit from window to window, disappearing for a few metres and then reappearing. They looked out at me, two faces framed in the glass. Shortly afterwards I saw them come out, going down the steps that separated the door of the house from the yard. The widow had a folder in her hand. They sat down on the plastic chairs, in the middle of the grass, and all the dog needed was to sniff his mistress's smell before getting up and moving away from me.

Olmo asked me if everything was still there, in Russia. He said it like that, with a little anxiety in his voice, as if he had been far from home and had sent someone to check things out. In the background, on the television, the woman who had first been crying was now laughing, as if before she had never wept. When Olmo repeated the question, I said nothing at first and then I told him that everything was there, and he said *Thank goodness* again. I didn't tell him that in reality Olga had accompanied me street by street, her map in hand, and that there was no longer any of the things he had marked for me. And that where the school had been before there was now a supermarket, and where he had drawn a house there was now a railway, and in place of the expanse of fields there was a swimming pool, in summer there was a queue every morning, some children already wearing armbands. And I didn't tell him that the church he had marked wasn't there, it had never been there, and that for every thing we didn't find Olga drew a cross over it in pencil, as if that were the point in which memory had died, shot in the back by time. And I didn't tell him that every time Olga made a cross on the sheet I had felt like calling him. Yet in the end I hadn't done so, and that cemetery had grown steadily bigger under the point of the pencil. So I merely told him that it was all the same as before, even though I hadn't seen how it had been before.

57

I SLEPT ALL NIGHT WITH A DRAWING ON THE BEDSIDE TABLE, a creased sheet of paper, yellowed with time, torn up and put together again with strips of sticky tape. It was a drawing made by a child. There was a gallows, a man hanging from it, and three men drawn below, each with two arms, two legs, and a head, as if they were men made from barbed wire. It was the same as the photograph Olmo had taken, only more frightening, I would turn round and feel it beside me. It lay there as if it had fallen by chance, a snowfall from the past, a drawing from 1943. The glow of the square poured over it, two street lights were out and the other four were flickering. I saw the gleaming of the strips of sticky tape, put there to stitch up the rips. The paper had been torn up and then they had stuck it back together, the pieces badly aligned, one part higher than the other, severing the legs of those barbed-wire men. It had been drawn by the man everyone was mourning. The widow had given it to me as if it were a gift. She had taken it out of a folder with other drawings. When Olga asked her about them, the widow was unable to answer. She said that she had seen those drawings her husband had made as a boy only once, many years before. We looked at one another, sitting in the middle of that grass left to grow wild. And there was a moment in which all of us, sitting there, thought to lower our eyes, but the widow instead raised hers to look upwards, beyond the gate. Because it was there, in that question, that her husband really died for the first time. For us, lowering our eyes had been both a sign of shame and decency. And so we stayed there for a while, without speaking, and I felt intrusive even in my silence.

Sara's telephone call found me with that drawing in my hand, still stretched out on the bed, I had dozed off again, my arm had fallen beside my body, lying on the sheet. All she said to me was *Ciao*, as if with that greeting she wished to open a window and look out of it. *I'm in Russia*, I replied, the drawing before my eyes, the back of my neck on the pillow. *I know* she said. Then I didn't say anything more. Outside the hotel they were cleaning the streets, the brush of the road sweeper lashing the tarmac and filling it with foam. A man was sitting in the machine, I could see him through the curtains, wearing a farmer's hat, looking like he was busy mowing the wheat in the middle of the main road. The man hanging from the gallows in the drawing had hair down to his shoulders, he looked more like a woman than a boy. But his head had been broken in two, then glued together, it was hard to find the gender in those torn lines. All the widow remembered was that perhaps the sheet had been ripped up by the soldiers who had hanged the boy, her husband had told her this. They had taken the sheet from his hand, torn it up in front of him, and dropped the pieces on the ground. He had had to get down on his knees to put them together again, collecting the pieces, his face among the boots, smelling the odour of the grease. He had picked the drawing up and taken it home as if it were a wounded man, with the surgical commitment of a small boy reconstructing a drawing, stitching its parts together. He had bent over it with anger and care, brought the pieces together, comparing drawing and memory to recreate it. That drawing had resisted the rising tide of the years, almost seventy years, to retrace the course of time and end up in my hands. No-one could say anything about it, except for a widow who said she didn't know.

And as I was looking at that torn drawing, on the other end of the telephone was Sara's silence, her *Ciao* unleashed in my room. From the floor below I heard the breakfast dishes, the cups rattling on top of them, the hoarse cough of a man who had coughed all night a couple of rooms down. Sara had told me that all she wanted to know was where I was, what I was doing. I told her that I was in Rossoš, in southern Russia, a few days and then I was coming back home. And when she asked me if I had found anything I told her I had found a drawing. She asked me what was in the drawing, and I told her there was a hanged man. She repeated *Hanged*. And I heard her open up into a violent silence and then burst into tears, a long hissing, like a feeble gas leak. And I lay there listening, the weeping from her eyes reaching me, her pain in a few instants had crossed all of Europe, kilometre after kilometre, and arrived there, her tears falling from my eyes, in that hotel room, running down my cheeks. And then Sara sniffed, took a breath, and asked me *Why have you never forgiven me?*

58

WHEN I TOLD SARA ABOUT THE DRAWING OF THE HANGED man, she let out a weak cry, a grief hissed between Italy and Russia, and then she said *We're going to bed now*. She hung up without adding anything else, not so much as a *Ciao* by way of a goodbye. With a *Ciao* she had opened the window of my hotel room, and now she wasn't closing it, all she had done was escape leaving it open, *We're going to bed now*. She said *We*, which was her and that body growing inside her belly, the child that wasn't ours. She would have stretched out on the bed making room for him, offering him her belly as a pillow. Outside, in the meantime, the man who was cleaning the street had entered the square. The square was full of the debris left by the fair, scattered everywhere on the ground. There were bits of paper, glasses, nylon ribbons, discarded posters, wooden planks, beer cans. A few men with brooms were sweeping up the remains, collecting them in heaps, wearing green plastic gloves and bibs. The man with the hat reached the monument to Lenin, then he walked on, but shortly after he was there again. I saw him turn and run around it like a dog does with its master. Then he stopped near the statue, switched off his machine, and got down with a jump and a twist of his back, holding his farmer's hat on with one hand. He went up to the monument with a white cloth, and then from below, on tiptoe, he began to rub Lenin's feet. Then he returned to his machine, clambered up onto the seat and moved away leaving a long wake of foam and water.

I, too, closed my eyes. Sara was doing the same thousands of kilometres west of me. Where she was it still wasn't morning, it was barely beginning to get light. In Rossoš it was the early hours. Every day, since I had arrived in Russia, on waking, I had thought of Italy still sleeping, I was like someone waking up in a house before the others and watching over their sleep, listening to their deep breathing from inside the room. And so to me, every morning, on opening my eyes there in the east, it seemed to me as if I were watching over all of Italy, listening to the heavy breathing of an entire country, and I would think about my mother, my father, Olmo and all the other condominiums and the flats in them, the empty kitchens, the televisions switched off, all those bodies sunk in beds inside the rooms, and from there in Russia it seemed as if I were watching over everyone's sleep. And with my eyes hidden beneath my lids I thought of Sara going back to bed because she couldn't stand all the suffering she felt.

When Sara had a pain too great to bear she would go to bed. First I would see her walking unsteadily, hugging the walls in the corridor, leaning against them every so often, sitting down as soon as she could. She would roam around the house as if that suffering were a man carried on her shoulders, his arms clutched tight around her neck, his legs squeezing her hips. Sara carried him with eyes half shut, as if she needed to concentrate to do it, bent forward to counter that weight which was so much heavier than her, pulling on her slim back. So she would move around the house slowly, her legs shaking with the effort. She would sit down, leaning forwards, so as not to crush him between the chair and her back, take him off her, lay him down beside her, then slump. Exhausted, Sara would stay like that, her hands drooping, their veins swelling more and more. I would watch her and near her I could see the pain, both of them worn out by that struggle. I would stay with her, take a chair, sit down beside her, look at her without saying a word. I would look for her eyes below those closed lids, I would see them moving beneath, shifting under the skin. Then every time she opened her eyelids, Sara would look at me with a defeated smile, without moving her head, only to ask my forgiveness for having fallen. Then she would tell me that it would be better if she went to sleep. And she would pick up that exhausted pain, load it onto her back again, and I would see them leave together.

I thought about her roaming round the house, thousands of kilometres to the west of me, with that pain clinging to her slim back, walking, hugging the walls of her new house, to carry the pain as far as the bedroom and lie down beside it. Yet that suffering she was now dragging along was the body of a man with a name and surname, and it was him she was now carrying round the house. It was the body of a man who had killed himself one day, they had found him hanging from a rope – a call had arrived one morning, the ringing of a telephone and then that silence. And afterwards there had been that sorrow I had seen explode in her face. She didn't stop crying for five hours, and for five hours I watched her. I didn't even know who that man was.

59

FOR THE YEARS WHEN THEY WERE ENGAGED MY MOTHER kept Mario hidden from my father. He didn't ask, she didn't tell, yet there was a photograph beside her bed, a frame and inside it Mario holding her in one hand, a newborn baby. My father had arrived like this, after a year spent ringing the intercom, and waiting for my mother to join him on the street, but then he had started to come upstairs. My grandmother offered him a chair, and when he sat down she said with a laugh *A man in this house at last.* Dinner was one long interview, every now and then my mother would say *Oh come on, Mamma,* and my father crossed his feet continually under the table, shaking one foot when he was asked something and keeping it still as soon as he began to reply. After eating for a while he was left alone to sit there at the table while my mother and my grandmother cleared up. My grandmother rested her hand on his shoulder as she took his plate, then she withdrew her hand. And in this way my father entered that house for two, a house that had only women's shoes at the door. But then those clothes emerged from the bottom drawer of the chest, one evening when my father arrived soaking wet, caught by a storm along the way. My grandmother gave the clothes to him and he closed himself in the bathroom, every so often sticking out a hand to give my mother his wet clothes. Then he came out wearing Mario's clothes, the overly long trousers and that military green sweater too broad for his shoulders. And my mother even took a photograph, my father standing and my grandmother in front of him. It seemed as if Mario had returned.

Mario remained a taboo for a long time, between my mother and father. She was sometimes not at home, and all my grandmother would say to my father was *She's gone to her father, she'll be back for dinner.* Yet, afterwards, my mother would say nothing, and when he asked about Mario all she would say was that he was living somewhere else. Then she would change the subject, and the week would come to an end without other surprises. And so time went by, my father continued to visit the house and to keep all questions to himself. He would sit down, eat, and then say goodbye to mother and daughter. Then one evening he had come and my mother was closed in her room, that afternoon she had been to see Mario. When she came back she had banged the door and had asked my grandmother not to let anyone come up, but my father had insisted and there was no stopping him. They had talked, the door between them, my father resting his ear against it and my mother on the other side crying, asking him to go away, begging him, he had even raised his voice. In the end my grandmother had put her hand over my father's hand. She said *Be a good boy*, and he allowed himself to be led into the kitchen. There, my grandmother had begun to talk to him more quietly, as a mother does with a child, she had asked him *Would you like something to drink?* and he had drunk a glass of wine. Then they saw my mother come out, and my grandmother went and held her by the arm. She crossed the kitchen in her nightgown, went into the bathroom, then crossed the kitchen again, and locked herself in her room once more. So my grandmother told my father everything, the clinic, the war, imprisonment, and that sometimes Mario was violent, in his head he went back to Russia, and they would calm him down a little, once he had slept for three days in a row. That day his head had returned to Russia once more and he had taken it out on my mother. He had struck her, her nose had begun to bleed, and it wasn't the first time. She yelled and four nurses came, they saw her face covered in blood and took Mario away. They restrained him and she started to cry, saying that it was only a slap, nothing serious had happened, and she cried out *He's my father, leave him alone.*

Afterwards, that evening wasn't mentioned again. My father hadn't shown up for a couple of weeks, my mother hadn't sought him out, and my grandmother told her *Give him time.* He appeared one afternoon, he rang and asked my mother to come down. *There's something I have to tell you*, he said. And she replied *There's something I have to tell you, too.* They sat down on a bench and he said he was afraid for her, he wanted to protect her, he had plans for them both. He had said this trying to instil the words with a little tenderness, but all that came out was something that seemed like blackmail. My mother looked at him and then lowered her face. Then she took him by the hand and said *He's my father*, the same words she had shouted at the nurses who had taken him away. But she said it quietly, without looking at him, almost like a sacrifice or a curse, and she felt alone, on the bench, and so she pushed his hand away. They had sat for a long time without speaking, and then they got up, my mother slipped her arm under my father's. Later, he watched her go up the first flight of stairs, she went up slowly, and she didn't turn round, her fingers on the banister. Hidden inside her belly there was a little thing that in the end she had decided not to tell my father about.

60

I MADE MY ENTRANCE INTO THE CLINIC WHEN I WAS THREE years old, a black-and-white photograph, the tunnel and my mother standing next to the pushchair. I was wearing a wool hat, on the back of the photograph was written 10 December, 1975. My father had also included the nose of the car in the photograph, it peeped out from the bottom right as if ready to sniff the air, the piles of snow in front of the entrance, and a man with a shovel removing it. My mother was wearing moonboots which almost reached her knees, and just above them a striped skirt, a fur hat over her fore-head. There were other photographs of that day, the white covering all the lawns, the branches of the trees buckling under the snow, the lowest touching the ground. Then there was a black dog, my father had taken lots of photographs of it, in one it was barking furiously at him, its lips drawn back over its gums. And there were others in which it was walking alongside people arriving, two ladies were escorted to the entrance and photo-graphed at the exit, the dog stopping on the threshold and then turning back, and the same dog with a man wearing a hat and a girl with a long scarf round her neck. In one photograph the dog was standing on its hind legs, its paws resting against the porter's lodge, the lady had slipped her hand through the open window, her face laughing, she was fondling the dog beneath its muzzle, and it was standing there as if it, too, were waiting for the piece of paper with the stamp, its tail up. Then there were three photographs taken at the tunnel. My father had come as far as the entrance, the black hole and in the background a white light. And in the centre of that white light I had appeared with my mother, two figures in the middle of that dazzling glare, as if we had come out of a fire, a mother and son in flight, her fur hat, and the pushchair leading the way.

Those photographs are all that was saved from my first time with Mario. My father had stayed outside to photograph all the rest; as time went by and we never came out, he got more and more irritated. The last shot he took was one of the building, a row of windows and two faces looking out. Then on the return journey my mother and father had argued, a few kilometres of silence, the sound of the engine and my father's coughing. All his anger at the wait exploded in a single phrase, *You're so selfish, he's still a baby*. At first my mother had tightened her lips, so as not to speak, then she had said *Yes, but that man closed up in there is his grandfather*. Suddenly she started yelling at my father, and I woke up and started to yell too. And it all ended up with my mother forcing my father to stop at the side of the road. Again, she shouted things in his face, sitting in the car, and then she got out, she opened the rear door and took me in her arms, pulling my hat down over my eyes. She slammed the door of the car. She began to walk with long strides at the side of the road. My father also got out of the car, he followed her, trying to hold her back by the arm, and then she turned and yelled even more than before, clutching me close to her breast. A few cars even stopped, my mother was asked if she needed help, my father said *Don't worry* and waved them away with a gesture of his hand. Then he let her go, he ran back to the car, two hundred metres behind. He followed her in the car all the way home, driving beside her at walking pace, the window down. He was apologizing to her, begging her to get back inside, and when we arrived below the house she said *Just go and park*, and she went into the building.

They didn't speak for a week, my mother slept on the sofa for days, my father eating his breakfast already dressed, as she lay there close by. There was also a photograph of that bivouac, my father had taken it while she was asleep. She was there with her head sunk in the pillow, her legs drawn up to keep all of herself on the sofa, a foot with a sock sticking out from beneath the blanket. And beside her there was a little table with a framed photograph on top of it. You couldn't see the photograph well, but it was of their wedding, the newlyweds' table, ties loosened over shirts.

61

I FOUND THE DRAWING ON THE PILLOW ONE EVENING, SOME-one had cleaned the room and had placed it there. The window was open, the curtains were billowing because of the air coming in from outside. Then the breeze suddenly stopped, and the curtains hung straight again. And a moment later a message from Sara arrived on my mobile, a vibration on top of the sheet of paper. I had left the mobile on the drawing. But the message was blank, no words were written, only a light flaring up. The screen stayed lit for a long time, even after the mobile had stopped making the paper vibrate, then it was snuffed out, as if it had never been. I sat down on the bed, I opened the message again, and once more I scanned its emptiness from start to finish. Then another one arrived, it was the same, the same nothingness, the same vibration as before on the paper, as if the hanged man inside the drawing was trying to say something before falling back into the darkness.

Sara continued to show up this way for almost the whole night, messages without words, a trapdoor that opened, the light visible then it closed again. Every time, I leaned over, trying to see the bottom of that hole, but shortly afterwards the lid would come down. It closed, the hotel returned, Rossoš, music from the floor below. The Texan was touting women to his customers, renting rooms so they could get undressed, a bottle of vodka to make everything easier. Then I received a new message from Sara and that hole of light opened up again, and all the rest would suddenly vanish. And I knew that at the bottom of that light I wouldn't have seen Sara but that man who had died one day. Half way through the night I turned the mobile off, outside all the cars had gone away. The last person to go was a youth, sixteen or only a little more, who had come to drink, to look for a woman, or both. His shoulders were broad and all the rest was narrow, it seemed like he had a clothes-hanger under his T-shirt. He pushed his moped for a dozen metres, the engine started and he jumped onto the seat and sped away, pulling his hair back, unlaced shoes on his feet.

That man had appeared in my life only in dying, one Sunday morning in late January. Sara had received a call, she went out onto the balcony to talk, she came back, sat down on the sofa and said nothing. I went up close to her, I saw her face lose all colour, the blood disappearing from it, like a beach from which the sea has ebbed. She just sat there, her back against the sofa. I asked her what had happened, who had called her. But every word I said fell to the floor. Then she put both hands on her belly, a grimace appeared on her face. A grief had climbed up along her breast from

186

her belly and she burst into tears. It was a violent explosion, like retching, her eyes and mouth opening to let it out. Not understanding, I could do nothing but take her in my arms, push her head against my chest and hug her, her every spasm a warm stream of weeping pouring onto my T-shirt. We stayed like that for an hour, she couldn't manage to say anything and I by that time had even stopped asking. All I felt was her breast trembling, its shuddering spreading out and dying down inside my body. There were these violent contractions and this spilling of tears against me, as if Sara were a severed artery, all the blood that her heart pumped ending up outside her body, wetting the body beside her. And so when she eventually drew away, she looked at me and you could see that she didn't know what to say. She ran a hand over my chest, as if she wanted to clean off the dirt she had left there. Then all she did was get up, and shortly afterwards the bathroom door closed. I was left there, drained, I let myself fall back against the sofa, my T-shirt wet, only a few dry islands and all the rest a drenched and sombre red.

On returning from the bathroom Sara sat down next to me on the sofa, to explain all the grief that deformed her face. And so that I could really console her, she had to tell me who that man was. In the midst of all that weeping, inside those eyes, I saw a man appear, someone who for years had been in her life, and in our life, a man whose name I didn't even know. Sara looked at me, lowering her face, the secret coming out like a stone thrown against a window. I was sitting on the couch, my T-shirt soaked in tears, and she was asking me to console her for the very pain she was inflicting on me And handing it over to me was the only way to punish herself and to tell me she was sorry.

62

THEN FOR WEEKS SARA DRAGGED THAT GRIEF ROUND THE house, she plodded along the hall, every now and then she would stop to get her breath back. I saw her exhausted, that man's body bowing her shoulders, crushing her against the floor, her closed eyes resisting the force of gravity, her legs shaking. I didn't know what else to do but look after her, I prepared her lunches and dinners, we would sit down at table and there was nothing to say to each other. I sat on one side, and on the other there were two of them, Sara struggling to swallow something, and the man who was slumped there in a chair. Sara never looked up, every so often I would see a tear fall, run down to her chin and drop into the plate. I looked at her head, she hadn't washed her hair since his death and it was full of splits and cracks. Every minute of grief amounted to years that dug themselves into her skin, and those bags that swelled under her eyes, as if all her suffering had drained into them. Every time she looked up, her face was a little older, as if all ages were passing across it, right to the last, which she had raised against me when lunch was over. She did this with a little ferocity inside, hurting herself by hurting me. She looked at me with a defiant air, that man's body still supine at her side. She stared at me, she wanted to punish herself by seeing the grief in me that she had caused, like taking the most precious vase in the house and hurling it against the wall with all the violence in her body, only to kneel on the floor and weep as she picked up the pieces.

For many nights she had embraced me, clutching me tightly from behind, seeking refuge by clinging to me. At first she said nothing, I would switch off the light and as soon as it was dark she would mould herself to me, curves against curves, she emptied herself where I was full and filled up my hollow spaces. I could feel her brow resting on my back, her hot breath that intermittently warmed a point on my backbone. Then the weeping would come with the first light, shudders apart from one another, the trembling of her breast, my body absorbed it and then it would vanish straight away. She would let herself go only when she was convinced that I was fast asleep, even though it was only the deep breathing that comes before sleep. So those violent shocks would begin against my back. Her entire body shot through by an endless tremor, and then that inconsolable weeping once more. And I would lie there, in the bed, and listen to her despair for the death of another. She had all the desperation of a castaway. I was her log, and she would cling to me with the strength of someone who doesn't want to drown. So both of us went down, that current dragging us along, resigning ourselves to being overwhelmed, hoping to come to the waterfall as late as possible. And in that grip there was all the hope of stopping in time, but also the certainty that the end would come in any case. The next morning we looked at each other, and our faces bore the surprise and the condemnation of having survived the ship-wreck, and to prepare breakfast, sit down at the table, share all that misery, that little thing that was us two.

Sara asked me if I wanted to go to the funeral, and I had merely turned my face away. She went out saying *I'm going*, as she crossed the courtyard she looked round at me twice. I had remained behind the curtains to avoid having to wave to her. When she returned, and that man's body had been buried, she sat down, asked me what I wanted for lunch, I said *You decide*. And so that body suddenly vanished, without my having the courage to hold her to account, nor she to respond. I knew nothing about that man, and I would never have known anything about him. We had put him away in a hurry, and a few weeks later there was no more trace of him in the house, only embarrassment when the two of us met someone who had the same name. Apart from that he was no more than a body placed in a bag and put away somewhere in the cellar. He stayed there under the ground, the metal door and a number written in paint, 38, and above the number my name. We passed in front of it to get the car from the garage, neither of us looked at the metal door, we went straight on, and when we heard a key turn in a lock, there below the stairs, we pretended nothing had happened, but Sara would take my hand.

So, in that meeting of fears, hers to speak and mine to question her, we buried everything under the sand. They had found him hanging in the kitchen of his house, without a note to explain the act, only a card around his neck with his name written on it, as if he were an article on sale. And this is how it all finished, with all this cowardice put together; the end of the silence after extreme unction, a normality seized at the last moment, making lunch, setting the table, and Sara switching on the television to see if something had happened in the world. In the meantime that man's body remained down in the cellar, wrapped up in a bag and stored away, among the things that were of no more use. It stayed there to grow mouldy with the jerrycans of wine, the mattresses, the bicycles, an armchair that neither of us dared to throw out. From inside the house sometimes we even seemed to hear him yell, that body hidden beneath the street. And clinging to each other in bed at night, crying out with the pleasures of the body, panting in each other's ears as we made love, was also a way of hoping not to hear him anymore, to deafen ourselves like that, and to long for a child who would have the courage to go down there, take him on his shoulders, and throw him in the river. But the child we wanted had not come, and I found myself with that man's body like a log in the middle of the road. First it had been Olmo's photograph, and now that drawing made by a man who had once been a little boy and to whom it was no longer possible to ask anything.

63

I WOKE UP AND ALL I NEEDED TO DO WAS OPEN MY EYES AGAIN for Sara to vanish, the pink room appeared to me like a liberation. I had held her hostage all night, her, her grief and that man they had found hanging from a rope in the kitchen one day. I had held them fast there behind the lowered blinds of my eyes, a light trained on their faces and their shadows climbing up the wall. And together with those two, there were the shadows of those who, when grief had exploded in Sara's face, had called to offer their consolation, all the people who knew about him. Telephones rang out like sirens in the house, I would sit squeezed up against a corner of the sofa, and at every call Sara would close the door and from behind its glass the desperation came. The last call was from my mother, Sara had answered. *Hello Giovanna* she said and she had tried to clear her throat, she said *Excuse me one second*, and she blew her nose into the handkerchief, one last burst of weeping. Then she picked up the telephone again, put it to her ear, she said *No, don't worry, it's only tiredness.* Then she said *I'll pass you Pietro.* She gave me the telephone looking at me, with an infinite sadness, with a silent request yet knowing that she could expect nothing. I gave a sigh and said nothing, only *She can't sleep at nights, but that will pass,* Sara lowered her eyes, drew her hair back behind her ears. Then I changed the subject, I went into another room and when I came back Sara said *Thank you* and I looked away.

*

Morning had come in Rossoš, the rubbish truck had woken up the houses along the street. So I opened my eyes, and those bodies came out in random order. Olga called me from the reception, I heard the other lines ringing. She told me that the widow had called her again. And while she was speaking to me someone knocked at the door, I asked Olga to wait a moment, I opened up and a little girl came in. She slipped under my arm and threw herself onto the bed. Her face was the same one I had seen on Olga's mobile. So I closed the door and told Olga that her daughter was in my bed, she burst out laughing and asked me to pass her. Saška took the handset, rearranged the pillow against the wall, stretched out as if she was going to talk for hours, and then she put the telephone to her ear. In the meantime I got dressed, embarrassed at being in my underpants and vest in front of a little girl I had never seen before. I picked up the socks scattered round the room, I placed my right shoe next to the left one. Then I opened the window to let out the intimate smell of the night, Saška was wholly inside the damp cloud of my body and my breath, and the odours flew away a little at a time, the outside air sweeping in and cleaning up the room. At first Saška was laughing, talking on the telephone with her mother on the floor below. When Olga was speaking to her she would keep quiet to listen, and would answer by laughing at the words she uttered. She assailed her mother with sudden bursts of laughter, sending every phrase flying into the air, like sneezing hard over a heap of flour. As she was speaking, she pulled the sheet over her head, she made it into a hut, and I heard her voice and her laughter coming from it. After a while the girl re-emerged, her hair strewn over her face, her cheeks red with the heat, and her voice had become brusquer and crosser, every sentence spoken between clenched teeth. I looked at her face, her eyebrows converging above her nose, she was beating her feet on the mattress. I imagined Olga downstairs ordering her to leave the room, even though she wanted to stay. Then she burst into sudden tears, banged the receiver down, and got out of the bed. I saw her put down one foot then the other, dragging the sheet away and pulling it over her shoulders, like a child bride, her train the last thing to go out into the corridor.

64

SHE WAS ALREADY ON THE SOFA WHEN WE WENT IN. SHE MUST have been eighty, the widow was sitting facing her on a straw chair, they both stood up to welcome us. The road was the one we knew already, the gate, the bicycle, the garden, and then the shoes among the shoes at the door. Olga, Saška and I went in the way a delegation makes its entry, and the widow introduced us moving her eyes from us to the lady and then back to us. She pointed at us, stretching out an arm, pausing first on Olga and afterwards on me, with an expression that became more serious. The lady who had also smiled looked at Olga, then she became more serious as well. Olga merely nodded without translating anything for me, a smile left there for the entire duration of those greetings, Saška, in the meantime, had lost herself in a thought. Olga pushed her forward, Saška put up a little resistance with her feet. The widow smiled at her, the lady put a large, slender hand on her face, a hand with veins on it like a river delta, Saška's right eye vanished behind that caress. Outside the wind was slipping through the branches, driving them as far as the window, the leaves caressed the glass and then pulled back. And I lowered my face, our feet in a circle, looking at one another, studying themselves on the floor. There were Saška's pink socks, Olga's bare feet, her long toes with varnished nails, and mine that I couldn't manage to keep still, my toes rubbing up against one another. And then there were the widow's feet, small in her nylon stockings, and those of this lady, large and gnarled. They looked like the roots of a tree, as if her extremities didn't end there, but entered the floor, and from there, down below the house, they met, intertwining, losing themselves in a single tangle, with all the other roots, including those of the tree outside that was lashing our window with its leaves.

Olga and I sat close together on the couch beside the lady, facing us was the widow on the straw chair, her knees close together below the hem of her skirt. The lady was called Irina, she sat there in a red velvet dress despite the heat. Our arms were bare, Olga's legs too, but the lady gave no sign of suffering from the temperature, her calm eyes of a rather opaque glass. On her breast she had three rows of medals and ribbons, and when she sat down we heard them tinkle. Saška hadn't taken her eyes off them for a second. You could see she wanted to touch them, and she constantly sought Olga's eyes to see if this was permitted. And Olga only laid a hand on her head, Saška took it away, Olga put it back again, Saška shook her head in irritation. Then the widow started to speak, her gaze jumping from me to Olga. She wanted to understand both of us. When she spoke to Olga her language didn't seem foreign to me, then when it alighted on me it suddenly became a forest of sounds. Every so often Olga would interrupt her, transforming long sentences in Russian into a few words in English for me. The widow nodded, without understanding, and I smiled in reply. And it seemed to me that I could see the things she had said lose themselves along the way, like carrying water in a plastic bag with holes in it. In the meantime Irina sat with her glassy gaze fixed on the widow, a face full of asperities, and yet those kind hands crossed on her legs, full of peace. And when Saška couldn't resist any longer and stretched out a hand to the medals we all laughed, her mother caught her wrist to stop her, Saška broke free, and Irina raised an

194

arm towards Olga, as if inviting the child do it because it didn't matter.

Before Irina could say anything, Olga explained that the medals on her breast had been awarded for mowing wheat years before, a heroine of socialist labour, every medal a record. Irina had been a tractor driver, the men had tried to give her a run for her money and she had beaten them instead, males who tried to be males in front of women, sometimes even employing the ruse of tampering with the radiators as long as they won. But Irina could fix everything, she repaired the reaper, mounted it in triumph, humiliated them all, and the men saw her win the prizes, clenching their fists. At Olga's every sentence I would look at Irina, smiling at her, trying to compliment her with my eyes. She looked at me from behind her glass wall, her face always turned towards the widow and her eyes turned towards me. Saška sat on the arm of the sofa beside her. One by one she studied every medal, absorbed by a design. She ran her fingertip over all of them. But then the widow came out with a curt phrase, pointing her finger at me, Olga instantly stopped laughing, and laid her hand on my leg to make me stop, too. And there was a moment of silence, and Saška carried on making the medals jingle against one another, the tree scratching against the window, and my eyes on Olga's profile. Then the widow had repeated that phrase, her finger pointed at me, and Olga turned, she told me that Irina's brother had also been hanged, in December, 1942, but he was only one of many who had met that end.

Then Saška fell asleep against Irina, on the sofa, reviewing her medals had been like counting sheep for her. Olga tried to move her, and Irina had merely raised an arm so as not to wake the little girl up. She then sat there, leaning against the sofa, her glazed eyes and her mouth that opened and closed to give form to the words.

The rest of her body was still, as if she were talking to us from under rubble, crushed to the ground after a house had collapsed. Every now and then the widow would get up, at a certain point she came back with a tray, little glasses placed around a bottle. Irina greeted the arrival of the vodka by closing her lashes tight over her eyes in sign of pleasure, on her mouth a smile that was like a scar, the faint memory of something that had happened a long time ago. In the meantime Saška had turned over, in sleep, she made her face more comfortable on Irina's dress, her hand running over the old lady to see where she ended, wrapping her in an embrace that was all dreamed.

The storm came suddenly, darkness fell in a moment inside the house, in the middle of the afternoon. There was Irina's silhouette against the window, Saška on top of her, and us in the darkness like outgrowths of the furniture. In that darkness Irina had talked: the thunderclaps, the dazzling lightning flashes, her brother hanged in the centre of the square. She spoke quietly, we could see her shoulders and the light from the window that traced their outline. She spoke slowly with Olga, next to me, gesturing that she would translate everything at the end, for fear that Irina might stop on hearing a voice following on from her, the risk that she might say nothing more. So when Irina sat back against the sofa once more Olga brought her head close to me, she began to talk to me quietly. The widow leaned over the table, rested a hand on Irina's knee, and Irina covered it with her own, larger hand. And Olga told me about that boy, who wasn't the one in the photograph or even the one in the drawing, but just one among many of those the soldiers took and killed. Olga talked, Irina remained in silence. I saw everything happen inside that room, in that house on the outskirts of Rossoš, nearly on the edge of the countryside. And I saw those boys, first they captured them and then they hanged them from a rope, and their necks broke, the feet below shook, seeking the earth, like the spasms of a fish caught and then tossed on dry land, searching for the sea to the last. Then the feet didn't shake anymore, the body surrendered to gravity, the feet all of a sudden were only shoes at the end of legs, some unlaced, their laces falling down, they too seeking the earth. Irina had said that they used to hang many young men from football goals, seven or eight per goal, like clothes on sale, and there was a town where they had hanged one from every lamppost, all the way along the road. Of an evening the light would illuminate the napes of their necks, people would pass by beneath and not look, walking straight on, quickening their pace, their heads alongside the knees of those murdered boys. On the afternoon they had killed her brother it was sunny, and after that day suddenly there was no more sun, lightning against the sky, thunder, and the sky that seemed to have come crashing down. It rained as if it were never going to stop, her brother's body, which at first didn't seem to get wet became drenched, hair like seaweed over his face, clothes clinging closely to him, darker, the water falling and pouring down from his feet. Below him, watching the water fall, there were some women, some wept, some inveighed against the soldiers, the invaders, they insulted them, spitting on their faces and uniforms. Some of the invaders let themselves be spat on, some laughed, one had slapped a woman, and she had hurled herself on his arm. She tore away at it, sinking her teeth in. And there was one soldier, Irina said, who was weeping too. He, had thrown himself to the ground, begging forgiveness. And her brother was wearing an elegant suit he had stolen.

65

IRINA HAD LET HERSELF BE TAKEN FAR FROM HOME, A SQUARE
with only one bench and four women seated on it. The women were
in the shade, above the bench there were two trees that seemed like
Siamese twins, the trunks that rose up parallel, close to each other,
their branches merged, a single crown of lighter and darker greens.
They all turned when they saw us coming, the nose of the car, our
faces in the windows, all of us pitching in and out of the holes. Irina
was in front with Olga, with one hand she braced herself, the other
was lying on her legs, the slender fingers and the velvet. At every
hole, the medals jingled and if the hole was a big one Irina held
them still by resting a hand against her breast, as if she wanted to
protect them or protect her heart from the fright. I was sitting in
the back, Saška a little further away in the child seat, her forehead
on the glass of the window, and her mouth making a circle beneath
it with her breath. Then every so often she would fill that circle with
a few words, talking through it. Olga answered her, turning her
head, slipping her response between the door and the seat, as if
she were passing it written on a sheet of paper, and Saška would
take it, read and fall silent. Then Irina had pointed to a dirt road,
Olga drove the car onto it and let it roll downwards. And at the
end of the road the square opened out, with those two trees and
the bench, the four women sitting, their feet tucked together in their
shoes. The rest was puddles of rainwater, some small, others you
had to hop across. The storm had suddenly stopped, as if bored by
itself, you could see a herd at the back of the sky, the last clouds
scurrying away. And now there were those women, who had come
out along with the sun, each with a nylon bag to sit on, one had an
open umbrella for the tree that was still raining on her head.

*

They saw Irina coming out of the car, her dress, the medals, they looked at her twice, at first to see her, the second time to understand who she was. In those looks there was a blend of amazement and suspicion, as if Irina wanted to hide herself, as if she were a traitor. But then Irina looked at them with her scarred smile, and the one under the umbrella said something to her. The other three started to laugh, Irina replied with a few curt words, pointing at me, blushing. Olga turned off the engine and got out, she opened the door for Saška, but she wanted to stay in the car. Olga went up to the four women on the bench, she greeted them with a smile, her head to one side. The first woman even gave her a kiss, and showing her to her friends, she added a few words. For a while the others remained in silence, listening, then they nodded and smiled, looking Olga in the face. One gave a shout of surprise, putting her hands over her mouth, as if she had come across her again after years of looking for her in vain. So Olga went towards the car, leaned over Saška, and after a bit she managed to persuade her to get out. We saw her emerge like a football falling out of a cupboard. She let Olga drag her towards the bench, her arm taut and Saška in tow a little behind. But it only lasted a few seconds, just enough time to let herself be seen, let her mother lift up her chin, let everyone comment, and then Saška slipped out of her mother's grip, to run back towards the car.

Irina didn't want us to accompany her all the way home, she indicated a vague point beyond the tree, a few hundred metres further on. It was a single procession of reinforced concrete buildings, parabolic antennas at the windows, some stifled by washing hanging down from the floor above. Before leaving, Irina came towards me, took my face between her hands, her eyes looking into mine, and gave me a kiss and a hug. We watched her leave, her gait lopsided, walking close to the edge of the buildings, staying in the shade. There were some youths outside the street doors, on the steps, some sitting on their bicycles. They were laughing behind her back at her and her medals, the thick velvet dress in all that heat. But she walked away erect, her handbag clutched to her bosom, one youth tried to hit her with his football, it flew over her head. Then Irina vanished at the end of the building, the last ricochet of the ball dying against a wall. We got into the car, the women waved goodbye as we passed by, the gravel accompanying us to the exit once more. And we, too, skirted the building, and after the building we also turned. And there behind it stood another building that looked as if it had been bombed, a block gnawed by rats, one window was broken. Irina was entering it, her red velvet dress for special occasions, her medals and ribbons, and yet that dilapidated house. Olga slowed down so we wouldn't be seen, Irina's shame at living in there, after having tried to hide it. And when she disappeared inside, Olga put her foot down on the pedal and we got to the end of the road very quickly.

66

WE REACHED THE RIVER LURCHING AMONG THE MUD AND the rocks, at every pothole the car would suddenly pitch to one side, as if it had sprained something. Olga and I went along with those sudden jolts by letting our bodies go, everyone to the right and after wards everybody to the left, according to the pothole. Behind, in the child seat, Saška was gazing out the window, her breathing broken only if the pothole was big. Every so often Olga turned to look for her face, if she found it she gave her a broad smile, if she didn't find it she merely took a peek. Other times, instead, she would take one hand off the wheel and stretch her arm out behind towards Saška, but without looking at her. She did this as if rummaging in a bag for keys, feeling in the back seat for a daughter who remained there in silence. When she found her, I would see Olga's arm remain motionless for a while and then return, her hand back on the wheel together with the other one that had kept us steady on the road. We left the main road after crossing a village, a sign with its name on entry, a dozen wooden houses looking onto the road, and the same sign as before, the village ending this way, with a line across the name. By turning my head in the window, I saw it pass, the houses appeared in the rear-view mirror and then were left behind, sown on the road already made, indistinct among the fields, suddenly lower than the grass. Olga pointed out a red building to me, she told me that it had been her school. From behind, Saška asked her something, and they talked in their secret language, which wasn't Russian but the vague tone in which they said things to each other, a few words in between the silences.

There was a road in the wood, a brown strip that ran down towards the river, and in the middle of it were holes full of sky, the clouds entered them every so often, changed shape and went away. We were going down towards the Don, Olga had seen it in one of my photographs and had recognized it. Olmo had asked me to go there, to look for that precise point. In the photograph there was an ordinary stretch of river, there was snow, a Russian soldier was walking on the far bank without concealing himself, Olmo had pointed the camera, taken the photograph, capturing him for ever in that gesture. But the Russian's smile was split in two, his mouth lent itself to the photograph but his eyes held a fear of something else, there was betrayal and pain in them, and in that same moment someone had shot him. Olga had looked at the photograph, her forehead disconcerted and her mouth disgusted. She pointed at the soldier with her finger, she told me that you can't betray a man who trusts you, killing him like that, while you're taking a photograph of him. All that was written on the back of the photograph was the Don River, January 1943. So now there we were trying to reach the river, Olga said that she wasn't sure if that was the point we were looking for. She said the water of those days had been gone for some time. As if to say that by now it had ended in the sea, and goodness knows how many times it had evaporated in the meantime, and goodness knows how many times the clouds had picked it up and let it fall on the earth, and goodness knows what fields it had rained on, which plants it had nourished, and who had eaten those plants, and whose body they had become, and inside that body what blood ran.

We came to the end of the road, we wound up the windows, because the water splashed us every time we ended up in a hole. There was a long dark stretch, the treetops closing over our heads, they had arched from one side to the other until they joined together. There were only a few patches of sunlight, a gap among the branches, then the river opened up in front of us, the light burst on the windscreen like a stone thrown from above. And so we came to the bank, the wheels sunk in the mud, and Saška asked where we were. We stopped alongside a car, all its doors open, music vibrating from inside it, the speakers too weak not to distort the sound. A short distance away, there was a family gathered around a grill, the barechested father smoking and spreading out steaks. The mother was holding out the plate from which he took the meat, and two overweight children were blowing on the embers to make the fire flare up, receiving a ticking-off. First I looked at that family busy around the grill, then I asked Olga if we had arrived, if this was the Don. She smiled with a hint of embarrassment and said yes. Her finger pointed at the far bank, there were two families identical to the one next to us, the grill, the car doors open, the smoke climbing up towards the trees. Olga turned off the engine, took out the key. There was a doll hanging from the rear-view mirror, it continued to swing for a few seconds, then it stopped.

67

I WENT INTO THE RIVER, JUST LIKE THAT, AS IF IT WERE THE only way to pass to the other bank. At a certain point the ground ended, I continued to put one foot in front of the other, and at every step I sank in a little more, feeling the stones, the mud, my feet in it, disappearing from sight. Olga stayed a few dozen metres behind, the car stopped where the path ended, the boot door up, the shade making a darker square on the grass. Olga was trying to get Saška into her swimsuit, but she kept losing her balance, she couldn't get her foot in the hole. She threw her head back and laughed. Beside them, a little further away, the father was scolding his children, they had dropped something into the embers, dark smoke rose up, the stink of plastic overwhelmed the smell of grilled meat. The children started to cry, Saška stopped to look at them, her mouth a little open, one foot in her swimsuit and the other in mid-air, like a hen unsure whether to take another step or not. Then the two children calmed down, their mother put the plate of meat on the grass, she took each of them by the hand and accompanied them towards the riverbank. So I found myself with them beside me, their mother fiddling with their caps to protect them from the sun as they tried to get rid of her. Their faces still had the crumpled look of recent tears and a desire to dive into the river. I saw them vanish under the water. Instinctively, I shielded myself, their splashing making my skin pucker into a rind of shivers. Their mother looked at me and smiled as if to apologize, shrugging. I restrained all the irritation I felt by closing my eyes for a few seconds, swallowing it, then I opened them again and returned her smile.

Then I saw the children move off towards the middle of the river. Their mother stood watching them from the bank, every so often she would draw a breath as if to shout, but then she remained silent. Every now and then the two children would turn round, the bigger one looking for his mother's face to see if they should turn back. Then, from behind, their father whistled, the whistle of a man who had kept dogs. The children stopped and swam back towards the bank. Not far from my feet, in the meantime, frogs were jumping, I saw them come out of the water and pierce it again a little further away, the water concealing them, the smothered croak of mouths suddenly closed. I continued to stand there hesitantly, my feet in the mud, wearing a pair of underpants with light blue stripes, the water snakes threading the river in zigzags, as if sewing the water up with themselves. Then I heard the ringing of my mobile coming closer and closer, growing louder behind my back. I turned and saw Saška holding it in her hand, her arm outstretched as she walked stiffly in her swimsuit. She called me only with her eyes, carrying the telephone as if it were a bomb about to explode. And on the telephone there was Olmo, he knew I would have gone to the river. He apologized, I told him I would have called him. He asked me if I was on the Don, and I said I was. He remained silent, then he asked me *Will you let me hear it?* I took a few steps forwards, the frogs jumping and the snakes coming and going between my legs. And after I took another two steps and the water was up to my knees, I bent them, and submerged myself up to my neck, the telephone against my ear, my breath suddenly heavier because of the cold, he holding his on the other end of the line.

*

Then there was nothing else but this swim we made together, breathing quietly as if we were wading together during the night, crossing without being discovered. That loud music was coming from the bank, emerging from the car windows, it passed over my head together with the smell of burned plastic, dispersed with the first gust of wind, sweeping down the current of the river. The two children were back close to their father, their mother had them sit on a towel, the smaller one huddled up against the bigger one's side. Olmo didn't speak, and I didn't ask him anything, immersed as I was in the water, only my hand and the mobile above the surface, my feet planted in the mud. And standing there, with his breath in my ear, it was as if I had hoisted Olmo onto my shoulders, to try to carry him to the other side of the river. He was fastened to me, his arms round my neck, his chest against my back, as I swam underneath him, moving my arms and legs slowly to prevent him from falling, fearful of unseating him when I wanted to save him instead. Olmo was clinging to me without a word, without any possibility other than trusting in me, the water carrying at least half of his weight. Until I stubbed my toe on a rock on the bottom, a stab of pain and I lost my balance, I looked for something to hang on to, grasping at the air, and the telephone fell in the water. And I saw it penetrate the green surface of the water and vanish, Olmo swallowed up in a second, without even a splash. In the meantime Saška was calling me from the bank, she had learned my name, she waved, her mother had put a pink handkerchief on her head.

68

MY MOTHER CALLED SAYING *GUESS WHERE I'M PHONING from*, and as she said that she laughed, repeating *Guess*. I was with

Saška and Olga, we had just gone into their house, my mobile was still working, saved by some miracle. Saška took me by the hand, dragged me out onto the balcony, and my mother was saying *It's not difficult, but if you want I can give you a little clue*, and when I said O.K., *give me a clue*, the line went dead. The building in which Olga lived was one like many others, but it was the last one before the city ended. On one side there were only buildings, cars, streets and people, and on the other there was the steppe, which came from too far away to be able to establish its beginning. Olga had opened a window for me, Saška had slipped in between us, she climbed up on a blue plastic chair and was the first to go out, her elbows on the parapet, her chin resting on it. Then they showed me the countryside, Olga showed it to me stretching her arm out and opening her hand, as if she had a butterfly in it that she wanted to release. So we stood there in silence for a long time, at that extreme point where Rossoš ended and the entire land along with it, and all of us thrust out a thought, each one a secret thought, certain that it would never come back but would have arrived somewhere anyway.

Every so often Saška would let out a yell and stretch her arm down below, as if it were the sea, towards a distant point that was coming closer, the sails furled. It seemed to us that we could see the flags, the ropes stretched tight. But every time they were cars or lorries, big and small, or a bicycle. They floated slowly towards us, catching what wind there was, then passed below us and disappeared. We went back indoors and after a few steps the house ended, only two rooms, linoleum with a parquet pattern on it, the kitchen, and the bedroom in which they both slept. Saška showed it to me, tugging me by the hand once more, a bare room, two single beds close together, divided by a bedside table. There was a doll on Saška's bed, while Olga's looked like a double bed cut in two by a hatchet, one half thrown in the fire, the other like a sacrifice in which she lay every evening.

My mother rang again when we were in the kitchen, on the fridge there was a drawing held up by a heart-shaped magnet. The drawing showed a house and a flower beside it, a daisy as high as the roof. In the middle of the kitchen there was a basin, on the floor, with a little water in it. Olga told me that it was for when it rained, the water ran down from the roof along the flex of the ceiling lamps, throughout the condominium, and every so often some flats would be left without power. When storms hit, Olga and Saška would switch off the light and sit in front of the window looking at the building across the street, in winter they would cover their legs with a blanket. They would stay there for as long as the rain lasted, sitting in the dark in front of the glass pane, every window an illuminated rectangle. In the darkness they would wait for one of those lights to disappear, the water running down the flex, the light bulb bursting and that sudden obscurity. They would stare at the building in front and at a certain point a window would go out, then another, like the targets in a firing range, aim, fire, and the black in place of the white. Then Olga asked me if I wanted a cup of tea, she began to heat up some water on the stove.

It was in that moment that my mother called again, Olga advised me to go close to the window. Her voice was finally clear, I heard the same laughter as before, she said *It's Mamma*, breaking off. There was someone beside her making comments. She said *Well, have you understood?* And I heard a cough erupt there beside her, she added *I could say that I'm calling from home*. So I realized that the person beside her was Olmo, my mother sitting in the kitchen of what had once been our house. So I laughed too, but with a touch of embarrassment, and she asked me *Why didn't you tell me before that he lived here?* Yet, as she spoke, her voice was light and she seemed to have become younger all of a sudden, she said *We're having a nice chat here.* Olmo was laughing in the background. I heard her moving around the house, the silence changed around her from room to room. She said *It's all different here,* and she said it as if it were a relief. Her voice then went out into the open, the balcony, the cars below, the tram passing by. Then she lowered her voice, suddenly becoming more serious, *Why don't you come home?* she asked me. And she added *Have you found something?* All I said was *Yes.* Then immediately after *No. No.* As she was speaking to me, Olmo arrived, I heard him say *Giovanna, there's a smell,* and, cheerful once more, she said *Switch off the gas, I'm coming.* So she went back indoors, *We've made some pasta,* she told me. And I heard plates and glasses. Olmo was setting the table, he asked her *Would you like some wine?* My mother replied *No, because it's hot in here.* Then she said *O.K., Pietro, it was just to give you a surprise, now we're sitting down at table.* Olmo came closer and shouted *Ciao* in the telephone. My mother hung up, and I closed my eyes to hold on to that telephone call for another moment. A telephone called filled with my mother and Olmo, and that light voice of hers which I had heard as if she had called me from a missing point many years before. In that missing point she was sitting in the kitchen, in our old house, and beside her was Mario, my grandfather, a plate and a glass in front of him. Mario used to accompany us as far as our building and then turn back as my father didn't want to meet him. The last thing I always saw of him was his back. And now, as a dead man, he had gone upstairs, crossed the entrance hall, then climbed five flights of stairs, and the door had finally opened for him. He had sat down at table with his daughter, and she had cooked for him.

69

BEFORE LEAVING, I KEPT THE PROMISE I HAD MADE TO Olga, to see her grandfather's house in the country. It was little more than a wooden box with doors and windows, an *isba*, in front and behind nothing but the steppe, hens coming in and going out of a big and broken sheet-metal door, on which someone had written numbers. Outside, there was a blue letter box, a large one pecked at by some bird that had wanted to make a nest inside it. On it there was a red cross made with a paintbrush. The paint had run out before the cross was finished, as if it had dissolved into the blue background. The door of the letter box was open, and in fact inside there was a nest, it looked like a bed someone had left unmade before going out. Olga had pointed out the place from the road as we passed, a distant point in the middle of the green, the electricity pylon standing out tall, and below it that little wooden house, the courtyard, as if forgotten, like a village that had disappeared, carrying off everything except that one house.

When the car stopped, Olga's grandfather came out the door preceded by a host of hens and they departed like majorettes, splitting up a bit to the right and a bit to the left. Then he arrived, a latecomer hen overtaking him and joining the others. He stood there, two crutches and only one leg, the short, squat body of a peasant, his face darkened by the sun and crossed by wrinkles so clearly marked they looked like engravings. We got out of the car, the pylon looming over us. Its triangle of shade passed above the house and vanished, it looked like a man standing above us, his legs apart, the position of someone with his hands on his hips, looking down from above. When we went through the metal door, the hens came back in too. And on the other side of the door there was a yard, two dogs on the ground against a wall, and a few cats were pestering the hens, making them run, wiggling in a flurry of feathers for a few steps. The rest of the yard was full of discarded things, left outside to be ruined by time, a mattress with holes, covered in stains, some rusty shovels, a bicycle without a front wheel, and heaps of other things, a broken chair, the legs of a table, a piece of the big door, and on top there was a shoe, open at the front. Those piles of remains looked like sacrificial pyres ready for the flames, to make towers of smoke rise up in the middle of the steppe, and watch them disperse in the sky. When we went in, Saška immediately ran to the dogs, Olga's grandfather tried to stop her by raising one crutch like the bar of a level crossing, but she ducked down and passed beneath it, and he was left off balance.

The hens also came into the house. The door was left ajar and they would poke their heads inside. There was one, in particular, smaller and plumper than all the rest, which came and went as if she were constantly forgetting something. She would appear in the kitchen, then vanish in the corridor. When she reappeared it was to leave through the door once more and go outside. We could see her through the window in the yard, joining the others. When she was outside she would run, but when she was inside she would walk warily, lifting her claw high at every step and putting it back down a little further on, taking aim, as if walking on a wire, never looking down, taking deep breaths. The other hens wandered in disorder round the house, meeting, bumping into each other on a tile, each after a thought, breathless, a blend of euphoria and panic, as if they had to take all that they could manage and then run for it immediately afterwards, reach safety as soon as possible. But the other hen would come in with a different gait, like a governess, we watched her make those deliberate movements, aiming and stepping forward, the rings under her eyes drawn in such a way as to resemble spectacles, slipped on to see close up. Olga's grandfather was sitting there in the middle, his crutches propped up against a small refrigerator, set between the sink and the stove. He sat there and it seemed as if he didn't even see those hens that filled his house, the floor covered with the signs of their coming and going. Every now and then some of them would get up on the table, take a couple of steps, and jump down again, using a chair as a stepping stone. We sat in front of him, Olga with Saška on top of her, on top of Saška a cat, and I lifting my leg to one side when I saw the governess coming by. It was nine in the morning, on the table there was some vodka, a bowl of honey, boiled eggs, an omelette. Olga's grandfather looked at me, he had prepared it all for us.

Olga had wanted me to meet him, the war had taken one of his legs, the house was what he had left. Olga had told him I was Italian, and that my grandfather had been in the war, with the Italians and the Russians things had gone as they had gone. All the Italian he knew was three words that for him were one alone. He had heard it said by the soldiers on the other side of the Don, it was cold, there was shooting and then that single word made of three, *Sacramento porca Madonna*. He shouted it, raising his glass in the air, those words unleashed, said there, struck him as a toast rather than a blasphemous oath. I too raised my glass above the table, *Sacramento porca Madonna*, and burst out laughing, and then Olga too, *Sacramento porca Madonna*, and even Saška said *Sacramento porca Madonna*, but she said it quietly, whispering it to the cat. After that it was all eating and drinking for hours, he started to sing, beating time with his crutch. Saška went outside, we saw her take a piece of wood, draw a road on the ground, carving out a track with straights and bends, and trying to make the hens go along it, getting angry with them, one even opened her wings out of her fear of the little girl. And then Olga's grandfather suddenly stopped laughing, his mouth closed, his eyes grew a little darker. Olga told me that vodka always brought him good cheer and songs, but the last thing it left him was this blue melancholy. The drink laid it on his shoulders, he would stoop, allow himself to be defeated. Even the hens sensed this, and in fact they no longer came into the kitchen, they kept their distance, the odour of another animal's pain, all the others running away. Olga stayed close to him, she laid her hand on his only leg. Her expression was torn, not sure whether to remain inside her grandfather's suffering, to slip into that private space, to leave me there outside to wait until it was over, or to translate all that grief for me. So they spoke in Russian for a while, tenderness in the eyes and violence in the mouth, and she was staring up at him as if pleading. Then Olga looked at me and said that he had no quarrel with me, but millions of them had died to free themselves of us. When she stopped talking, her grandfather pointed outside, beyond the window. And Olga told me that the land there was full of dead, the fields, the trees, this house and her grandfather's brother, he too was under that black earth.

Before saying goodbye I wanted to take his photograph. Olga's grandfather raced out of the kitchen on his crutches, then he came back in with a jacket with medals and ribbons on it. He struck a pose, standing beside the fridge, at attention on only one leg, his face serious, his expression concentrated. Olga asked him to smile and he didn't. His face was that of a man who knew that, in this way, in a photograph, he was passing on beyond death. Then he accompanied us outside, to the car. In the meantime, a white pollen had begun to fly everywhere. The yard was already full of it, the hens ran around, making it fly up. We shook hands, he asked Olga when I was going to leave, I pointed at my wristwatch to signify very soon, the first flight there was. We waved to him from behind the car windows, he raised one crutch, the one on the same side as his leg, the gesture of someone shooting in the air. He stayed there for the whole time it took to cover the dirt-track, Saška looking out behind watching him disappear. He stood there, whitened by the pollen, his jacket and medals already white, and his head turning white too despite the fact that he no longer had any hair. And that pollen fell over all of Russia, it fell on our car, and on the road, and it fell on the fields with all the dead beneath them, over all the steppe, and the animals, and the women pedalling their bicycles in the countryside, and on the pylon, and the sky was full of those white flakes, yet it was blue, in the middle of that summer snowstorm, the warm snow alighting on all things.

70

THEY ACCOMPANIED ME TO THE COACH JUST AFTER DAWN had broken, Olga had wanted Saška to come with her, to see me off. I had slept in their house, my luggage taken away from the hotel before dinner, a goodbye with Olga in the middle, a handshake with the Texan, and that disappointed look of a missed opportunity on his face. He made me a present of a bottle of vodka, drink it in Italy, maybe with a woman I wasn't afraid of. Saška stayed with me as I packed my suitcase in the hotel, her mother on the floor below. She sat on the floor watching me. I felt her eyes following me, as if casting light on me from behind, going in and out of the wardrobe, taking all the shirts off the hangers, folding them on the bed, putting them one on top of the other in my bag, an extra layer that rose, another colour. She stayed there for a long time, without ever coming closer, only looking at me in that vindictive way, making me feel that my every gesture was the gesture of someone who was leaving. She sat still, her back against the wall,

all huddled up in the niche below the window, a votive chapel with an angry little girl inside it, the pink drapes that hung down to the floor serving as a curtain. For the entire time she stayed sitting under there, Saška covered one eye with one hand followed by the other side, first the right then the left, to see things move a few centimetres while remaining in exactly the same place. She did it with me too, shifting me at her pleasure as if seeking revenge, the power to move me, without my noticing anything. But then she went away, I heard the door slam, the anger, and the votive chapel empty, the saint escaped.

Then there was that night spent at their house, three of us around a table set for dinner, eating and saying little, the cloth napkins, theirs bound with a red ribbon stolen from a present. Olga had dressed up, and she had wanted her daughter to do the same, and she had done so against her will, and in fact as she ate she had taken off her shoes, and put her feet up on the chair. And for the whole dinner Olga got up and sat down, so as not to burn the things in the pot, to serve me and take my plate, to show Saška how the house would look with a father in it too, doing this even though she already had a father, goodness knows where. In the end Olga cleared the table, the dishes in the sink, and she wanted to take a photograph of us all, placing the camera on the stove and running to sit down beside us. But twice the self-timer went off before she could sit down and strike a pose, the flash caught her in the back twice, photographs of a woman escaping. In the end we managed, Olga put Saška in my arms, and she held both of us from behind in a single embrace. But then in the photograph Saška had her face turned away, Olga instead was looking at the lens, her lipstick, her smile, I had my eyes shut and Olga's arm on my chest. That's how we came out, a family for only one photograph, the crumbs on the tablecloth, the glasses still on the table, and those napkins, two with a ribbon and one without. The rest of the evening was joining their two beds together to make a bigger one, but they were still two beds, two blankets and two sheets. Saška went into the bathroom and then came back wearing a really tight nightdress, her bare feet poking out at the end of her legs. None of the three of us slipped under the blankets, so as not to create partitions. I was in underpants and a blue T-shirt, with all my bashfulness regarding Saška, and a touch of shame, the hairs that covered my thighs climbing all the way up beneath my boxer shorts. Then in sleep everyone had gone their separate ways, and the alarm clock caught us like that, divided. Olga together with Saška, the sheet pulled over their bodies the way you cover a sofa before leaving for the summer. I woke up in the other bed, my head on a pillow full of faded fairies, pointy hats and wands in their hands, my mouth having breathed all the breath of the night over the fairies.

When we arrived, the engine of the coach was already running, the driver on board, his dark glasses ready for the sun. A few minutes in the car and Saška had fallen asleep again, even though she hadn't really woken up. Then the coach left, Olga waved goodbye with her child in her arms, then she put a hand on her daughter's head once more. Afterwards there was nothing but fields. I dozed off and found the fields still the same every time, hours of road all the same, the tarmac, the sun, the green grass, waiting to see Moscow. And on one of my awakenings, in the middle of the fields, there was a bronze monument, a tank aiming at the sky, and before and after the tank nothing but fields. Beneath the monument there were two cyclists, two men with sunburned faces, technical gear, calf muscles like professionals, They were sitting on the pedestal, handing each other a water-flask, their bicycles leaning against the tank tracks. They sat there, elbows on their knees, both bare-chested, their coloured T-shirts hanging over the cannon, flapping as if hung out from the window of a flat block.

71

THEN MOSCOW REMAINED ON THE GROUND, THE VIBRATION suddenly finished on the runway, and the recoil of the under-carriage swallowed up soon after, the dull thump and then that different silence, the air on the wings, looking for a hole to go up through. I peered at Moscow from the window, I saw it standing there like a refusal, as if it had first run after the plane and then had suddenly given up. As the plane gradually reached the sky I saw the city grow smaller, looking down to see it, and in the end the whole of it was inside one window. Then we went into a cloud, and I saw Moscow grow fuzzy and disappear. Above the clouds there was only us, a few people in a half-empty plane. Beside me there was a man with a moustache, he had sweated all through the take-off, then as soon as the plane had become horizontal again he had stopped. First he had stared at the back of the seat in front of him, as if his whole life were running through it, reviewing it in sequence before plunging down. He had these drops of sweat, they started at his temple one at a time and then ran down, the path was always the same, and when the drop reached his cheek he would press his fingertip against it, collect it, then dry it on his trousers with his finger. As soon as the first drop ran down, another would start, like skiers at the starting gate, hurling themselves down with a shove, and he would always instinctively skewer them at the same point, extinguishing them on his thigh, his eyes still fixed on the headrest in front of him. Then the ascent was over, we emerged into the blue, the seat belt light went off, his face suddenly became dry, And he tightened the knot of his tie, as if his job had finished there, getting the plane into the sky, and his eyes searched for the hostess, a salty streak on his cheek.

The journey was a long broken sleep, opening the eyes every now and then, looking down to the end of the aisle and falling into darkness once more. The hostess came by only twice, put a tray on the fold-down table, took it back after a while with the plastic cup upside down, lip stains on its rim, the napkin stuffed inside, the last mouthful of sandwich. And it seemed to me that I was going away and losing everything, with each patch of sky losing something that I had brought on board, which I hadn't found after going all that way, and what I had found without looking for it, and every metre of air held something less and something more. There was a moment, during the flight, in which I looked down, I sought a point between the fuselage and the wing, I looked towards land. There were no clouds, only an expanse of fields, Germany, Austria, maybe Italy already. Every so often a built-up area would appear, a town or a city, tiny in the distance, Monopoly houses and hotels. Outside those houses, in the courtyards, on the balconies, lying on the grass, along the streets of the town, stopped at the traffic lights, there were people who lived their lives, too small and too far away to be seen from up there. Some of them, tilting their heads backwards, saw us passing, the white wake we left behind us. And suspended at more than thirty thousand feet, it seemed to me I was losing things, abandoning them in the sky, like a plane attempting a desperate landing, first emptying the fuel tanks in flight and then seeking land. And so I left Olga and her daughter in the sky, it struck me that I was scattering them like ashes in the air, above Germany, Austria, or Italy. And as well as them I also scattered Olga's grandfather, his crutches, the hens, and the gold teeth of that woman whose name I had never known, and her grandson Kolja, and the statue of Lenin, the Don into which I had dived, and even that drawing I still kept close in my pocket, a boy hanging from a gallows, and the ashes of the man who had drawn him, his face in the frames.

Thirty thousand feet below there were those people, some were looking up, some were pointing out the aeroplane to the person beside them, and some still were shading their eyes with their hands to see it despite the sunshine. And the things I scattered in the sky were the wake of the plane as it dissipated, disintegrating, at first a compact white wake, and little by little wads that broke off, lingering behind, the shoes left at the entrance, the medals on the woman tractor driver's breast, the photograph of Olga's grandfather, the water snakes, the Texan's hat, the dead buried under the steppe. Everything fell down and I was left with nothing. My things descended on those towns, from thirty thousand feet, like planes that fly over and toss leaflets on the beaches. Maybe someone would have run to see them fall, or caught them in flight, caught them in their hands, taken them home, and all the while the aeroplane carried on its course and disappeared.

Thirty thousand feet below, but I still didn't know that yet, there would be Sara to welcome me. The automatic doors of the arrivals would have opened and we would have all gone out together, like athletes from round a bend, each pulling a trolley. Among the others I would have seen Sara, my gaze called by hers. She would have broken away from that backdrop of waiting people, she would have come out of there and then straight towards me. We would have left the airport and seen the lights of the taxis coming towards us, and the car boots opening for relatives, everyone welcomed back, the hugs, the mothers checking the faces of the children in the summer that was ending there, school beginning a few days later. Sara would have said that my mother had told her the arrival time, and we would have headed for the underground car park. For the whole time we wouldn't have said anything else, heard only the sound of our steps, the wheels of the suitcase and the sound of the automatic till. And we would have got the wrong floor, looking for the car in the same place but one floor below. And Sara would have said *It was here*, and then *What an idiot*. And when we would have found it she would have said *There it is*, as if it had returned. She would have given me the keys and said *Will you drive?* And she would have sat in the passenger seat, while I put the luggage in the boot. And she would have put on the safety belt, I would have watched it pass over her breast, I would have stretched out my hand towards her belly and then I would have withdrawn it, and I would have asked her *Are you sure about the safety belt?* And she would have said, *Come on, they're flashing their lights at us, let's go.*

ACKNOWLEDGEMENTS

This novel has many homes. In the course of writing it I found great hospitality and comfort. In some houses, I received warmth, support, intellectual and human consideration and discussion. In others I had the gift of precious and painful accounts, which I tried in every way to look after and care for. Other houses were authentic refuges. These places, and above all the people who live in them, have made this novel what it is. I want to thank them all this way, adults and children, without naming them, leaving them in the intimacy of their own homes. They have meant, and still mean, so much to me, each in his own way, that the thought moves me. All of them will be able to recognize themselves, with all the modesty and affection they deserve.

These places are: in Turin in the strada Consortile del Salino, via Belfiore, lungo Po Antonelli, via Fratelli Calandra, via Vincenzo Gioberti, via Carlo Alberto, via Fidia, via Sant'Antonino, via Biancamano and corso Siccardi; in Torre Pellice in vicolo Dagotti; in Milan in via Cappuccio; in Trento in via Francesco Petrarca; in Camogli in piazza Don Bosco; in Bologna in via delle Fragole; in Genoa in via Assarotti; in Voronezh, Ulitsa Michurina (V.G.A.U.); in Moscow, Ulitsa Pyatnitskaya; in Paris in rue de l'Université and in rue Becquerel; in Fontanelle by Reano; in Cuneo in via Beppe Fenoglio and via Luigi Teresio Cavallo. This is my embrace.

ANDREA BAJANI is a novelist, playwright and journalist living in Turin. He writes regularly for the newspapers *La Stampa*, *L'Unita* and *Il Sole 24 Ore*, as well as for the radio and theatre. Previous novels have been winners of the Premio Mondello and the Premio Brancati, and for *Every Promise* he was awarded the prestigious Premio Bagutta in 2011.

ALASTAIR MCEWEN is the translator of novels by Alessandro Baricco, Roberto Calasso and illustrated works by Umberto Eco, published by MacLehose Press.